TALINDOR'S GUEST

Charles McGarry

ISBN-10: 0-9861419-1-7
ISBN-13: 978-0-9861419-1-1

*This book is dedicated to my wonderful wife Kellie who
puts up with dragons,
To my amazing kids John and Briana, who love dragons
as much as I do,
And to all my friends who believed in me.*

ACKNOWLEDGEMENTS

I am deeply indebted to many people throughout this project, not the least of which are my amazing wife and kids who encouraged me and put up with my frequent periods of zoning out in front of my computer. I could not have done this without them.

I am immensely grateful as well to my beta-editor Tracy Nakatani. She read over this work, pointing out anything from typos, to ideas that needed expanding, and also things that just really did not work. She is largely the reason that you have anything remotely worth reading in your hands, and I cannot say enough how much her assistance means. She is also an extremely amazing writer, and I look forward to seeing her worlds published at some point.

Cheers go out to my amazing friend Ruth Calder Murphy for her spectacular crafting of the poem Here There Be Dragons at the beginning of this book. Ruth is an amazing artist, no matter pen, brush, or song, and I am delighted that she was willing to lend her incomparable talents to my work. She also happens to have an inner dragon just like me.

Much thanks to Lindsey Burcar, for the amazing cover art design. Her attention to my story, and her inspiration have made Talindor's Guest stand out remarkably.

And last, but definitely not least, my heartfelt thanks and appreciation goes out to all my friends, fans, coworkers, managers, debt collectors, etcetera, etcetera, who believed in me and kept pushing me to get with the program and finish the darn thing. I did it!

HERE THERE BE DRAGONS

Gentle reader, please beware
- and so proceed with utmost care;
within these cunning pages, here,
are things you might be wise to fear...

For, within your hands, you hold
the bits that slipped into the folds,
uncharted lands and unmapped ground
- the bits where magic can be found.

Here there be (as old maps say
around the edges, shaded grey)
Here are dragons - fierce and bold
as ever ancient stories told.

Here are scales and fiery breath,
talons, treasure, pending death
and dragons who are mainly good
- and therefore, quite misunderstood -

and where the dragons pause and rest,
keep up your guard: it is a test;
for just when things look safe at last,
that's when other stuff slips past:

There's magic, mystery and more,
forming just beyond the door
- waiting for the page to turn -

where even chilling words can burn...

So turn the pages, but with care,
and feel the magic breathing there;
For here there be, undoubtedly,
Dragons:
Read on, if you dare.

~ By Ruth Calder Murphy (Arciemme)

CHAPTER ONE

THE TRAVELER

Flashes of light and chaos erupted in the recesses of his subconscious as he quickly and violently came alert. Quaking chills ravaged his body, slowly tapering off into mild spasms and twitches, and he could feel the drench of sweat on his skin. He blinked several times, begging his eyes to regain some semblance of normal sight. Blurry images flashed before his eyes, and gradually became clearer after a few more blinks.

He found himself staring at a brilliant purple sky adorned with a bright gas-star beating down upon him. To his left the remnants of a fissure rippled out of existence. He squinted at the light, and slowly pushed himself to a sitting position.

A gust of wind blew dust in his face, and he coughed and spat trying to clear his lungs. His long robes, normally smooth, elegant, and the color of the deepest parts of the sea, hung loose and tattered on his person and the color had faded severely. His long raggle-wood staff, bedecked with the shimmer-stones of his order, lay in tact on the ground beside him. Save for a few scratches, it had at least survived the journey. Traveling the void currents always left him in such a mess.

The Traveler touched the staff, uttered some syllables, and his appearance was righted once more. He looked again at the giant star in the sky long enough to get a sense of time. It was final peak, before the decent of the day into darkness. He noticed a large and imposing mountain in the distance. It stuck out like a beacon in the otherwise barren desolation before him, and he resolved to make his way toward it.

He stumbled across the open plain toward the mountain, wind continuing to whip at his hair. He lifted his cowl to shelter his face from the debris being flung by the wind. The sun was beginning to descend behind the mountain, casting a multitude of fantastic colors across the sky as it did so.

The Traveler had dark hair with flecks of white and gold, cropped off at his jaw line, and tanned olive skin. He was a young man in appearance, yet ancient by any standard reckonings of age. He had seen many journeys, and experienced numerous different realities, but he sensed that he may be in danger of coming to the end of his journey.

As he tripped and compensated, he noticed he was walking through what had once been an expansive forest. All that remained was a vast valley of stumps; many of which were charred as if having been set on fire. A hint of pine was carried along a slight breeze through the air as he moved.

When he finally reached the mountain, he noticed a large rectangular door set within the rock. The door was beset with runes along its outer edge fashioned of pure gold, with an inscription in a long forgotten language in the center of the door. Fortunately for the Traveler, he had encountered the language in his travels. The script read simply, "Beware the Winged Beast."

He inspected the rune patterns closely, tracing his finger along the edge of each one to determine their value. As he did so, something in the patterns awakened a sensitivity within him that he had not felt for hundreds of years. He instantly saw the pattern for what it was, and spoke the ancient words carefully in slow humming murmurs.

Closing his eyes, he ran his hand from the bottom left corner of the door, up along its edge until he reached the other side. All the while, the power ignited within him took hold with the ancient words as his hand glazed over the runes. He slowly stepped back and sat down to watch the door.

The golden script came alive as if with fire, and lit the edge of the door. He gazed in wonder at the spectacle, and all of a sudden the door creaked, shuddered, and moaned. It began opening slowly, spraying dust out of the opening. No doubt the effects of having been sealed for ages untold. Numerous smells wafted from the dark cavern beyond the door. The Traveler noticed the familiar smells as that of pine, velum, and pressed papyrus among others.

He got up slowly and walked toward the door. He ran his hand along the inner edge of the door. It was fashioned of a metal that he felt he should know, but could not place at the moment. He turned and stuck his head inside the doorway. The smells were stronger the closer he got, and he also noticed a faint metallic tinge to the air. "Treasure," he thought to himself.

He stepped inside, cautiously taking one step and then another. Once he was well inside he raised his staff, and a spark of light flew up into the center of the room. It grew in intensity, and illuminated his surroundings. What he saw before him took his breath away, and he wondered how such a spectacle existed in such a remote world.

He stood in a grandiose octagonal room that had been carved into the mountain. From the ceiling of the cavern to the bedrock floor was easily twenty fathoms, and the other seven walls in the round were fully adorned with wooden bookcases that stretched all the way from the floor to the dome, except for the center wall opposite the entrance. The bookcases were filled with books too numerable to count, and on the floor itself sat a scattered pile of more books.

Under the books could be seen assortments of various different coins and other treasure. The smell of pine was heavy in the room, which left no doubt that the bookcases had once belonged to the forest. Great cracks had begun forming in the walls, and there were places where the stone had been completely eaten away by the passage of time.

In the center wall, where no bookcase stood, there was gaping hole twice the size of the entry door. It was obvious the hole led somewhere, but the pitch blackness beyond gave no hint of how far it led beyond the room.

He was just contemplating exploring the hole when the door slammed shut. The light winced out as whirled to face the door, his focus obliterated, and he was left in utter darkness. His growing unease, combined with a light, chilly breeze that wafted by him, caused him to shudder. He rushed to the door to open it back up, but the runes on the outside of the door were absent from the inside. He tried various different enchantments, but to no avail.

All of a sudden his prison grew warm, which he knew was not normal, and he had the growing sense that he was being watched. A low rumble followed by the sound of steady breathing filled the room, and he began to turn slowly around. Two large eyes lit the hole in the opposite wall, obviously staring at him, and steam was escaping from the hole as well to dissipate in the air as it rose.

"Ahh, I have a visitor," came a voice. It was a deep, booming, bass toned voice, yet somewhat coarse and gravely. "I do love good company. Especially company that…smells as savory as you do. Come closer…human."

Beads of sweat began to trickle down the Traveler's face, triggered by the rising heat in the room. He stepped forward cautiously, still unable to see anything but the eyes. "Who, or what are you?" He asked as he took the next step.

The voice came again. "I am Talindor, the last of my kind. Who or what are you, human. If indeed you are human."

"I am but a simple Traveler, and I am human, yes. Of a kind anyway. I stumbled upon your keep as I looked for signs of civilization. My apologies for disturbing you."

"A Traveler, hmmm? Well, Traveler, you are now my guest. I have not had a guest in many ages. Those that come do not…er…last for very long. I often wonder if my reputation precedes me."

He stopped in his tracks at the statement. "So, Talindor, I take it that you are not human?"

"Most certainly not," he said with obvious amusement. "Allow me to light the room, so you may gaze on my grandeur."

Seven recessed candles in the walls, which the Traveler had not noticed before, suddenly came alive with fire. The library was lit with a brilliant array, more so even than the Traveler's own illumination spell had done, and born of a magic at least equal in power to his own.

An enormous dragon then crawled out of the hole and perched itself upon the pile of books and treasure in the center of the floor. His coat of scales was a brilliant golden color laid over a richly colored turquoise skin. He stretched his long and impressive wings, fanning the room once, and then folded them against his body. His long forked tail wrapped round and came to rest in front of him, slowly twitching.

Talindor extended his long neck, bringing his great snout within breathing distance of the Traveler, who by this time had stepped slowly back towards the door. He held his staff ready to defend himself if necessary, but thought better of it when the dragon looked at it as though it were a twig to be blown away.

"Oh yes, you shall make a wonderful addition to my collection of bones. Would you like to see it, Traveler? It is just through here inside my lair."

After a short time, the shock wore off, and the Traveler gathered his wits about him. "Though I'm sure your collection is truly a wonder to behold, oh great beast, I'm afraid I cannot stay. I really was only passing through."

"Then you should not have let your curiosity best you, for now you are my captive. I will not let such a delectable meal escape me."

He knew it could never be so easy, but had felt he should give it a try. As the dragon eyed him with a hungry look in his eye, the Traveler gazed around at the multitude of books.

"Ahh, do you like my collection, Traveler?"

"I do indeed, Talindor. Many of these I have read, and many I have only heard of. Still others I am not familiar with."

"I have read each one so much that I cannot read them again. They have become utterly mundane."

"Perhaps you would fancy a new tale? I have traveled many realms, and I am sure that you would be sufficiently amused by the accounts I have to tell."

"Why yes, spin me a tale Traveler. In fact, let us strike a bargain. You will regale me with your stories, and if I am sufficiently pleased you will be free to go. Do we have an accord?"

Knowing full well that the dragon would never let him go he replied with a bow, "It would be my honor, Talindor."

The dragon made a low rumble that sounded quite like a laugh, settled himself down upon his hill of books, and reared his head back in eager expectation.

The Traveler sat down on the cold stone floor, crossed his legs, and began, "Oh great dragon, lend me your ear, and I will take you with me into the empire of Cartissia...."

CHAPTER TWO
THE SUNWIELDER

To chronicle the civilization of Seyn would be no small undertaking. The largest of three major provinces in the Cartissian empire, Seyn was home to the royal seat. The other two provinces, Terrn and Ryst, were home to the minor nobles of Cartissia, and their families. There had been a fourth major province as well, but it was now only spoken of in whispers among the shadows. It was spoken of as the province of the dead.

The throne was held by High Lord Dallan and Lady Renella Aerstwind, who had ruled the land for nearly forty years on current count. Lord Aerstwind ruled his people with a firm but gentle hand, and his people trusted him beyond measure. The people also trusted the power which protected their land, which the royal family held mastery over; the Sun Sapphire.

The Sun Sapphire was a rare gem, so rare in fact that it was thought to be the only one of its kind. If others had existed, they had seemingly vanished from the world. A translucent blue, the Sun Sapphire was said to harness the power of the sun. The limits of its power were not known, not even to Lord Aerstwind, and even he feared its potential. Only a powerful mage could channel its power, and Dallan was indeed powerful.

He was said to have been the lust child of a Sol Shaman and a Rue-Witch who had then abandoned him at birth. He was taken in and raised by a noble couple who were unable to bear children. His mystical powers had made him the ideal candidate for the throne. He always wondered if his son Trant would display a knack for the magic, but so far he had not displayed anything of note.

Young Trant Aerstwind, a boy of sixteen years, was cunning with both words and a sword. He could shape a tale, or an insult, as surely as he could wield a blade. The young prince was eager for battle, and had sparred regularly with his father's man-at-arms, preparing himself for the day when the shadow might fall upon his home.

The shadow had been advancing over the realm of Cartissia for a decade now. Slowly brooding, and moving. Rumors of wars within the realm were plenty, but no hard facts had come to light. Every once in a while a missive would arrive bearing news from a minor province that had been laid waste the prior eve, but details were always few and scattered.

On the first day of the fourth month, word came from the nearby village of Hyrn that hundreds of dark forms were advancing at rapid speeds with what seemed to be the citadel as their destination. The city guardians streamed through the city, sounding the alarms and pressing upon every man, woman, and child to remain barricaded indoors.

When the commotion finally arrived at Trant's door, he quickly suited up in battle gear and donned his blade. He grabbed an apple from the basket on his window table, and flew down the flights of stairs as quickly as he could. He was determined that he would be with his comrades to address the unknown forces. When Trant reached the armory, one of the legion commanders was waiting for him.

"What word commander?"

"Yer grace, we have received another missive. It says the creatures that are advancing on the citadel are shades; beings of the underworld who merge with living flesh!"

"Commander, I know what shades are. I have heard the stories."

"These are more than stories, and these shades are different yer grace. For some reason, the flesh of choice is that of dragons."

It was unclear exactly what to expect once laying eyes on them. One thing was for sure; if shades were involved then there was something at work giving them life.

Lord Aerstwind had already taken ten legions beyond the outer wall to set up formation, and wait for the coming onslaught. If anything were to breach the citadel of Seyn, it would not happen on his watch. As Trant rode out to the battlements, he could hear the sickening screech of things not of the natural world. He knew that the attack had begun. As he drew closer he could see waves upon waves of the creatures in the distance, forming what seemed similar to an enormous black cloud.

As he came within earshot of the camp, the cloud began to dissipate. The creatures were returning to whatever abyss they had come from, and when Trant arrived at the battlefield, he could see why. Virtually nothing was left of the reckoning force of the city. The ground was littered with the carcasses of horses and their riders. Trant dismounted and ran over to a scraggly group of legionnaires who had just barely escaped the wrath of the shades and lived to tell about it.

"What happened here soldier?!"

"My lord, we had no chance whatsoever. The creatures came on us in a torrent. Black, unworldly things they were too. They moved so fast that I could scarce get a good look at them, but it wasn't just them. They had riders too, and the riders looked as deathly as the beasts."

"Thank you soldier. What of my father?"

"I saw him felled my lord, but regretfully I am not sure where his body lies. Everything about this day has left me in a bit of a fog."

At that moment something died inside Trant. He felt a choking of emotion welling up inside him, as if his entrails had been ripped from him. *My father...dead.* When it seemed he would collapse under the weight of his emotion, he realized he needed to be strong for those around him.

"Fair enough soldier. How many remain alive?" Trant asked.

"A battalion at best, my lord, and many wounded among them."

From ten legions to a battalion Trant thought. *How can we possibly stand a chance?*

Trant picked his way through the carnage of the battlefield, and finally saw the spot where his father had been struck down. Something shrouded in blackness left his father's side as he approached. He fell to his father's side quickly, and looked over his wounds. Nothing would save him now. Trant was overcome by waves of emotion as the sobs erupted and tears poured forth.

Lord Aerstwind grabbed hold of Trant's jerkin, pulled him in close, and between blood curdled coughs he said, "The power is in you, son...waiting to be unleashed. You must find a centering point within you. A point at which you can see clearly and all else fades away. Then, and only then, will the magic come. Then...you will be a force unequalled." With those words Trant's father passed him the sun sapphire and breathed his last. A tremor of power coursed through Trant as he laid hold of the gem.

He reached up and closed his father's eyelids, and remained by his side for what seemed like an eternity. Finally, he rose up and strode to his horse. As he slowly mounted the animal, he was mindful of all the day's events, and he knew that plans must be made for the sure return of their enemies.

He made haste for the citadel, riding as hard and as fast as his mount could possibly take. When they reached the citadel, Trant went straight to his mother's chambers.

"Mother!"

"Here son! What news?"

Trant summoned every ounce of strength to be able to tell his mother of the day's events. He sat her down on the bed next to him.

"Mother, I am not sure how to say this, but father has been slain in battle."

Instantly his mother came apart. As he held her in his arms, a realization came to him. He was now the Lord and ruler of Cartissia. He commanded the legions of Seyn. He stayed with his mother for a long while, until finally she rose. Lady Aerstwind smoothed out her dress, wiped her face with a cloth, and retired to her bedchamber. As he watched her go, Trant stood fixed to the spot where he stood, lost in thought. There had to be some way to destroy the hordes of the underworld, but as of yet he had no idea what it was.

He called a special meeting of the warlords that evening. They met in the chamber of Syst, the patron god of war.

"Gentlemen," he began, "as most of you now know, my father is dead. Being his only child and heir to the throne, it is time for me to assume my duties. However, any ceremonial recognition will have to wait. There are more important matters to attend to. The nether-dragons have vanished, but I fear it is not the last we will see of them. We must make plans to fortify our city, and protect our land."

Brynn, man-at-arms to the throne and longtime friend to Lord Dallan and his family, spoke thoughtfully. "How shall we defeat something not of this world my lord?

Shades are near impossible to defeat. I myself know none who have tried to and survived."

"My father spoke of a power in me, Brynn. Now I do not as yet understand it, or even believe it necessarily, but I trust my father's word." The words sent a shudder through Trant even as he spoke them.

"Your father was a powerful man, my lord. A powerful mage at that. Everyone feared his power, though the love and trust they had for him outweighed the fear. As for you though, you best not trifle with powers you know nothing of."

Mindful of the truth of Brynn's words, Trant replied, "I share your concerns, Brynn, though I am not sure what options are available to us. What of the Rue-Witches of Ryst? What do you know of them?"

Brynn paused, studying Trant to discern whether he was serious. When it seemed that he was, Brynn lost his words. His color changed, as if all the blood had drained from his face. "My lord, surely you are not serious! Rue-Witches are unpredictable, and extremely dangerous. No one knows the limits of their power, and they are loyal to no one; at least not to mortals. They put up with the royal seat more than anything. Their power is said to feed on the aura of those who have passed to the next life. Some sort of strange necromancy."

"I have heard rumors of my father's begetting Brynn, and they must be more than rumors for my father to have had powers beyond that of the standard mage. Is it true that he was born of a Rue-Witch?" As he spoke the words, Trant leaned forward to gaze intently into the eyes of his friend. He would have the truth of it one way or another.

One of the other warlords, one of advanced age by the name of Tenn, spoke up. "Lord Trant, though he was not proud of it, your father knew the truth of it. He shared it when he first came to power, for those of us who remember it. He had been studying the census reports of Cartissia and happened on information that led him to the eventual discovery. He would tell you the rumors were true; may he rest in peace."

"Do the witches know of my lineage?" Trant asked.

Tenn replied with a wary look in his eye, "It is doubtful my lord. Nor would it matter. They would not pay heed to you if you were their own child, let alone the child of one of their sisters. They bed out of wanton lust, and any children sired are seen as an unfortunate side effect."

"To what good fortune do I owe having such wonderful creatures in my kingdom?" Trant replied with a heavy air of cynicism.

The warlords all let out a mighty bellow of laughter at that. They needed a good laugh after all that had transpired that day. Night was falling, and their meeting had not accomplished anything of significance. A great fatigue settled over Trant, and he decided it was time to call it a day.

Drawing everything to a close Trant said, "Gentlemen, the day has been long and I am spent. I will speak no more of the witches of Ryst for now. I want a count of our remaining forces delivered to me on the morrow, once I have broken my fast. I fear we will need every man we have left. Also, summon the mages from Terrn, and together with our own mages we may stand a chance of victory this time."

Trant bid the warlords farewell, and exited the chamber. He passed through the armory to a door that led up the spiral stairwell of one of the citadels many turrets. As he reached the top he went to the lookout and stood, gazing at the star studded canopy above him. If only his legions could number as the stars of the sky. Then their chances would be greater, he thought.

He looked down into the courtyard, and as he did so he was suddenly aware of something strange. A presence that had no business being there. The courtyard was very well lit, and he could not see anything unusual. He decided it was his exhaustion getting to him, and he quickly descended the turret. He collapsed on his bed, garments and all, and was instantly asleep.

Dreams came fitfully that night, filled with the dragon-shades of the day. After only a few hours of sleep, Trant woke with start. He was drenched in sweat from the intensity of the dreams he had grappled with that night. He sat up on his bed besieged with thought. He considered the shades again. The dragons had riders. Had the shadow advanced so slowly for a time to gather corpses for their army? Perhaps the Shade riders were some of his own people. How could he destroy them with that knowledge? He reasoned with himself that they were not the people they once were. This must come to an end.

He descended the stair, and entered the feast hall. He would break his fast alone this day. The kitchen-master brought him a bowl of porridge and a serving of maple sap bread, along with a side of peach mead to wash it down. Thankful for the refreshment, he greeted the kitchen-master warmly, and chatted with him between bites. Finishing quickly, Trant rose and went once again to the chamber of Syst.

The warlords were assembled and waiting eagerly for him. The only one absent was Brynn, but he entered shortly after Trant. Their countenances told a tale of dismay. It seems their resources were slim.

"What do you have for me my friends?" Trant asked.

Tenn was the one who spoke. "My lord, we have barely 20 legions of troops left. Some of those must defend the citadel if our main defense should fail. The Archmage of Terrn has dispatched two of his conclaves to our aid, but even he is wary of our success. He suggested that we summon a host of the snow-dragons of Marth. That may be to our advantage, but the dragons are wild, and may not care that we are perishing. What would you have us do my lord?

Trant thought for a long while. He pondered what his father would do. He knew that answer. "We must do everything we possibly can. We must stand our ground! Tenn, summon the snow-dragons. If they will heed, so be it! If not, so be it! We will stand with or without them. Leave five legions to guard the citadel. The other fifteen will go with us to defend the wall. My father died with ten, we will live with what we can."

The warlords rose with Trant, each clasping their right fist to their left guard plate, and nodding in respect for their King. Whether they lived or died, he was the man they would follow as proudly as they had his father.

Trant immediately went to his mother. She had been holed up in her chamber for days, only rising to eat and drink meagerly. She was sitting in her solar when Trant bid to enter, staring stoically down into the gardens. She gazed at him expressionless, but Trant knew that her longing gaze held one unspoken request. *Make them regret the death of your father!* She kissed him gently on the forehead and wished him good fortune in battle, and then turned her gaze back to the garden. He wondered if she would ever be herself again.

He made haste to the main stable, which set just adjacent to the main armory. The foot soldiers were gearing up for battle, and the horsemen were preparing their steeds. Some were sharpening swords and spears, while others were preparing their bows and quivers. Pots of ash had been prepared, ready to be set aflame for the igniting of arrows. The men-at-arms were barking orders and testing the preparations. All seemed to be as planned, yet there was a heavy weight among the armies. They knew they would not return with as many as they went out with.

As the late morning sun approached its zenith, the trumpets of the guard towers sounded forth the sickening song of doom. The shade army had appeared on the horizon, and the time for battle had come.

Trant mounted his steed and crested a four-foot mound in the courtyard. He summoned his army to audience, and a hush fell over the crowd. "I am Trant Aerstwind," he began, "son of High Lord Dallan Aerstwind now fallen, and heir to the throne of Cartissia. Today we seek to rid Cartissia of the stench of Shades, both dragon and rider! Many of you will not return, but the cause you live, or die for, is the protection of our people! Your wives…your children…your elderly, they will live to see another day when we win this battle! Follow me as you did my father, and Cartissia will not fall under an eternal shadow!"

As his words ended, a roar went up from the crowd that could scarcely be equaled. Swords clanged against shields, horses reared and squealed, and helms were banged together in a ruckus that could have reverberated across the empire. This day would be a day of liberation.

Trant turned facing the great wall, lifted his sword in the air, and cried out "to war!!"

The armies of Seyn charged toward the battlefield like a great carpet being rolled out for the procession of a king. As they reached the wall, the great iron gates were fanned out to allow their passage. Once the entire army had passed through, the gates were pulled shut and barred in place as a precaution against possible defeat of the protectoral force.

Trant drew his forces to a stop once they had travelled a league from the great wall. He directed them into battle formations to prepare for the onslaught. Two legions of foot soldiers in the front prepared to march, with yet another legion behind for a second offensive. Five legions comprised mounted spearmen, another five mounted archers. Flanking the sides were the two legions of warrior class carrying massive war hammers. The forces were at the ready. They would hold their ground, and await the arrival of the dark forces. They would not wait long however.

The first wave of shades came on them like a swarm of locusts. The first legion on foot fell within a matter of minutes, charred beyond recognition by the abysmal flames of Shade-Dragons.

As Trant and Brynn fought side by side against a legion of human shades, Brynn was worried. "My lord, were we not supposed to receive aid from Terrn? What of the conclaves promised us?"

Trant nodded without answer, but was silent and focused as he felled warrior after warrior, not knowing how. It was as if the power his father spoke of was fueling and empowering him. Perhaps it emanated from him as well, for there were those close to him who pressed on with success as well.

All of a sudden the sky was littered with great eagles from Terrn, swooping down with great speed. Upon their backs rode powerful mystical warriors in long flowing robes, who could only be the mages of Terrn.

From the east came two dozen great white beasts, with wings that fanned the winds of the heavens. The Snow Dragons of Marth!

The Dragons descended, spewing flames the like of which none in Cartissia had ever seen in the present age. The flames were as blue as the oceans of Trinia, the small harbor town to the south. The flames must have had arcane properties, for all shades that came in contact with the flames were instantly turned to ash.

One of the Dragons landed in a clearing before the armies of Seyn. "Who is Lord Aerstwind?"

Mounted on his steed once again, Trant strode forth. "I am Lord Trant Aerstwind, my father Dallan was felled in the first battle against these creatures. What are you called?"

The Dragon spoke mightily, "I am Voth, ruler of Marth. I received your summons, and we arrived when we could. I must warn you, do not mistake this token of our help as an alliance. We do not ally ourselves with the likes of men, but we also will not suffer Cartissia to burn. Do we have an understanding?"

"It is understood, Lord Voth," Trant said. "You have my respect. Let us go now, and finish this battle."

With a curt bow, Voth rose to join his warriors.

The mages of Terrn had joined the fray and were pummeling the shades with blankets of white hot light, brighter than the light of day. As the battle drew on however, one whole conclave of mages had already fallen.

The sky was growing black, the color of smoke, as flames faced off against flames. Numerous shade dragons had fallen with their riders, though a dozen of the Snow Dragons had also fallen.

Half of the warrior class of Seyn were all that was left of the army's legions, save for an assortment of scattered battalions who had managed to escape with only minor wounds. Brynn was the only man-at-arms left standing.

When the afternoon sun was blaring, the battle had ended. The battlefield was colored a deep crimson. The bodies of mages, snow-dragons, and shades as well lay scattered upon the blood soaked soil. Those of the aiding forces lucky enough to have lived, fifty mages and only five Snow Dragons to be exact, bid their leave and returned whence they came.

Trant stood on the open plain amidst the carnage of battle. The beasts that had ravaged his comrades had dispersed as if vanishing into thin air. Perhaps they did. He could not make sense of anything right now. He could still see their ghastly forms, as if they were made of the nightmares that plagued little children.

They soared in upon their prey with wings that would span a quarter mile, spewing fire and wanton destruction from the bowels of their throat. When they walked, if one could call it walking, they walked on two legs. The speed at which they progressed was too fast to really tell. Their lizard heads were serpentine in appearance, like that of a great emperor cobra. Their upper torso, chest, and arms were littered with bony spikes jutting out from the flesh that instantly impaled any who got too close.

That was how many of the mighty warriors of Cartissia had died that day. The rest had their hearts or throats ripped from their bodies with inhuman precision, or turned to heaps of burning flesh at contact with their flames. Snow dragons had been blasted from the sky, engulfed in black flame. As if it were not enough, the creatures then began to feed on their prey.

As he stood surveying the devastation, Trant thought back to the last words of his father. The words he heard his father utter as he lay dying on the battlefield in much the same way as those that littered the ground now. He could hear the words echo in his mind. *The power is in you, son...waiting to be unleashed. You must find a centering point within you. A point at which you can see clearly and all else fades away. Then, and only then, will the magic come. Then...you will be a force unequalled.* All of a sudden something else brought him back to reality. He was in the presence of.... Something. Something eerily familiar.

He now stood frozen, as if time was standing still, and there was only this moment. Perhaps this was true. Perhaps this creature could do even that. Trant noticed it when all the beasts had taken their leave. One solitary figure; dark and abysmal. He had seen this creature before of course. The day his father had died this *thing* caught his eye as it left the remains of his father to die.

Trant's gaze was fixed upon the creature. Dark flowing robes that seemed to swirl viciously around. It moved lightly on air, no lower appendages to be seen. The being was incorporeal save for its garb and the dark sackcloth gloves which gave the appearance that it had hands. Trant knew the tales. The Demon Sorcerer of Pelle, province of the dead.

The appearance, freakish as it was, was not what disturbed Trant the most. Within the darkness of its cowl something stared back at him. The reason he was so transfixed, was that he knew the face that stared back at him, eyes boring into his mind.

The face...

Was his own.

This thing...was a face-changer. Perhaps this was how it controls people. Was this how it gained its power? Did it make people believe they were looking at themselves, and then they would do whatever it wanted? Perhaps the face-changer's hypnotic gaze served as a hex.

Trant thought of his father, slowly drowning in his own blood. He willed himself to press on, to resist, to...unleash his power.

Nothing happened.

The voice came, not so much audible as internal. A voice reverberating in the confines of his soul. "We are the same...you are me...I am you...there is no difference. I have destroyed...you have destroyed. We are one. Destroy yourself, and you destroy us."

Was this his father's fate? Did his father look into the sorcerer's cowl, and see his own face lurking there as well? Still Trant resisted with every fiber of his being. Then the face upon which he was transfixed changed. No longer his own face, it was the face of his father. Drained of blood as it were. His face scarred, his lips blue, a deathly white in his eyes. His father's eyes pierced his own, and the specter began again. "You are done for my son. End it now before a worse fate befalls the remainder of our people."

Suddenly Trant came to his senses. This was not his father. His father would never allow such cowardice. Not even at the end of his life."

A profound clarity came over Trant. This demon thrives on sight; the window to the soul. Its faces require such a connection.

Trant dug deep within himself burying everything that he was, every deep emotion, every ounce of his humanity. As he became another self, his resistance was complete. The young man who now faced this sorcerer was faceless, an impenetrable mask having formed from the deep magic that he unleashed within himself.

He now stood on equal footing with his enemy. Though the specter could not gaze into Trant's eyes, Trant gazed long into the cowl and found nothing but darkness within. He had found his power. The centering point was the clarity of his enemy's weakness, and it had given him the upper hand. The creature no longer had control over him.

The sun was his power and his body the channel. Trant raised his hands over his head facing out, his thumbs touching and his index fingers touching to form a triangular shape. The clasp of his belt was fixed with the Sun Sapphire, which began to glow white and suddenly appeared as though there were flames writhing within it. Where the creature once gazed into Trant's eyes, only deep red flames could be found as the power of the sun began to possess its summoner.

Ecstatic shrieks escaped from somewhere in the abyss of the sorcerer's being as it realized the peril of the moment. The sky went dark as the creature chanted in guttural tones trying to regain control of the young summoner. An immensity of solar energy burst through the triangular orifice Trant had created and careened into the Demon Sorcerer with a raging force.

The thing was prepared, but not completely. The force of the burning light enveloped it to the point that it should surely have vaporized, however it only served as a deep wound. The thing came back with a vengeance. From within the folds of its sleeves came blasts of dark energy which encircled the young man, threatening to choke the life out of him. The cords of darkness wrapped him like chains, pinning him to the ground and tearing at his flesh. A deafening cackle of satisfaction echoed from within the specter's being as victory was apparent.

From within the sapphire came a force of energy that completely eradicated the chords of darkness, and as they dissipated Trant raised his hands again crying out with the sound of hundreds of voices "Solaiav Vix!" This time, as if a thousand suns had come to his aid, there came a flare of power which even he could not bear. It surged through the orifice, dragging him with it, and pierced the core of the sorcerer. Thousands of wailing screams could be heard, as though souls trapped by the face-changer for countless years were suddenly released. The blackness of the creature's robes became a crimson light as they burst into flames and vaporized into nothing. The sorcerer had met its match, and was no more.

Trant's seemingly lifeless body lay in the dirt for hours. Upon the fourth hour following the ordeal, he woke in a fit of screams. A soft rain began to fall, slowly rinsing the dirt from his now almost naked body. He tried to stand, but failing to do so he began to crawl. In the near distance he noticed a horse standing by its fallen rider. Gasping in breath after breath, he desperately crawled toward the horse. When he finally reached it, he pulled himself up into the saddle in excruciating pain, and gently prodded the horse into a trot.

They arrived at the castle gates hours after sunset. The guards rushed him to the healers. The soft rain had now become a torrent, as if symbolic of the events of the day.

Trant woke the next morning in his Mother's arms, her tears streaming down onto his bedclothes. They made gentle small talk for a while, and then she left him to rest. He tuned his head to the window. The sun was streaming through it, as a light breeze was unsettling the curtains. "The sun," he thought to himself, "the sun was my power, and with it the darkness has vanished." The thought brought him comfort. His losses were many, and yet hope was still shining.

~

As the Traveler finished recounting the tale, he stole a look at the dragon who was staring at him, casually licking his chops and salivating as he did so. When the dragon saw the Traveler staring back, he stopped and nodded his direction.

"Oh yes, that was a delightful story. I especially liked the part about the carnage after the big battle. So much to…clean up. You are such a brilliant storyteller, you simply must stay and tell me more."

"What of the agreement we struck?"

"I will decide when I have been sufficiently entertained, Traveler. Now, do go on."

"Very well. The next I shall tell you is of a remarkable young man I encountered in my travels."

CHAPTER THREE
A RELUCTANT ALCHEMIST

Maak had discovered his ability when he was ten years old. He was playing chance sticks with his friends when he tossed the winning play. What happened next came so fast he didn't have time to think. His friend Dolen, who was a rather sore loser, jumped him and tried to drive him to the ground.

Trying to brace his fall, he touched his left hand to the ground and grabbed Dolen's shoulder with his right. Instantly the young boy crumbled into granules of dirt and became one with the ground.

Screams of horror erupted among his little group, and they started running away. All of them that is except a young man named Anruk, who just stood there staring at the ground in utter shock.

Panic coursed through Maak and propelled him into a run as well. He ran and ran for what seemed like hours until the initial horror subsided, and he passed out along the service road close to the market.

Half of an hour passed, and a local textile merchant came down the road on his way to set up shop for the day. When he saw Maak collapsed on the ground he pulled his horse up close and dismounted. He knelt beside the boy and placed the back of his hand on his cheek. Maak's skin was cool and sweaty to the touch, and his body twitched slightly every few seconds.

The man knew the signs of fainting when he saw them. Something had traumatized the boy laying in the road, and someone was most certainly worried about him by now too. He grabbed a cloth from the saddlebag, doused it with water from his water skin, and began to dab it gently on Maak's face.

After a few seconds Maak shot up, and when he caught sight of the man in front of him he scooted away frantically shouting "Stay away from me!"

"What is it lad?" The man said.

"I'm dangerous! Don't touch me! Who are you?!" Maak babbled nervously.

"My name is Berdok. I sell fabric at the market down the road."

"I'm…uh…Maak. I live in Day Haven."

It was clear to Berdok that young Maak was terrified of something. He wondered if it would be wise to probe further, but he couldn't contain his curiosity.

"What troubles you, young man?" He asked.

"I hurt someone," he began to sob. "A close friend of mine. He turned…I just turned him to…he," was the last thing he said before breaking into uncontrollable tears.

"I will take you to your home," Berdok said.

As they made their way along the traveler's road toward Day Haven, Maak kept withdrawn from his companion.

Berdok was a well-built man of medium height. Though only slightly grey, his worn features set him at least three times as many years old as Maak. He wore a long velvet robe, which he had likely made himself, and a matching cap. His hands and his feet were enhanced with jewelry, some of which jingled when he walked.

Berdok chanced the occasional look back at Maak. The boy walked cautiously a few steps behind him, with his arms wrapped tightly across his chest, and his eyes focused intently on the ground. It seemed like he was in another world.

They reached Day Haven at peak light, and Maak took the lead. He walked notably faster, and Berdok watched him look from side to side obsessively as if hoping he wouldn't be seen.

As they neared his home, however, it became obvious that keeping a low profile would not be possible. An angry mob of townspeople surrounded the modest little house he called home, and when Maak came into view the mob rushed him.

"Don't let him touch you!" Someone screamed.

From out of the crowd came a young man about Maak's age. He was short and stalky, and had wiry red hair. When Maak saw him, and heard the words come out of his mouth, his heart sank. It was Anruk, one of his closest friends. Anruk had been playing with them when Dolen turned to dirt.

Anruk parted the crowd and walked slowly up to Maak, looking him up and down as if he didn't recognize him. He stopped a few feet in front of Maak and just stared. After a couple of minutes, he looked ready to speak.

"Maak, what did you do? Dolen is gone! He just…turned to dust! What have you done?!"

Maak began yelling, "I never meant to hurt him Anruk! I don't even know exactly what I did, or how I did it!" He collapsed on the ground and began wailing.

Anruk took a couple of steps back, and spoke again. "You need to leave Maak. You need to leave and never return. I want to understand my friend, I do. But…I'm afraid of you. So is everyone here."

The crowd had quieted down and began backing off. Maak's father pushed through the crowd and ran toward him and embraced him. "Everything will be ok son," he said. He pulled Maak off the ground and they walked toward the house.

As they closed the door the Law-bringers arrived, and just in time as the mob began to go hysterical. They began beating at the door of the house, screaming for justice.

Berdok kept his distance from all the commotion, but watched with great interest. He pulled some dried meat from the saddlebag and sat in the dirt against the wall of a stable nearby. He knew there would likely be a long wait, but it would be worth it. He had seen this sort of thing before.

It was well into the night before the crowds came under control. The law-bringers had directed them to go to their homes to await further news. The parents of the young boy Dolen had been called in for questioning, as had Maak's parents. Maak was no doubt confined to his house.

Berdok tied up his horse and approached the house. He knocked gently but firmly on the door, and Maak's voice came softly afterward. "Who is it?"

"It is Berdok. Please, Maak, open the door. I can help you," he said.

"You know nothing about my situation!" Maak said forcefully.

Berdok grinned in amusement, "Actually, that is where you are wrong Maak. I know a great deal about your situation. I have seen your abilities before, and I know someone who can help you."

The door slowly opened a crack, and then a little more and a little more, until Maak's tear reddened face stared out at him.

"There is someone you need to meet with."

"Is he a friend of yours?"

"More like a friendly acquaintance, but I know he won't turn you away. You will be an outcast here, you know. Do yourself a favor and leave tonight. Say goodbye to your family, and leave quickly."

"I can't just leave, people will know."

"Your family will protect you, you must believe that. Pack light, and travel under night to the market. I will meet you there in the morning."

"Where will I be going?"

"Gerrenholde."

Maak sensed trouble the minute he heard the name. Gerrenholde was the city of smiths and bankers; the wealthy elite of the realm. Commerce was all they valued. What good could come of going there?

"Thank you Berdok, but I will stay here."

"Don't be a fool Maak! If you stay here, you cannot guarantee your safety. Go to Gerrenholde. I promise you, no harm will come to you if you go there with me."

"What good will it do me to go to a city such as Gerrenholde? Who are you taking me to?"

"It is not best to speak of him here Maak. He is not well liked, as are many who dabble in the areas of commerce that he is involved in. I will explain to you as we journey there. Now, no more questions. Will you go with me?"

"Ok, I'll go with you." Maak was too scared to stay behind, not knowing what his fate would be in Day Haven.

When Maak's parents arrived home from the interrogation, the pain of the day's events was written on their faces. They sat him down to explain to him the judgment of the Law-bringers. It had been decided that Maak would be banished from Day Haven for life. He would never be allowed contact with anyone in the town except his parents, and even then only if they went to him. Also, if word came of any more trouble in the realm that resembled what had happened that day, there would be no choice for the Law-bringers but to go public with his name and what he had done.

His parents had also decided to leave Day Haven. The shame would be too much for them. Maak's father was on the high council, and his mother was an herbalist. The day's events would serve to ruin their reputation.

Though he felt horrible about the impact on his parents, the news came as a relief to Maak, as he had already planned to leave with Berdok. He knew that he would have to either subdue his abilities, or learn to control them. He made up his mind from that point on that he would subdue them, because he did not know how he would learn control.

He gathered his shirts and underclothing into a shoulder sack, and spent the next few hours sharing memories with his parents and crying with them about the separation. They told him that they would not be leaving for several months yet, and that he should send word immediately once he settled in Gerrenholde. They assured him they would visit often. They also stressed that he should watch his back. Apparently Dolen's father had sworn vengeance for the death of his son.

When night fell he grabbed his shoulder sack, and a bag of dried fruits, nuts, berries, and dried meat that his mother had put together for him. He also took what little money he had and secured it in his pouch to buy food along the way. He said his final goodbyes to his parents and snuck out the back entrance to the house.

He made his way down the traveler's road, being careful to move through the high thick bushes on the sides of the road so that he would not be seen.

The trek took longer than anticipated, and the sun was already peaking over the mountains by the time he reached the Marketplace. Maak spotted Berdok, who was looking around anxiously for him.

"What took you so long, lad?"

"It was further than I planned, and it was hard leaving home."

"We must leave immediately."

Berdok had secured a young horse for Maak that was a fitting size for him. There was also a saddlebag for the horse that contained extra food and oats.

Maak mounted the horse and followed Berdok as they set off to a slow trot. The new morning sky was crisp and clear. The scents of fruits, and tarts, and mild perfumes wafted lightly in the brisk breeze. As they rode, Maak began to feel impatient about what lay ahead of him.

"So, are you going to tell me more about your friend?" Maak asked.

Berdok was silent for a few minutes before answering with his own question. "Are you familiar with the word *transmutation* Maak?"

"Not really, no. I may have heard someone say it."

"It refers to the act of changing something from its essential material form to a completely different form. For instance, a person may change a piece of metal into a diamond. To do this, you must be able to alter the essential elements of something."

Maak sat dumbfounded in the saddle as the horse trot bounced him up and down gently.

"I can tell by the look on your face that you have had a realization, Maak." Berdok said as an amused laugh broke his lips.

Maak just nodded, but as he was still in shock, he said nothing.

Berdok started to say something and then suddenly pulled up short.

"What is it?" Maak asked, but Berdok simply put two fingers to his lips and gently guided them off the road and behind a hedge of high bushes.

Two men walked by dressed in dark apparel. Their garments were of one piece, tightly wound around their body. A separate binding was wrapped around their heads, with the eyes only vaguely visible through a small gap in the wrapping. They each had a Zitar at their side. A deadly double bladed sword with a two hand grip separating the opposing blades.

Berdok knelt close to Maak and whispered, "The Shadow. They are mercenaries for hire, and not for a small sum either. Your friend…, is his family wealthy?"

"Sort of I guess, although Dolen never showed it."

"It is too convenient that they are on the same road we are. They're no doubt looking for you. Who hired them is the question. They specialize in stealth, and they can appear and disappear at will, so they are extremely dangerous. The fact that they are out in the open says that they probably don't know they are so close to us."

They watched for a few moments as the mercenaries slowly meandered along the road looking at the prints left by the horses' hooves. One looked at the other and shook his head, and then they were gone.

Berdok sat down and continued, "So, as I was saying. There are those who will pay handsomely for the services of someone with your abilities. However, that particular kind of commerce is frowned upon, because it tends to attract the more malicious segment of the population. Now, we must move on. Gerrenholde is an easier place to blend in, but if those…things find us here, you are as good as dead."

They got back on their horses and rode for a few more miles in silence. Berdok wanted to make sure all of this information sank in for Maak.

"So…the man you are taking me to…, he's what exactly?" Maak asked, finally speaking after a lengthy silence.

"He makes a profit off of those who perform transmutation. Most people call them Alchemists, and he recruits them to service his clients' needs."

"What kinds of things do his clients require?"

"Anything can be changed given the right circumstances and the right amount of mental effort, or that is how I understand it anyway. I am not an Alchemist myself. I understand that some of his clients sell weapons of war, and need people to create them and fortify them. Others simply want their coin to be multiplied on short notice, and want people who can create coins from something else."

They rode for another hour before pulling off the road by a small stream for the horses to drink. Maak stared out across the open fields of hay while the horses watered themselves. He could not believe everything he had heard, and was rather unhappy with himself for agreeing to go with Berdok.

Dusk was approaching fast, and Berdok signaled that they should begin again. Maak had never made the journey to Gerrenholde before, and wondered to himself how much longer they might be traveling. He pulled out a strip of dried salt pork and started to nibble on it. He must've not eaten in a while, for the more he ate the hungrier he got.

Unable to contain his impatience, he blurted out "How much longer will it take us to get there Berdok? I am getting very tired."

"Another day I believe, although it has been almost a year since I have had to travel to Gerrenholde. One loses a sense of timing for the trip after a while."

The groan that escaped Maak's lips must've done the trick. Berdok reined in his horse, and signaled to Maak to do the same.

"Forgive me, I am not used to traveling with children. I forget how quickly you expend your energy. We will camp over there for the night."

He pointed to a meadow a short walk from the road that was overgrown with willow trees, which made it perfect to conceal them while they slept.

By the time they fed the horses some oats and laid out their bedrolls, night was already on them. They both retired immediately, though Maak lay awake for a while staring into the star lit canopy above them. *Who am I?* He thought to himself. *What kind of monster turns people to dust?* He was beside himself with confusion, and even sleep seemed to fear him. Somewhere in the turmoil of his mind, sleep finally seeped in.

He woke to a firm pat on the shoulder from Berdok. "It's time for us to be on our way Maak. Gather your things up quickly. We have a long journey yet."

Maak was barely awake, and still sore from the previous day, when they started back on the trail. They still stuck to the deep ruts in the sides of the road for concealment, fearing that they might encounter the masked men again.

The journey was long and arduous, and the day was unusually hot. Maak found himself constantly gorging water. He kept looking to the sun to get some sense of the time, and wondered when they would stop to eat and rest.

After about four hours they pulled just off the path and sat under a pomegranate tree to eat and cool off. Maak was enormously grateful for the break, as was his buttocks.

They feasted on fresh pomegranates from the tree, and some of the dried pork from their stores.

"We will need to find a spring to replenish our water," Berdok noted.

"Is there one anywhere close?" Maak asked.

"There are several as we approach Gerrenholde. We must hope our supply will last until then."

"How much longer would you say we have?"

"Well, the terrain is beginning to look more familiar. I would say six to eight hours at most."

That was a bittersweet answer to Maak. He was glad it was not longer, but frustrated that it was still as long as it was.

They mounted their horses and started off again. A slight breeze had picked up that took the edge off the heat, and Maak's mood livened a bit at that. He closed his eyes and let the soft wind glide across his face, and somewhere in the experience he leaned forward on his horse to sleep in the mane.

They arrived in Gerrenholde as the twilight of evening was approaching. Berdok had taken the liberty of stopping to refill their water supply just outside the city. After securing the horses, he roused Maak. "Wake up lad, we are here."

Maak casually rubbed his eyes and looked around. Gerrenholde was a sprawling city bustling with trade and excited activity. Anyone seeking to make a name for themselves started here, and many only started. The slums were reserved for those who failed.

The first street they came to was Bathe street, and Berdok and Maak took it eastbound toward the city center. The Central hub reminded Maak of an amphitheater, or a giant funnel. All the smithies and finance guilds were arranged side by side in a massive circle that dropped in tiers down to a central gathering point.

They approached a large stone building on the northwest curve of the circle. It had had a large oak door set inside an alcove, and there was a sign above the entryway that simply read "Master Alchemist."

Berdok knocked firmly on the door, and they heard a voice from inside say, "Come!"

Upon entering, Maak thought to himself how quaint the building was. From floor to ceiling on each wall were shelves filled with bottles. The bottles contained all manner of powders, potions, and other liquids. All were simply labeled, and some were dusty while others were not. In front of the far wall there was an ornate desk that looked as if it had been chiseled out of a single mound of rock. There were no windows, and the lighting, though brilliant, didn't seem to have an exact source.

There was a man standing behind the desk, hunched over a few miscellaneous bottles and making notes so vigorously that it seemed his quill should break. He was dressed simply in a long sleeved, collarless shirt that cuffed his neck. The only other garment visible was his long, and extremely thick leather apron that hung down from his neck and cinched around the waist.

Curiosity had not got the best of him, as he had not looked up to see who had paid him a visit. All he said was, "Can I help you?"

"Callister, it has been too long." Berdok said.

The man who had formerly been rather disinterested in them, suddenly dropped everything and looked up from his work. His expressionless face completely changed demeanor. "Berdok?! Berdok, my friend!" He hurried around the desk and came quickly to stand before us. "To what do I owe this long overdue pleasure."

"Callister, I have brought this lad here all the way from Day Haven to meet you. He is a, shall we say, very unique young man."

Callister eyed Maak with a patronizing grin, and then extended his hand. "Callister Stinne is my name, young master. Who would you be now?"

The name sounded somewhat familiar, but Maak couldn't place it. He quickly shook the man's hand and answered, "Maak Calfrey, sir."

"A pleasure," he said, and turned back to Berdok. "So, unique you say? How so?"

Berdok produced a gold galleon from one pocket and a smooth penny stone from another. He gave Maak the galleon saying, "Ok Maak, hold this stone open in your other hand."

Nervously Maak obeyed, and as he did so the stone was instantly transformed into the same material as the coin. Maak was holding a stone sized chunk of gold.

Callister was gawking at Maak by that time, and when he became aware that he was making Maak nervous he looked back at the stone. It wasn't long before he looked at Maak again though.

"Young man, when did you first learn about this gift of yours?" Callister asked.

Maak was obviously at a loss for words, so Berdok answered for him. "Maak paid a terrible price for the learning, Callister. A few days ago, a comrade of his was transformed to dirt in the middle of a scuffle between them. He is very confused, and scared as well. I thought perhaps he could apprentice under you to get control of his ability, and hopefully be more comfortable with it."

Callister turned to Maak. "How do you feel about that Maak?"

Maak was not sure how to reply. "What is it that you do Mr. Stinne? Berdok told me earlier that you are not well liked by many."

"He did, did he?" Callister turned an upraised eyebrow and smirk toward Berdok. "Yes it is true, there are many who do not like me. I balance the scales, so to speak. I am an Alchemist, Maak. I can do the very same thing that you just did, and more."

An Alchemist, Maak thought. "You said you balance the scales. What do you mean?"

Callister laughed buoyantly. "My services are available to whoever wants them Maak. Whoever can pay the even price, and there is always a price. Some of my clients are wealthy, and want more wealth. Some are poor, and want to be rich. They will be in debt to me for most of their natural lives. There are still others who want other….eh…. less honorable options. I turn no one away Maak. Our powers put us in very high demand."

"I don't want to be part of anything dishonorable," Maak said, eyes fixed firmly on the ground.

"You are free to choose your path Maak. I will simply guide you toward a more comfortable use of your gifts."

Maak nodded wordlessly, still staring at the ground.

"Very good, it is settled then. I have an apartment in the upper level of my establishment here that I have never used. I sleep in a hidden alcove behind the wall as a safety measure."

"One more thing Callister," Berdok said. "We encountered the Shadow on the road. I think someone hired them to hunt down Maak."

"Very well, I'll stay alert," Callister said.

Maak took his things to the apartment, and then came down to say farewell to Berdok. He was less than happy to see him go. In the short time he had known Berdok, he was now comfortable in his company. Something about Berdok made him feel safe, and he wasn't sure about being around another complete stranger. He also feared for Berdok's safety on the return.

They stepped outside together, and Berdok clapped Maak firmly on the shoulder. "Callister really is a good fellow Maak, a little rough around the edges, but good. He will train you well. Just never forget who you are Maak. Just because you learn from him, does not mean you have to emulate him." Maak nodded, and waved as Berdok left.

Maak progressed quickly the first few months. Most of his time was spent learning different mixtures for making various materials. Callister was sufficiently impressed, and began helping Maak learn to focus his Alchemy and even suppress it when necessary. This was the biggest challenge for Maak. Fear inhibited his self-control. He did not want to harm someone else.

As the years passed, Maak got to know the types of clientele that Callister catered to. Some were beggars from the slums who had once been prominent, and wanted that chance again. All they needed was a little coin to get them by. Others were the corrupt of the banking guild, wagering their customers money against a fee for obtaining more.

Every year, Maak was also party to a gathering of other Alchemists from all over. Most of them had been trained by Callister, though there were a few that had made his acquaintance in other ways. It seemed they were all as morally ambiguous as he was, and Maak did not really care for any of them. Callister was always very proud to announce the progress that Maak had made in harnessing the power.

From time to time Maak would see what happened when patrons could not pay their debt. Trivial situations would result in reverse Alchemy, which would seek out the remaining money and return it to its original state. Callister happily taught Maak the incantation for it. Other situations would result in the transmutation of a finger or a limb into gold in order to pay for the debt.

Maak grew increasingly tired of being present for things like that. He hoped that his apprenticeship would soon be done. Callister was much different than at the beginning. It seemed that the last few years he had gotten especially greedy, and also more barbaric.

Everything changed one day, when a patron came to beg more time from Callister. She was only a few years older than Maak, but very attractive in a simple way. She had come about three weeks back needing money to buy an herbal tincture for her ailing mother. She was certain that once her mother was well, she would be able to work to earn enough to pay the fee. She had brought several penny stones for conversion.

She had returned, because her mother had not recovered, but instead become worse. What little compassion Callister toyed with when Maak first knew him had faded. He grabbed the woman's arm, and touching one of the gold chunks he had been working with, he began turning her arm to gold.

As she wailed in pain, Maak rushed to the woman. He grabbed her arm and spoke the incantation to reverse the process. She ran screaming from the establishment.

"Mr. Stinne, what has come over you?!" Maak shouted.

"You will pay dearly for that boy! I am your master, and you should not have interfered with my business transaction!"

Callister grabbed a quarter staff from the corner of the wall, and rushed from behind the desk. He clearly intended to teach Maak a lesson. With one hand on the staff, Callister reached out for Maak with the other.

Maak barely escaped his grasp, not to mention almost being transformed into a piece of wood, and began frantically looking around for something he could use. Finding nothing he rushed for the door, adrenaline coursing through his body. As he laid hold of the wood bar on the door, he turned on instinct as Callister came at him. Maak reached out his hand in desperation, and without even touching him Callister's arm became one with the quarter staff and started forming into wood.

Callister roared with the pain, and his face was purple with blood boiling anger. Maak released his focus on the magic, heaved open the door, and ran from the city center into the congested streets of Gerrenholde.

The afternoon sun was hot and blazing, and Maak felt as if he was soaked with sweat, but he kept running until at last he felt far enough away that Callister would not find him for a while. He was an emotional wreck, still unable to believe what the power had done to his once tolerable master. Lust for power and greed for gold had consumed him. He had no doubt that the same was true for most, if not all of the other Alchemists.

His mind settled on the others for a moment. Callister would no doubt enlist their help in finding him. He had to leave Gerrenholde, and fast. The thought of running and leaving the other citizens of the city helpless made him sick to his stomach. How could he abandon them? How could he abandon others like the woman he had just saved?

Maak feared his own abilities now too. He had not even touched Callister, and yet the power was still manifested. Was he so powerful that he could change elements without even making contact? If he could do it, Callister and his friends may be able to as well.

Meanwhile, Callister had indeed called on the other Alchemists for support. He was determined to hunt Maak down and make him pay for what he had done. He also wanted to preserve Maak, however. He had never known any Alchemist who could transform matter without making contact with both subjects. He certainly was not able to. That made Maak extremely valuable to him, and time was running thin as it was only a couple of hours before the approach of sundown.

Callister did have an advantage as well. Two of his fellow Alchemists were also high ranking Law-bringers in Gerrenholde, and he had told them to notify watchers around the city to be on the lookout.

Maak turned down an alley, and crouched near a well-worn door. He sat there for a few minutes before the door came flying open. A small boy emerged and went running out into the street and disappeared around the corner.

Maak calmed himself down, and went out of the alley and around the corner. A few streets down he found a tavern that seemed fairly empty, and went in. He found a seat at a table tucked away in the corner and sat down. He ordered a pint of ale, and sat alone with his thoughts.

He had been there for an hour, when he heard the tavern door open. Nervously, he jerked around to see who had entered. To his great relief, he saw Berdok standing in the doorway and looking around the place.

When Berdok saw Maak in the corner, he quickly walked over and sat down next to him.

"Maak, is that you?! My how you've changed lad! I've often thought of you. What are you doing in here, Maak? I went by Callister's building, and no one was there. There was a parchment on the door that said an urgent matter had come up. I paid it no mind until now. What has happened?"

Maak wasn't sure how much Berdok knew about Callister, or how much he could trust him now, but he needed help. He told Berdok everything.

Berdok could see the fear in Maak's eyes. "Blast it! I should've known better. Maak, we need to get you out of here."

"No Berdok, I can't just leave the people of Gerrenholde at the mercy of these people. I've got to do something." He hesitated for a minute before saying, "Berdok, I found out today that my powers are stronger than I thought. I started to change Callister without touching him. I didn't know that was possible, and he looked as shocked as I was."

As they were talking the tavern door opened again, and this time Maak was anything but relieved as he looked toward the door. Callister stood in the doorway, as did some of his associates. Apparently Berdok wasn't the only person who had talked to the right people.

"Berdok, please leave. Maak and I have some unfinished business." Callister exclaimed in a forceful tone.

Berdok quickly got to his feet and stood his ground. "I'm not going anywhere Callister. What has happened to you, old friend?"

"A friend would respect my request Berdok. My business with the boy is mine alone."

"Apparently not. You seem to have brought a few friends with you."

While Berdok was making conversation, Maak gripped his pint glass tightly. He had seen a stairwell which no doubt led to the cellar. He focused his entire will, and extended his other hand in the direction of the tavern floor at the feet of their assailants. The floor immediately turned to glass at their feet. Quickly, Maak threw his pint glass at the floor. Not only did the glass shatter, but so did the floor.

Callister and his minions fell through to the cellar below, with looks of astonished anger on their faces as they fell. Callister scrambled frantically to get up, obtaining all matter of cuts and gashes in the process. Three of the five that came with him survived the fall, but were immobile due to broken bones. The other two had died in the process. One had been impaled on a large shard of glass, and the other had snapped his neck on the way down.

Maak grabbed Berdok by the arm and rushed him out the tavern door. As he rushed to run away, Berdok halted him and turned to the tavern door. He placed his hand on the stone doorway, and his other hand on the door, and instantly the entire entryway became a slab of stone.

Maak looked on in shock. "You're a …, you're an …, an Alchemist?"

"Yes, Maak I am. I am sorry I lied to you. The doorway will only hold them temporarily, so we must hurry from here. I promise to explain as soon as we are safe."

They ran to where Berdok had tied his horse, and quickly deserted the city. They found an old inn about an hour outside Gerrenholde, and took up board for the night. When they had settled in, Maak just sat on the floor and stared at Berdok.

Berdok spoke first, "Maak, again I'm sorry to have kept my powers from you. I should've realized that you needed someone to relate to after you discovered your powers, and I was not willing to provide that."

"Why is that, Berdok?" Maak asked.

"Maak, you have to understand my experience with the power. When I first discovered it for myself, it was less traumatic than it was for you, but I was still very confused. Callister heard about me, and took me under his wing. He was much different then. More sensible. His intentions were better. He helped me hone my focus, but I never worked for him. I was already doing then what I do now, and I was happy. Besides, even then his reputation was not good. I knew enough to stay away from that way of life."

"That still doesn't explain why you withheld the information from me. You surely put the power to use after that?"

"No, I didn't. My line of work did not require it, and I knew that there was more potential for harm than help with the power, so I stayed away. Oh, I did use it on rare occasions, but I was very inconspicuous about it. I wanted to keep it hidden away. If I were you, I would do the same now. But, that must be your choice."

Maak had so many questions, but decided to hold off. "Berdok, I think Callister probably has a lot of local Law-bringers on his side. Do you think we could convince the Law-bringers at Day Haven to get involved?"

"I think it's an excellent idea, Maak. Since Callister is not well liked, it is likely he has not bought off any of the law-bringers at Day Haven. We will make haste there at dawn."

True to the plan, they left early the next morning and made the journey back to Day Haven. They arrived two days later as evening approached. Maak wrapped his cloak tightly around him and stayed with the horse, while Berdok went to meet with the high council.

It had been dark for a couple of hours when Berdok returned. Maak's father was with him. The townsfolk in Day Haven had convinced Maak's parents to stay despite all that had happened. After a long embrace they discussed the plan.

"Your father has agreed to send a contingent of Law-bringers to Gerrenholde to apprehend the Alchemists. It may be difficult to detain them long, because he brings much wealth to the city."

Maak thought for a few minutes before finally speaking. "I want to address the town. I know everyone has reason to fear me, but I want to convince them that they have nothing to fear."

"Maak," his father said, "you would only make matters worse. Let the Law-bringers handle this. It is bad enough that you have come back. The town may push for you to be executed."

"I need them to hear me father. After that, they can do what they want."

The high council called a meeting in the town square for the following day. The whole of its thousand inhabitants of all ages flocked to the event.

Maak stood in the middle of the stage, he noticed the Shadow appeared at various different hidden spots close to the center of town. He turned to Berdok, and Berdok nodded. He had seen them too.

People all around were shouting hate and venom his way, and calling him all manner of accusatory names. The Law-bringers rushed the crowd, and quickly brought order. When all had quieted down, Maak spoke.

"I know I have no right to stand freely before you. The memory of what happened to Dolen sickens me, and not a day ends that I don't wish I could bring him back. I never meant any harm. However, I have come in contact with people in Gerrenholde who possess my abilities, and they do mean harm. I have seen it with my own eyes. My power was new, and since I didn't know I had it, I could not control it. Now I can, and I want to help bring these men to justice for the crimes they have committed.

They have corrupted many of the Law-bringers of Gerrenholde, and so the High Council is sending some from Day Haven. They will know which of those at Gerrenholde can be trusted. I plan to go with them, as they will need my power to help bring them down. Think what you will of me, but you must grant me this time. After all has been done, you have my word that I will leave and never come back.

There was a loud uproar as the crowd resumed their hate-mongering. Then, all of a sudden, there was silence as Dolen's father approached the stage. He walked up to Maak, and with tears in his eyes he slapped Maak hard across the face. He stared at Maak with pure hatred for a few moments, and then his face softened. He pulled Maak into an awkward embrace. The years had softened his resolve to destroy Maak.

Maak was stunned beyond belief, and full of confusion.

Dolen's Father turned and spoke loudly so all could hear, "I am not the only one who lost Dolen. We all lost him. But, nothing can be done about that now. I will stand with Maak today. I have no desire for someone else to lose a son." He then said something in a language Maak did not recognize, and the Shadow disappeared.

They all stared on in disbelief, and finally a murmur of reserved approval began sweeping the crowd.

The next day came all too quickly and Maak left with the Law-bringers, despite stark disapproval from his father. He knew he had to be part of whatever happened. Berdok also went with them.

Traveling with a large caravan is slower, and the journey to Gerrenholde took four days. Upon arriving they marched their contingent straight into the city center.

The law-bringers of Gerrenholde were nowhere to be seen in the hustle and bustle of commerce.

Maak pointed to where Callister maintained business, and Drakkis, the chief law-bringer, approached the establishment and pounded on the door. There was no answer, and he pounded again. After a couple of minutes Callister opened the door. He glared at Maak.

"How can I help you today?" He mocked.

"Callister Stinne," the chief began, "you stand accused of assault and intent to harm. By the laws of the realm I hereby take you into custody. You will stand before the High Council of Day Haven."

"Are you quite finished?" Stinne said with a sneer in his voice. As he said it he grabbed the stone archway of the door.

"Get away from him!" Maak shouted, seeing what Callister intended to do.

It was too late. Before he could get the chief away in time, Callister had laid hold of the man's arm and turned it to stone. He then slammed the door, and it became a solid piece of stone leaving no entrance visible.

Maak muttered the words to reverse the transformation of the chief's arm, and then rushed to the next building looking for a different material to change the door.

Just as Maak arrived at the building, the door of Callister's shop turned back to glass and Callister and two other men burst through the glass attacking Law-bringers left and right. They began channeling the stonework of the streets to do battle. Callister must have known he was beaten since these weren't *his* law-bringers, and he would try to get away no matter what the cost.

Maak wheeled around, and in a fit of panic he ran to a nearby fountain. He reached out for the fountain and concentrated, but instead of the stone of the fountain his hand hit the water. Before he could break his focus, Callister and the other two men turned to bodies of standing water and spilled instantly to the floor.

Horror coursed through Maak as he saw what he had done. His hands went clammy, his legs went out from under him, and he passed out.

Maak finally came around half an hour later. Berdok was wiping his face with a damp cloth. His head was throbbing due to hitting the fountain on the way down.

"We lost you there for a while, lad." Berdok said with laughter in his voice.

"Please tell me I didn't…. didn't…, please?"

Drakkis spoke up, "You did what you had to do, boy."

"But I killed them, I…just like Dolen."

"Think of how many people you saved today, Maak." Berdok said. "If I was more in practice, I would've done what needed to be done. Just like you did."

Maak was starting to feel sick. "Berdok, please take me home. Oh, wait I can't go home can I?"

Drakkis answered again, "Yes you can, we'll work something out. Hell, your father is on the council after all. They allowed your parents to stay, and maybe things will be different now."

After a grueling trip Berdok and Maak arrived in Day Haven a couple of days later. They had forged ahead of the law-bringers.

Maak's father ran to him, grabbed him, and embraced him tightly. Maak was sure he would suffer broken ribs if his father continued.

Gradually all those who lived in Day Haven were filing out of their homes to see Maak. Once word came of what had happened at Gerrenholde, the simple folk of his home town began to think better of him. Not all was water under the bridge, but a mending of the nets was taking place.

Thirty days passed, and word came that there had been a cleansing among the Law-bringers at Gerrenholde. Those loyal to Callister had been purged, and the ranks filled with those who were loyal to the realm.

The high council of Gerrenholde eventually sent an official request for Maak to resume the duties of City Alchemist, but Maak declined. He had no desire to ever be part of that line of work again. He was satisfied to fill the coffers of his family and closest friends with gold transmuted from stone.

Berdok went back to his usual work of selling his wares, and Maak joined him as an apprentice. He was glad to live a simple life, and put the troubles of his past behind him. It seemed that for once everything was right with the world.

~

"So Traveler, answer me this. Why ever would the boy not take advantage of such power? The master he was apprenticed to clearly had the right idea about how to use it."

"My guess would be that he wanted to be a force for good. There are those that say negative actions bring negativity to one's life, and positive actions bring positive outcomes. I would imagine he preferred the latter."

"Hmm, yes. Well, that was an entertaining tale. Don't dawdle now, Traveler. Tell me another."

The Traveler knew immediately the next tale he would relate. It was one of the most unique encounters he had experienced in his journeys, and he was sure Talindor would be fascinated.

CHAPTER FOUR
THE INKMASTER

Words have power…written words can weave a story…but in the hands of the Inkmaster, words can alter the very fabric of human existence. They can weave a new thread into the tapestry of a person, changing the direction of their life.

His patrons would come from all over the seven realms, sometimes traveling for many months just to see him. Each one had his or her own story, sometimes painful and sometimes successful, but each one was dissatisfied with life. They sought out the Inkmaster in hopes that things would be different.

He was an enormously tall man, and wiry as well, about forty years from his name day. His long brown hair, were it not tied back and bundled, could stretch to his calves. He sported an intricately curled mustache under his long pointy nose, and a tuft of hair in the crevice of his bottom lip. His spectacles consisted of two glass disks set in a rubberized frame which wrapped around his head and tied in the back. He dressed in a long dragon-hide trench-coat, a shimmering crimson in color. It was a gift from one of his patrons who had slain a dragon a few weeks after sitting under the needle.

He used a penetrator and ink to infuse words into the skin of his patrons. His skill with the penetrator was much more than ordinary. He had learned that early on as a young man. His father had worked the penetrator before him, and his father before him, but the Inkmaster was different. His skill was arcane, otherworldly, a skill that tampered with the fabric of reality. His father had feared him, while his mother swore he was special. Ah mothers…they always see the best in their child.

When someone came to see him, it was more than an appointment. It was a journey. Something within him allowed him to see into the person's very soul. He could see portions of their past, their present, and incoherent smatterings of their future. What is more, he knew why they had come. In fact, he probably knew better than they did why they were there.

His first patron of the day was a young man of not more than twenty-five years. He not so discreetly peered through the window of the parlor off and on for the span of an hour, before he finally developed the courage to open the door. He was of average height, slightly stalky, and obviously well decorated already. What hair might have adorned his head was gone, and instead appeared haggardly about his face. He may not have slept for several days judging by the dark puffy circles under his deep blue eyes. He bore a signet ring on his right hand which would have indicated either nobility, or high class thievery. The power of the Inkmaster told him it was the latter.

The Inkmaster studied him for several minutes with a very stoic look on his face, all the while his hands busy arranging his workstation to prepare for his first event of the day. His piercing gaze obviously made the man uncomfortable. The man averted his eyes several times, and each time he would look back to see if the Inkmaster had stopped staring.

Finally, the Inkmaster spoke to him. "What business shall we transact today?" His voice was gravely and gruff, but not overly pushy.

The man was silent for a time. Either he was carefully choosing his words, or he was simply afraid to speak.

Clearly intimidated, his first words came out in stutters and stammers. "S-s-sir, if y-y-you will permit m-m-me, I.... uh...."

The Inkmaster grew impatient. "Get the words out please, we have much yet to do. Let's start with your name."

After several more seconds the man got out what was obviously an expertly constructed alias. "My name is Baris, lord of Larimer Keep."

The Inkmaster thought on this for a few seconds. Yes, to be sure he was a lord, though only self-appointed. He lifted his hand slightly in gesture towards the seat in front of him. "Kindly remove your tunic and sit, *lord* Baris. You will excuse me while I set things in order for the session."

Baris gave a slight nod, and it wasn't long before things were ready. He sat forward against the back of the chair facing the Inkmaster. The merchant was a very odd looking character. Many questions ran through Baris mind. What sort of individual was this? What stimulants might he be on to make him so eccentric? Will he understand more about me than I would like?

The Inkmaster spoke gingerly. "So, tell me about yourself lord Baris. Specifically, tell me what lord you plundered and assumed his title, and also tell me what has possessed you to seek me out this day?" Noticing the look of horror on Baris face, he continued. "Oh come now, surely you did not think that little ruse would escape me? You sought me out, so you must have been told about me. I do not post notice at any of the local alehouses."

Baris collected himself before replying. "In respect sir, my name is Duric son of Barsh, and I belong to the thieving guild. You have spoken true that my false title was not gained, but stolen. His name is not important. The reason for me comin' be the need of a fresh start."

At once the purpose of the ruse was clear. Duric wished to be in truth what he claimed to be with lies. When he spoke, his words were carefully chosen. "This direction is a noble one, however be warned. Fate is the great reckoner." With those cryptic words the Inkmaster grabbed the penetrator, dipped it in his ink basin, and set to work.

There was a burning sensation like none Duric had ever known. It was as if the needle were extracting portions of his soul and embedding them in his skin. Though at times he felt like crying out, the sound would not come. He was trapped it seemed.

The Inkmaster worked as if in a trance. His eyes, normally a soft purple in color, were completely white. It was as if a strange force had wiped away his eyes. He wove intricate patterns of script across the upper back of his patron, regularly dipping for more ink. The language was unintelligible, but something innate in each patron always knew what was written.

After half of an hour had passed, the pupils of the Inkmaster returned to his eyes. His masterpiece was finished. He fetched a bottle of spirits from a cabinet adjacent to his workstation, doused a cloth with it, and laid the cloth on Duric's upper back.

Duric flinched and squirmed. The discomfort of the needle had been enough, but adding the alcohol had thrown it over the top. When the pain had finally subsided, he stood, donned his tunic, and reached for his bag of coin. "What do I owe you sir?"

A slight grin lit the face of the Inkmaster. "You may deposit five gloon in my canister there on the shelf." He studied his patron for a few seconds. It seemed that something had already changed. "A word of caution if I may," the Inkmaster continued. "When you return to your point of origin, go straight to sleep. The words need time to do as they are intended to do … *lord* Duric." With that he smirked, and turned his back to begin preparing for the next patron.

Lord Duric paused for a moment, and then strode out of the parlor. He resumed cautiously looking from one side to the other in hopes that no one had noticed him.

A few minutes later a young girl, who could not have been more than twelve years from her name day, strode into the parlor. Whatever speed she had possessed upon entering was quickly squelched when she looked at the Inkmaster. She was petite and demure, and when he looked at her she blushed and turned away. She wore a dark green satin dress, covered by a black hooded cloak. Her appearance made it clear that she came from nobility. She had arrived by carriage, albeit an unmarked one, and the driver was shrouded as well.

"What might I help you with, child?" The Inkmaster said as gingerly as possible.

The girl was a stammerer too. *What is this?* He thought. *Will all my patrons be stammerers?* "Sir I - I have h-heard that you are able to ch-change people's destinies."

He motioned her to come closer. Hesitantly, she obeyed. When she finally stood about a hand grip between them, he leaned down with his hands on his knees and gazed intently into her eyes. She could've sworn she saw a faint flicker of red light in his eyes. All of a sudden she felt curiously different. It was as if there was a deeper connection between them now.

"Tell me child," he began, "do your parents know you are here?"

"My parents were killed by a thief sir," she said. "I live with my uncle now. He cares for me…I know he does, but he is not a father, and he cannot be of much help to me."

He eyed her sternly for a moment, and then motioned to her and said "do sit here young one." He then proceeded to look her over to determine the best option for the inking. Due to her modest nature, he thought it best to use her right forearm, so as not to draw too much outside attention for her. The Inkmaster had never dealt with adolescents much, but he had much experience with the modest types.

"So you want to change your destiny, do you?" He said mildly. "Tell me more about the changes you seek."

"I have always been a quiet person sir, and…well…, I would like to be more confident. I wish to be more of a risk taker, more of a free spirit. I want to make my own path." Her forthrightness was a far cry from her original demeanor.

The Inkmaster studied her for a moment, and then spoke carefully. "You are afraid miss. You are afraid of what your background may cost you. Also, you have ulterior motives for this change. You want to hurt someone don't you?"

The girl's unease made an answer unnecessary.

"Not to worry, young one," he said. "Your secret is safe with me. Take care, however, not to underestimate fate. Please remove your cloak, and raise your right sleeve."

Though she was uneasy about what to expect, she did as she was bid. He was far too intimidating for her disobey him.

"What is your name?" he asked.

"My name is Netta," she replied.

He bowed slightly in affirmation, dipped his penetrator in the ink, and went to work. His eyes glazed over to a pure white as he worked, immersed in his typical trance. Netta winced while he poked and prodded, watching his eyes as they twitched excitedly and his head as it shook nervously. The ink was transformed from blotches to an intricately woven design upon her skin. Tears welled in her eyes as the burning sensation increased. When at last he was done, her eyelids were red from the trauma. The Inkmaster's eyes returned to normal, and he cleansed the creation with spirits. He then rubbed a gentle salve made from tree oil on her forearm, and wrapped a cotton cloth around it.

He took her chin and lifted it so that she looked into his eyes, and then he said "Remember young one, I have altered possibilities, but only you can alter your destiny."

"I'll remember, sir," she said. "What is your fee?"

Having never inked a child, he had to think on this for a moment. The nobility did not use gloon, but she had brought some with her for the sake of discretion he knew. "Two Gloon will be sufficient miss Netta," he said.

She dropped the payment in his jar, smiled slightly, and hurried out of the parlor. As she clambered into her carriage she glanced quickly from one side to another, to make sure no one had seen her.

There seemed to be a lull in the traffic today, and so the Inkmaster took the extra time to prime the penetrator, and make sure it was in pristine working order. As he was cleaning the door was quickly opened and shut.

The Inkmaster looked over in the direction of the door and saw a man who was obviously very agitated. He was of equal age to the Inkmaster, and though not of equal height he was very tall. His hair was neatly cropped, but wet from the sweat that was pouring off him. His noble robes were newly tattered, and the olive skin underneath bore several cuts and gashes in various areas. Someone had obviously attacked him.

"I need your help, and quickly!" The man demanded, apparently accustomed to ordering people around.

"With arrogance such as that, what help do you need from me?" The Inkmaster replied.

The man looked at him aghast, "How dare you! I am the Duke of Therrenell, and I demand respect."

"Oh do beg pardon…your grace." The Inkmaster mocked with an accompanying bow. "How might I serve you this fine day?"

The Duke had not noticed the air of mockery in his tone, and simply gave a curt nod. "I need protection. I have guards, but they are useless. I understand you provide some unique services."

"I am an…artist, not an assassin." As he said this, he set his piercing eyes in a stare into the Duke's, and seconds later the Duke's countenance fell into a fearful grimace. "However, there is something I may be able to do for you," he said looking him over again, "yes indeed. Remove your tattered robes and sit."

Perplexed at his loss for words, the Duke simply nodded and did as he was told. The Inkmaster gave him coverings for his lower body, and helped him sit properly in the chair.

The Inkmaster turned to prepare his instruments, smiling devilishly as he did so. This would be a fantastic work of art.

When he turned around holding the penetrator, the Duke cringed. "What is that! What are you doing?"

The Inkmaster chuckled lightly, "What did you hear about me? Look around my parlor, and think about it. I decorate the skin. Surely you're not afraid of a little needle."

"Um…alright then. As long as it works, I suppose I will do anything. But make haste!"

The Inkmaster nodded, smiling as a hint of the arrogance returned to the Duke. The pure white glaze set into his eyes as he was consumed by his arcane powers. His mouth settled in a strange rictus with the teeth set firmly together, as though he was achieving some sick pleasure, and just looking at it terrified the duke. Once again the unknown script began to appear where the penetrator touched.

The pain was excruciating, and though he tried to pull away, the Duke was fixed in the seat by some unseen power and could not move. Tears streamed down his face as though he had never wept before, and touched on the various cuts on his body causing them to burn and itch.

Pore by pore the needle penetrated his skin, and pore by pore the ink was embedded until at last the Inkmaster was done with his latest masterpiece. Normality returned to his eyes, and the smile dissolved to a faint grin as he turned to the shelf and grabbed a bottle labeled Lightning Liquor. His grin became wider as he doused a cloth heavily with the libation, and rubbed it roughly on the Duke's scripting.

Following a voluminous wail, the Duke barked, "THAT HURT! This had better work for all the pain you've caused me."

"That will be ten Steeds, your grace." The Inkmaster said.

"You'll be lucky to get one. Now tell me what I can expect to gain from this nightmare."

The Inkmaster loomed over him like a giant all of a sudden. The Duke's arrogance left him, and all he could manage was a deep seated fear of this intimidating man.

"Your grace, you are a man who is hated by your constituents, and disdained by your servants. Now you can rest assured that no one will ever bother you again. Fate is the great reckoner, your grace, and I hope that you enjoy what Fate has dealt you. Now," he said in a very calm, business-like manner, "you will pay me ten Steeds, and then you will leave." The Inkmaster held out his long fingered hand palm up.

With a begrudged look on his face, the Duke retrieved ten Steeds from his purse and handed them over. He then went quickly out the door and was gone.

As if nothing out of the ordinary had occurred, the Inkmaster turned nonchalantly back to his workstation and began cleaning up and preparing for the next visit. After a few minutes of silence, he went over to the sundial that was lit by a small skylight in the roof. The shadow fell on the northern node; the mid-day hour. He went to the entryway and hung a simple wooden sign which read, "WILL RETURN FOLLOWING A MEAL."

He grabbed a small clay cup from the shelf in his pantry and went outside the shop to a small solitary well on his property. He drew up the bucket, dipped the cup in the fresh water, and gulped it down quickly. He repeated several times more, and then let the bucket drop. The day had grown warm, which made his parlor even warmer.

He went back inside, and into a small sitting room adjacent to his parlor. The room consisted of a well-worn lounging cushion, some low lit sconces, and a brick fire well. He had set a cooking pot inside the fire well before opening for business, and the little alcove was steeped with the aroma of his stew. Off to the side of the fire well was a decanter filled with an ample amount of dark wine.

The Inkmaster poured some wine in his clay cup, ladled some stew into a clay bowl he had brought in as well, and leaned back on the cushion as he ate. He ate slowly and methodically, savoring every bite. After every few bites he drank liberally from his cup of wine. All through his routine, he thought about the patrons he had serviced thus far. He grinned giddily as he thought again of the Duke, and laughed coldly to himself.

After finishing his meal, and draining a second cup of wine, he returned to his workstation and surveyed his preparations. He had apparently overdone it with the Duke, as the ink was running a bit low, but he assumed he had enough to last one or two more sessions. The needle was as sharp as ever, in fact it had always puzzled him that it never seemed to dull.

A knock came at the door, and he realized that he had forgotten to remove the sign. He saw a young couple at the door, holding something in their arms. He walked over and took down the sign, and then opened the door and ushered them in.

He walked back to his work area with his back turned to them and called over his shoulder, "How may I help you today, Mr. and Mrs. Wittigrew?" He knew their stories, but he sensed that they were not here for themselves.

"You know who we are? How?" Mr. Wittigrew answered. He had a look of pure shock on his face, and the Inkmaster amused himself noticing the man did not stammer.

He turned around, grinned, and said, "I have my ways, lad."

"Well, sir. Me and the Mrs. Here, we're of low birth ye see, and where we come from you really never rise much in the ranks if ye get my meanin'."

The Inkmaster nodded, "Go on."

"Well, we brung our infant boy here. We wan' a better life for him, a more prosperous one. I'm not meanin' rich er nuthin, just that he get every opportunity to have a better life than we can give."

A newborn child! The Inkmaster thought to himself. *That explains it.* The Inkmaster's power had its limits. Not many, but they existed.

He took care as he replied, "I cannot help you, Mr. Wittigrew. I do not do young children."

"But you've got to help, don't you understand? I know yer powerful, see? That is why we came here."

"Mr. Wittigrew, all magic has limits, and mine is no different. My artistry has power, yes, but it is a power dependent on the reading of the potential fates of an individual. Even if I did ink infants, which I do not, it would do you no good. I cannot read a child, as their soul energy does not settle until they are older. I cannot do this thing you ask of me. Your child is innocent, and it is against nature to tamper with the fates of the innocent."

The young man flushed, as he was obviously distraught. His wife burst into tears, and began to berate him for his foolishness. She stopped abruptly though, as the baby began to cry.

The Inkmaster walked over and opened up his purse. He took out five of the ten Steeds that he had received from the Duke and walked back to the couple. He took the young woman's hand in his, and closed the coins into her palm.

Addressing both of them he said, "This is all I can do for you. Use this to make the best life you can for your son. Let his fate shape him. When he is older, perhaps he will happen by my door. But, it must be his doing."

The couple looked down at the coins, more money than they had ever heard of even in stories, and through smiles and tears they thanked the Inkmaster. They promised that they would do as he said, and then left for home.

The Inkmaster normally saw a lull in the early midday, but today was more than a lull. The sun was blazing at its final peak before the next patron entered. He was a much older man. Roughly seventy years by the Inkmaster's estimation. He was an able bodied man, full of vigor, and did not seem to require even the assistance of a staff. As he fixed his intuitive gaze into the man, he gleaned that he had been a mercenary in his younger days. This would explain the way he carried himself.

"I've heard about you," he began. "I've heard that you can alter the course of one's life."

The Inkmaster knew what the old man wanted, but he wanted to hear more. A person's point of view about themselves tells a great deal. "You were a brute for hire in your younger years were you not?"

"Well m'boy, there are many things in life an old man finds to regret. I have many such things. I have taken many lives in the course of my years, some for profit and some for protection, and I simply can't live with the anguish anymore." He paused with the faintest hint of tears appearing in his eyes. When he spoke again the emotion was startling. "I remember each face, and the look in their eyes as they died. They haunt my dreams at night, what few I have when I can actually sleep."

The Inkmaster nodded gently, and walking over he guided the man to the chair.

"I must prepare you, grandfather." He said. "The procedure may be painful for you. Though I don't doubt that the pain that you have carried these many years is far greater."

The old man simply nodded, his eyes flushed with red, and removed his tunic. His back was riddled with whipping scars, and his spine was bent into a smooth bow.

Tool in hand, the Inkmaster settled into his work and into the familiar hypnotic power of his craft. As the ink flowed, words spilled from his mind into the man's skin.

Words rich with forgetfulness, laced with peace, and exuding tranquility. The words would form a foundation of restful reflection for the man in the twilight years of his life.

Many patrons found the pain almost unbearable, some even went mad under the torment, but not this man. As the Inkmaster twisted and turned, weaved and painted, the old man did not flinch at all. Hardened by years of extremes, he was as impenetrable as a barbarian fortress. Though his eyes were clear as day, and those of the Inkmaster driven white by the power, they were at one with the power together.

The procedure came to an end. The Inkmaster's face was riddled with beads of sweat, and his breathing was labored. The whites of his eyes, though normal again, were bloodshot. He pulled over a wooden stool to sit down. It was as if something in his power fed off the pain of his patrons, for the resilience of this elderly man had left him drained.

The old man stood and donned his tunic again. Something already had changed about the man. His visage was summarily enhanced, as if a great weight had been lifted from his shoulders. As he stood there it seemed his back was as straight as an arrow. He reached into his pocket, retrieving two Steeds which he laid on the shelf next to where the Inkmaster sat. He looked at the shop-owner and raised an eyebrow in silent question. The Inkmaster nodded with a smirk in silent answer. With a wider stride in his step, the old man left.

The Inkmaster was racked with exhaustion. He waited a while, and when no other shadows darkened the entryway, he unrolled the shades, crossed the chains, and made for the sitting room. Staggering to his cushion he collapsed on it and stared at the ceiling. He thought to himself how odd it had been. He had never had a client who drained him so completely. Though their powers were different, it was as if they were equals. While he had the power of sorcery at his side, the old man had the power of sheer strength of will. That indeed was a force to be reckoned with.

Gathering his thoughts, the Inkmaster got up and filled his clay cup with wine. The warm tingle of the alcohol as it trickled down his throat was a soothing tonic to his weariness. With sip after gentle sip, the tension in his body faded. He removed his spectacles and his dragon-hide coat, and as he reared back on the cushion he fell asleep.

His dreams had an intense lucidity. Clarity was something he had grown used to in a dream state, but this was different. Each of his patrons from that day appeared eerily present in his visions. The thieving lord, the naive young woman, the arrogant ass of a Duke, the destitute young couple, and the remarkable old man each circled round him in a dizzying fanfare as if he were caught in a whirlwind of responsibility for the lives impacted by his trade. Darkness was all around them and their eyes blazed with green light as they reached out to him. It seemed their souls desired to forever remind him of the consequences of his power.

He woke in a hot sweat on the floor by his lounger. He picked himself up and headed for the washroom. Once inside he stripped himself, stood under the wall faucet, and pulled the chain letting the ice cold water gush over his body in cooling waves. He unraveled his hair and let it mat against his skin under the water.

When the water sent his body into chilled convulsions, and he could bear it no longer, he turned it off. He restored himself to some semblance of order, clothed himself, and returned to his sitting room. He quickly ate a meager breakfast of oats mixed with Zillow milk and honey, and made for the parlor.

He peeked through a broken spot in his shade, and saw that two people were already waiting for him. He sighed, and let a slight thoughtful grin wash his face, and he turned to make his preparations. As he did so he thought heavily on the events of the previous day, and the souls that had darkened his door. He felt emotions of anxiety and sorrow begin to pull at the edges of his mind, but he fought them back. He had to be about his business, and let Fate deal as it would with those he worked on.

It proved to be a long, laborious start to the day. He still felt the effects of his encounter with the old man, but he did his best to work past it, and he finally finished out the day with little consequence.

As the weeks rolled by, and clients came and went, the Inkmaster began to learn some of what Fate had dealt to those who came to him on that unique day in his work. Some he learned from reading the daily missives that he found, picked up when at the market, but he pieced together most of it from the loose lips of those who frequented his ink parlor.

Lord Duric, it turns out, had gone mad with the pressures of authority. He wanted a change, and was sure being a dignitary would provide that, but apparently he was not prepared for the responsibility. He had confined himself to his suite, steeped with depression, and was only seen by his servants who took him food. It was said they had to feed him, but that is only what was said. The affairs of his authority were handled by a former colleague he had appointed, and who was more than happy to *handle* things. Upon hearing it the Inkmaster smiled and thought to himself, *It is one thing to become a lord, and quite another to actually be one.*

The maiden Netta had definitely made a name for herself. The death of her parents had brought her a considerable fortune, which she used frugally under careful supervision of her advisors of course. One of the advisors was her uncle who, though somewhat distant emotionally, had quite a good head for ledger books. She had appointed him over her advisors for just such a reason. She had set up several promissory funds for the care of orphans in her province. She had become quite outspoken on the matter as well, having written several theses for public consumption.

The high and mighty Duke of Therrenell had got exactly what he wanted, and also a little of what the Inkmaster had desired for him. Not only did thieves and disgruntled constituents avoid him, but everyone in his employ and all those who supported his Duchy abandoned him. His entire regime fell apart, as it relied on other people to maintain it. The last time someone had happened to see him, he was milling around a refuse yard in the tattered remains of his finely tailored robes hoping to find food, as there was no one who would come near to help him.

"Really?!" The Inkmaster replied to the young woman who enlightened him with this little piece of gossip. "Are you serious?" He let out a great bellow of laughter so loud that his client jumped back two feet in surprise. The reaction was hardly what she expected from such a seemingly stoic individual.

In the first month of the final cycle of the year, the Inkmaster sat reading a missive at a local tavern. As he perused the headlines, he ran across an entry about a young couple who had come out of poverty and taken ownership of a large wheat farming operation. Looking closely at the drawing he saw it was the Whittigrews. He looked up from the paper, and smiled thoughtfully. He had, after all, given them a reasonable fortune. One Steed was worth an average four-year salary for a middle class regent.

His time was running short, but as he got up from his seat to leave another headline caught his eye. There was a death notice set in obscurity in the corner of the second page. An untrained eye may have missed it entirely, but not his eye. A familiar face looked out at him from a hand-sketched portrait in the notice, and he staggered trying to find his seat again. A man of about seventy years, whose visit had haunted the Inkmaster for months, had died peacefully in his sleep. It was said he was only known briefly by those who lived close to him, and though friendly, he had kept to himself. "Well, well, perhaps whatever life he meets now will be kinder to him," the Inkmaster said rather loudly to himself.

As he made his way slowly back to his shop with the dirt kicking at his heels, he began to wonder how many would bother paying their respects to the old man. The Ritual of Ash was in five days, and he decided he for one would be there.

No one was there when he arrived, so he closed up and pulled the heavy shade. He then placed a freshly scrawled sign in his window, slung a rucksack full of necessities over his shoulder, and set off down the road.

The quiet little shop had several attendees over the next few days. Upon reading the sign, they all turned away, disappointed at his absence. The sign was direct but vague. It read, "Visiting the dead. Do call again."

~

"Do your kind truly embed art in their hide? What a strange practice. I've never heard of such nonsense."

"Indeed they do Talindor, and for various different reasons. For some the drawings represent magical properties, for others acceptance into various sects, and there are other reasons as well."

"Very well then, carry on Traveler."

"Talindor, it occurs to me that you will never honor our arrangement."

"Oh no, Traveler. I fully intend to…er…take good care of you," he said with a sparkle in his great cat like eye.

The Traveler rolled his eyes, and thought for a while. He could see Talindor growing impatient…and hungry.

"Ah, yes," he said. "Next I will tell you of a young girl from a world known as Antharos."

CHAPTER FIVE
THE UNDOING

The Aether, the source element, is full of pure living energy. At the time of the emanation, the Aether produced the four great distinct elements of fire, earth, air, and water.

The planet Antharos is a lush world, made up of one massive continent surrounded by oceans. The continent is inhabited by both human and animal races, as well as the Twykk. The Twykk control the elements of Fire, earth, wind, and water and their use in the realms of human and beast.

The Twykk are not more than six inches in height, and the texture and color of their skin is closest to the element which they control. To look upon a water Twykk, for example, one would see a lithe creature of pure blue skin which might be smooth and oily or wet to the touch. The Twykk connect themselves to the young, whether man or beast, and form a symbiotic relationship fostered by a telepathic and empathic link. It is a relationship of mutual benefit, as they learn about the planet's inhabiting races, and they also divulge information about their race.

Not all creatures are given the privilege of this connection, however. Those that are ushered into the Symbiote Guilds. The masters of the guild travel Antharos in caravans along with the Twykk, seeking out humanoids who are suitable for the joining. The choosing of beast kind is left solely up to the Twykk to discover.

Shara Daro was a young, pleasant girl of ten years. Her parents were common folk, who were fishers by trade. It was a sustainable life to be sure, though much depended on the bounty of the oceans. Shara had learned to read at a very early age, and much of her knowledge came from the tomes of parchment that she read as much as was possible. The schoolhouse provided a basic education, but higher education was unheard of in the seaboard towns. Leitha was a very small town compared to other seaboard towns.

The guild masters had not visited Leitha in many years, not since before Shara was born. In fact, she rather doubted their existence. They could be an imaginary group made up by the scribes to exercise some measure of control over the populace. It was truly a shock, to her as well as the rest of the town, when news came that the masters would be arriving for a visit.

The rains had been good this year, and the waters were high. Shara immensely enjoyed sitting on the end of the dock and dipping her feet in the lukewarm water. She was sitting on one of the docks doing just that when the masters arrived.

Their caravan arrived on a massive trireme. The caravan consisted of six masters and six mistresses. Each wore a long, dark flowing robe made of satin. The closure of their robe was highlighted by a strip of colored velvet. The color was determined by the element they commanded. Each master's Twykk was riding in a small leather pouch strapped across their backs.

The trireme pulled into one of the docks on the other end of the town, and the caravan exited immediately. They made their way quickly and fluidly through the main part of town. One of the guild masters pulled a small veiled carriage, the contents of which could not be seen.

A multitude of people had gathered in the town square. They looked out in amazement as the caravan drew closer, and eventually came to a stop a few yards from the large group of people. Shara had come to join her parents in the crowd, and hung safely behind her mother's gown peeking out ever so slightly with great curiosity. The veil to the small carriage was all of a sudden lifted, and a small group of Twykk emerged.

The Twykk scanned through the crowd for several minutes, until finally one of them paused. It floated quickly yet cautiously through the crowd, and came to a halt directly in front of Shara's mother. It gazed at her for a moment, and then lowered slowly and peeked around to gaze into Shara's eyes. She was unable to control the urge to move closer to the Twykk, and when she did it leaned forward and touched its forehead to hers. A flash of excruciating pain went through her head, as if she had been hit with a blunt instrument, and she collapsed.

She had the sensation of floating on a large expanse of water, lit by the gleam of five moons. It seemed she was being watched. Suddenly she felt dizzy, and in fear of drowning.

She awoke as the lights of the sky were changing cycles. Her head felt like an avalanche had ravaged it. She pushed herself to a sitting position on her sleeping mat and brushed her thick chestnut hair away from her face. As she looked around, the Twykk was looking at her.

"Hello Shara," it said in a voice that sounded like a gentle current of water. The Twykk had light blue skin covered with intricate designs, and what might be considered hair was shimmering like a soft fountain.

It continued, "I am sorry for the pain I caused you, but it was necessary to increase your frontal lobe to make the joining possible. All will be explained in due time, but I am pleased to be a part of you. I am your water symbiote, and you are now of a prestigious race known as the Water Kynd."

Shara realized that the being had no mouth, none that was visible anyway. The Twykk was obviously using some form of telepathy.

"Am I dreaming?" she asked.

Her symbiote floated closer to her, and poked her arm. She flinched, and all of a sudden began to laugh heartily. All the Twykk did was stare at her.

When she had collected herself, her symbiote spoke again. "I can see why you would think this a dream, but I assure you that this is all very much real. Perhaps it would help if you knew me better. The Twykk do not practice naming in the way that humans would understand, but I would be pleased if you would call me Mek."

Shara nodded and said, "Thank you Mek, I am glad to know you."

"And I you," he said. "There are some things here for you. They were left here at the foot of your mat by the masters. You collapsed after the joining, and one of them carried you home."

The joining. So, it was real. It had happened to her. Shara had heard much about it, even fancied herself that one day she might be privileged enough to be joined. She never thought that it would ever happen though. She knelt at the foot of her mat and stared at the items in wonder. There was a shimmering blue cloak, made of a material that she was not familiar with. It was fastened at the neck by a turquoise brooch in the shape of drop of water. The other item was a long narrow staff made of intricately wrapped coral. At its crest there was a single blue water crystal, as clear as the purest ocean.

Mek spoke again. "These are the vestments of the human Water Kynd. The cloak to set you apart, and the staff to channel your power."

Somewhat confused Shara stammered, "M-m-my p-power?"

"Yours is the power of the water element. The power to control tides and currents, to communicate with all manner of water life, and even to travel on the surfaces of the oceans should you desire. Water is very mercurial, constantly changing. Yours is the power of that change. It is a responsibility that you and I bear together, as I am the one who grants you this power. Worry not, for I shall train you to harness it."

"How many are there like you, Mek?" Shara asked.

"Many hundreds of thousands, actually." It replied.

An awkward silence hung in the air for a while before the Twykk finally spoke. "It is time to leave Shara. We must journey together to the Symbiote Guild. Now is the time for you to take the first step in your learning."

Shara became excited. "We will be riding back with the masters?" Shara had always dreamed of meeting a master, and she had so many questions for them now that she was joined.

"No Shara," it said. "We will be traveling by ourselves across the vast expanses of water toward the mainland. Please gather your things and refresh yourself. We must make haste."

Shara broke her fast on blueberry infused porridge and a drink of freshly pureed watermelon, and then quickly gathered her belongings into a shoulder sack. She donned her new cloak around her neck, drawing the hood over her head, and took the staff in hand. She was amazed at the lightness of the staff, though she sensed it was virtually unbreakable.

Shara turned to face her parents. Sorrow and pride mingled together in the tears that streamed down their faces, for though they knew the great work she would accomplish, it was clear they would scarcely see her as much as they were used too. She rushed to them and embraced them for what seemed an eternity, until Mek made it clear that they must be going. Wiping the tears from her eyes, she looked back one last time, and then exited the cottage.

Mek led Shara down to a particularly shallow inlet. This was purposeful, so as not to overwhelm Shara. Mek stopped at the water's edge and turned to face her.

"Shara, the time has come to harness your powers for the first time. Please step forward and place the top of your staff in the water. Make sure you fully immerse the water crystal."

Shara moved slowly, hesitantly, toward the water. As she began to lower top of the staff in the water, she cringed as if waiting for some catastrophic event to take place once she did so.

She squinted her eyes, and submerged the water crystal fully in the rippling waters. Immediately, she felt cool waves of power coursing through her body. It was as if she had stepped out of the blistering heat of a desert and into an arctic arena of cold crisp air. Though instead of being unpleasant, the feeling was exhilarating. The irises of her eyes, normally a dull brown, turned completely blue with the power of the water magic.

When the power had fully immersed her, she heard Mek speaking loudly as if talking over a torrent of crushing sound. "Now Shara, step out on the water!"

The minute she did, she was surrounded by a cyclone of water that could have sucked any normal person in and drowned them. She, however, floated effortlessly at the center of the torrent. She looked around herself, amazed at what was taking place. She would've thought that the water would completely drench her, but instead she remained perfectly dry as drops of water danced around her shimmering cloak.

Either the cacophony was fading, or her ears were becoming acclimated to it, for she heard Mek clearly as he spoke again. He had joined her now in the small pocket at the base of her hood.

"It is time, Shara. Raise your staff and point it toward the eastern horizon. That is the direction of the Guild Regime, and it is time we made our way there."

She did as Mek commanded, and the cyclone began spinning like one of the wooden tops she had played with as a young child, and it advanced forward on the water as if some unseen force were propelling it. It was not an unseen force however. It was her, and she knew it. Never before had she experienced the kind of rush and thrill that she was experiencing at this moment.

The hours passed quickly as she traveled toward her destination. Fatigue evaded her, and hunger was far away. She seemed to be nourished by the very power itself. As the daytime lights began to wane, and the evening lights to rise in the sky, the Guild Regime came into view far in the distance. Even as far away as it was, there was no mistaking its brilliance.

The structure was outlined all around with numerous spires that rose so high they seemed like they could pierce the clouds above. The corner spires each flew a brilliant golden flag, with one of the four elements emblazoned on each one. On either side of the water channel adjacent to the city were legions of Triremes helmed by various warriors of the elemental Kynds. The chains began whirring through the portcullis as the great iron mouth of the citadel opened to receive Shara.

Her cyclone flew into the forward hall of the city. She quickly lifted her staff from its horizontal position, and just as quickly regretted her haste. The cyclone of water vanished, and she landed flat on her face on the stone floor.

There was no damage, and the pain was minimal, but then she realized something. She had made her grand entrance in front of at least three dozen new recruits, who instantly began snickering and laughing. The noise quickly came to a halt, however, when their Twykk had finally had enough.

One of them, whom Shara would later find out was called Syt, invaded the minds of all of the recruits with one word. "Respect!" He continued by saying, "The girl is still just learning about her new abilities, as you all are, and I demand that you show her the proper respect."

Shara picked herself up, brushed off her garments, and attempted to regain some of her composure after the embarrassing assault on her pride. Syt was looking intently at her, and finally he simply nodded. She nodded back and smiled as if to say thank you.

Mek nudged close to Shara, easing her tension, and said, "Shara, it is time for you to meet the high Elders. I will take you to them now."

"Who are the high elders, Mek?" She inquired, puzzled.

"No one knows of the high elders except the Kynd. They are the founders of the guild, and they are the only ones of this world who possess the power to wield the Aether. All this will be explained to you in due time, but you must come with me at once. All newly joined initiates must appear before them."

"Very well," Shara said, "I am ready."

As the mouth of the citadel was closing, they made their way from the forward hall down a long corridor. Shara and Mek were in the lead. The other recruits, ashamed for their behavior, trailed closely behind with sheepish looks on their faces. The hallway seemed to go on forever. There were no doors lining the walls on either side of the hallway. It seemed to Shara that they were all being sucked into nothingness, when they finally arrived at what she assumed was their destination.

Two large oaken doors stood before them. The doors were notched with all manner of strange symbols and runes. The archway was lined with five crystals; two on either side and one at the peak of the archway.

One crystal on the left she recognized, for it was the same as that upon her staff. The crystal two feet below it was a flowing reddish orange, much the same as that upon the staves of her new comrades. On the opposite side was a light brown, rather grainy crystal, and another that had the appearance of a cloud contained within glass. These, she noticed, also resembled those of some of the other initiates.

The final symbol at the peak, however, was one she did not recognize. It was a luminescent gas filled orb, with colors that constantly fluctuated. She guessed it must be the source element, but she could not be sure. Mek must have read her thoughts, because he spoke briefly and said, "You are correct Shara. That…is the Aether."

One Twykk representative from each of the four elements approached the door. Each hovered to its respective crystal and placed both hands on it. A stream of light creased the edges of the doors, and they slowly creaked open. The Twykk led their groups through the doors and into a large throne room. At the far end of the room stood a dais with six simple wooden thrones upon it. Three women and three men occupied the thrones. All of them appeared to be well advanced in age, but they possessed a vitality that clearly defied it.

One of the men stood and addressed the Kynd. "I am Voltanis. I was the first to be chosen by the Aether as an ambassador to the planet Antharos. You have been given a great honor, in that you are all bearers of one of the elemental powers crucial to the protection of our planet and our race. To be sure you must all have many questions, and I promise you they will be answered in time. Know that this is an extremely crucial time. Just as the Aether is a force for purity, there is another force at work in our world. The only word that we have found to best describe it is The Undoing. I know you are all new, but you will have an equal part with all those who have come before you in eradicating this great evil. As I said, more will be explained to you when appropriate."

Voltanis made his way to the far left end of the dais and spoke again. "I want you all to know us and feel comfortable approaching us, so the first step in that direction will be to introduce my fellow elders. Please follow down the line in order as I introduce you. This is the lady Ellandra. Next is lord Mavrell, and then we have lord Crispin, lady Marina, and lady Celestia. You will treat them with the same respect you would treat me, and with which you should also treat each other. Though we possess the power of the Aether, we are no different than any of you. The only difference you will notice is that we do not engage in symbiosis with the Twykk."

Shara looked up and down the line of elders, and yet she kept coming back to focus on lord Mavrell for some reason. His stately form, and his deep brown hair that tumbled to his shoulders was disarming. Yet there was something she didn't like about him, and she couldn't understand why. Mek sensed her discomfort, though he said nothing. Perhaps now was not the right time.

Voltanis spoke one final time in a very clear and precise tone. "You will now retire to your quarters. I know that what has happened will make it hard to wind down, but you must get sufficient rest tonight. Tomorrow begins your training, and I am afraid you must make haste. The Undoing is growing stronger by the day. Good night."

As the large group left the throne room, Mek escorted Shara to the east wing of the citadel. They came upon a large door with a single large water crystal in the center. Mek touched the crystal, opened the door, and they proceeded down a long hallway adorned with doors on either side. They approached a door which bore her name in the ancient script of Antharos. When they had come within a couple of feet from the door, it opened for them of its own accord. There was a thick down feather mat laid in the center of the room. Next to the mat was a circular discus of some sort, no larger than the size of Shara's hand.

"What is the disc for?" Shara asked.

"It is for me," Mek replied. "Twykk sleep sitting up, if you would call it sleeping. We enter a trance until precisely the time to awaken our symbiote. The trance allows us to connect with the mind of the Aether."

There was no lighting in the room except for what came from an expansive window in the ceiling. This was no doubt to guarantee that sleep would be adhered to at the proper times, thus making sure that bodily rhythms were at their peak efficiency.

Shara laid down on the mat and pulled the comforter over her. Her whole body and mind were completely exhausted, and it was only minutes before she was soundly asleep.

She was floating on the expanse of water again, although this time it was more than a sensation. The experience was so vivid that it was difficult to tell whether she was dreaming or awake. The light of the five moons reflected off the water and illumined her skin. It gave her skin a translucent appearance that amazed her. The stars danced in her eyes as she saw them in her hands and arms. Suddenly, without warning a dark red pallor enveloped the five moons, and the smell of smoke and ash filled her nostrils. It was as though the moons had caught fire, and any minute she expected the lights of the world to turn to ash as well and leave the world in darkness. A hideous cry erupted from all around her, and she woke hyperventilating in a feverish sweat.

"A troubling experience to be sure Shara," said Mek as he softly touched her mind.

When she finally calmed down, she ran to the washroom to wash the sweat from her face, and then returned to sit by Mek. There was no way she would be sleeping again this night.

After collecting her thoughts, she spoke weakly to the Twykk. "It seemed so real Mek! What happened? What caused the whole scene to change?"

"That…was the undoing, Shara," Mek replied. "There have been few who have dreamt of the undoing, and far fewer who have recovered their mental acuity after doing so. You are extremely resilient Shara."

"Can you tell me more about the undoing Mek? What is it, and how does it happen?"

"I do not fully understand it myself Shara. I know it has to do with intermixing of the elemental powers, but that is all I could tell you. Master Voltanis will be giving a discourse after the daybreak meal. He will no doubt explain more at that time."

"Master Voltanis mentioned training. What will it involve?"

"The training is limited Shara," Mek replied. "We simply teach you how to control your powers and tune in to your personal energy. You will intuitively know what must be done in a given situation, so that is something only you can harness."

Shara quieted her mind and spent the rest of her interrupted morning in meditation and connection with Mek. When day broke, they made their way to the meal hall.

There was a large stage in the middle of the meal hall, on which Shara assumed Volantis would later address their group. The tables were decorated with large platters piled high with all assortment of fresh fruits and vegetables. Most Shara was familiar with, but there were some that were completely new. Especially among the fruits. She grasped a long cylindrical fruit that was purple in color. When she broke it in half, the inner flesh was yellow, and smelled like fermented plums. She stood looking at it in wonder.

Mek noticed her expression, and spoke up. "That is called a royal pear. It is native to the citadel region. It is said that earth kynd created it."

She bit into the fruit, and a cavalcade of flavors danced on her tongue. Honey, lemon, and a hint of cinnamon were some of the many participants in the dance. The taste was amazing, and yet perplexing.

After the meal had ended, a hush washed over the crowd as High Elder Volantis took the stage. He looked out over the group, and they could all feel his eyes on them. It was as if he could see the deepest secrets of their souls.

He began and got straight to the business at hand. "I know you are all anxious to begin preparing yourselves for your role, but before you can confront your enemy you must better understand your enemy. It is time for you to learn as much as we know about the Undoing. The elements that you have been entrusted with were meant to balance each other. Water keeps fire in check, just as fire can be conducted to heat water. You get the idea I am sure. The Aether is the central balancing element that maintains the balance of the other four, and the four in turn maintain the Aether.

"The Undoing has created a corruption in the essential nature of the elements, and by the corruption has created an unnatural blend of the elements. You could look at this corruption as a kind of anti-aether. The Undoing has been growing and evolving over many years, and we have been fighting it, but whenever we take one step forward we end up falling behind two steps. It is crucial that we double our efforts and eradicate this corruption, for if we don't all of Antharos will be laid waste. The elements sustain our ecosystem. Without the pure elements no life can be sustained for long."

Shara sat still as a stone, soaking in the words she was hearing. *A tainted Aether. Who or what would have done such a thing?*

She thought about her family and friends back in Leitha, the people she knew and loved. Their entire existence depended on the seasons and the living planet. If all that were laid foul, the results would be catastrophic.

Mek had been resonating with her thoughts. "Yes, Shara. You know all too well the implications of the task ahead of you."

"Your job," Voltanis continued, "is to become one with your Twykk, and with your element. This will prepare you for a battle which we feel will come soon, because you will be able to feel the energy shift when the time comes."

The group of initiates were immediately led to ready rooms devoted to each of their elements. Shara took a cushion alongside another Water Kynd, a young man named Rudan. He looked as nervous as she was, so at least she was in good company.

Lord Crispin had been put in charge of their initial instruction. He spent an ungodly amount of time on information that Shara felt was unnecessary, and then finally got down to the essentials. However, Shara did not hear any of what he talked about. She felt a fluctuation in the elemental energies that seemed unusually close, and it completely distracted her. It was as if she was in another world.

Lord Crispin noticed, and called her out. "Miss Daro, perhaps you feel this is a waste of your time?"

His reprimand jerked her awake, and she looked at him in despair. "I'm sorry Lord Crispin, but something is wrong. I was feeling something just now. Something…well…I can't explain it, but something feels imbalanced, and it just started feeling that way to me."

He could tell that she was greatly unnerved, and then Rudan spoke up. "I felt it too sir."

The other initiates in the room let go of their reluctance and affirmed what their two comrades had said.

"Tell me more, miss Daro." Crispin said.

"Well, it felt like a vibration of some kind inside me, but it was more than that. Something very wrong is happening, and it seems to be very close to us. Maybe even inside the Citadel."

"That is impossible! The Undoing could not possibly go unnoticed here. What does your Twykk have to say of all this." He turned toward Mek with a piercing and insistent gaze.

"Lord Crispin, Shara and I share the same mind and the same connection to the element. Something is indeed wrong."

"Have you felt it before miss Daro?"

"I feel like I have, but I can't place it." She turned to Mek, hoping for his help in remembering.

"Yes Shara, you are right. However, I believe it would be best to discuss it in private sir."

"Very well," Crispin said. "We will break for one hour, but you must all use your time wisely. Practice using the strength of water on each other, and remember to join your mind completely with your Twykk." He motioned to Shara and Mek. "Come, we will go to my private quarters."

They wound up several floors along a spiral staircase in the northern tower, until they came to a man sized archway with a door set back several feet into the arch. The door had a single glass pane set in a small square of the upper part of the door. Lord Crispin took out a large metal key to unlock the door, and guided Shara and Mek inside.

The room was sparse and simple. A chair and desk here, a small cot there, and also a single large candle on a tray upon the desk.

"The instruction must be completed, so make haste with what you tell me."

"The last time Shara felt anything similar to this was at the introduction of the Citadel leadership yesterday, Lord Crispin." Mek said.

A flicker of light came to Shara as she remembered and said, "Yes, that was it. Lord Mavrell. I had the most awful feeling when I looked at him. I felt like something was not right with him, but I couldn't figure out what it was."

"Lord Mavrell?!" Crispin exclaimed as he rose to his feet. "Surely you are not serious! Mavrell has been part of our order since the rise of the Symbiote Guilds."

"Lord Crispin," Shara pleaded. "If there is even the slightest chance, don't you think we must take every precaution?"

He was silent for a time, and then looked on Shara and smiled. "I suppose you're right, Miss Daro. Will you recognize the feeling if it comes again? Perhaps if you are closer?"

"Yes…but…why?"

"Mavrell will be in his quarters in the southern tower now. The southern tower is dark and brooding, as the light from the sun never reaches that part of the citadel. If something is amiss, he will likely do it where he is most comfortable. I know I would."

The afternoon sun was bursting through the windows in the tower as they left, and as they approached the southern tower it seemed they were plunged into darkness. They climbed a similar stairwell to that of the other tower, and as they came closer to their destination the same feeling of dread hit Shara and her Twykk like a tidal wave of her own making. She was so taken back that she stumbled and tripped on the stair.

"Lord Crispin!" Shara squealed.

He looked back, and noticing her ashen face he charged the stairwell and began to open the door to Lord Mavrell's quarters. Just as he had opened the door a few inches wide, a force like nothing he had ever known or felt before careened into him from inside the room, and he toppled over the stairwell. Before he could hit the stone floor below, he called upon the wind which propelled him up again with a great force and he grabbed the edge of the stairwell and pulled himself up.

A huge crowd was gathering in the center arena of the citadel as initiates and veterans alike formed a sea of onlookers. Shouts and screams erupted from the crowd as they looked upon the freakish man towering over Shara, Mek, and Crispin. It was definitely Lord Mavrell, but yet it was also not him. The figure that was dressed in his cloak and covered with his skin was like nothing that they had yet seen. His eyes seemed lit from within by a living green flame laced with rifts of black that pulsed within. A ghastly purple haze emanated from him, and writhed and swirled all around him. His staff was enveloped in the haze as well, and it climbed up and down the length of it with a mesmerizing rhythm.

Crispin climbed weakly to his feet. "Mavrell, you fool! What have you done?!"

He opened his mouth and the swirling green flame erupted from his mouth and began writhing through his teeth and around his lips as he spoke. "I have amassed power! That is what I have done Crispin! Voltanis has kept enormous power from our grasp. Enough power to control Antharos, and yet more still to bring other worlds under our control. Limitless power, Crispin!"

Shara cowered in the corner of the stairwell as if a nightmare had become reality. Mek touched her neck to calm her, and fixed her gaze with his. She knew she had to do something.

Crispin was speechless for minutes on end before he finally spoke. "This is power that was never meant to be had Mavrell. It is a corruption of everything that sustains the universe." Crispin raised his right hand, and on each finger a single particle of each element rested. "These were meant to work together to sustain existence Mavrell. What you have created will destroy us all!"

"This will not destroy us all, Crispin. It will only destroy those who are not resilient enough to appreciate the power. Starting with you!"

The power swirling around Mavrell's staff moved faster and expanded. He lurched forward and touched the head of his staff to Crispin's chest, hurtling him toward the wall with uncanny speed. Upon hitting the wall, he burst into ash.

Panic erupted in the arena as people ran screaming from the epicenter. Shara stood her ground as if she was frozen in time. Mek touched her consciousness saying, "Shara we must retreat!" She still didn't move.

The remaining high elders arrived in the center of the arena just as Mavrell began slowly approaching Shara. In a mocking tone he said, "Clever little one, aren't you? I saw you gazing at me when we were first introduced. I had no idea one young girl could discover me so easily, heh heh. You are not worthy of the Undoing, so now you must cease."

"Now Shara!" A shout from Mek that reverberated throughout her consciousness.

She snapped alert instantly, and slammed the head of her staff against the stair. The force of her will joined with the properties of the water crystal and flashes of blue spilled skyward out of the crystal sending her spinning away from Mavrell in a massive tornado of water. The torrent of water ripped and pulled at her cloak, twisting it around her. If the power had not gripped her so fiercely she might have suffocated. Mek was gripping her hair as he was enveloped in a trance brought on by the joining of their souls.

Voltanis and the others cleared a path as the rush of water deposited Shara among them, and they crowded around her determined that they would bear the brunt of the Undoing.

An unworldly screech of anger bellowed out of Mavrell as he flew to the arena on a wave of flames and ash. The sheer force of the heat was so intense that it forced the huddle of elders back several paces.

"Voltanis," he screeched again. There was a loud and menacing echo that accompanied the screech. "You cannot protect her from me. I am more powerful than the lot of you combined."

"Mavrell, listen to reason!" Voltanis shouted. "An intermixing with the Aether is completely unstable. It was not meant to be so, and it will consume you."

Mavrell laughed in derision. "I want it to consume me! Only then will I know its true potential. The scales have been tested, and your ways have been found lacking. I will spread the Undoing across this planet, and into the universe. It is only an undoing of your ways, but it will spread order throughout all that exists."

Mavrell raised his staff, pointing it straight at Voltanis. The putrid purple emanation leapt from it and began crawling up the taut frame of the high elder. As it did all color began leaving his skin, and after turning a deathly white he collapsed to the floor in a fuming pile of ash.

Mavrell spit green trails of smoke from his mouth as he guffawed in triumph, but the rest of the elders continued huddling around the young girl.

All of a sudden, as if filled with rage at the death of Voltanis, youths and adults who had once ran screaming from the arena began piling into it again. Their hoods were pushed back, their staves were raised, and shouts of rebellion caused a deafening clamor that made Mavrell cover his ears.

Shara turned as Rudan came up beside her and placed his hand on her arm. Others of the water Kynd gathered to her as well. All around the arena the masses were congregating into formations according to their element, and with their Twykk by their sides they all crowded in until they surrounded the high elders.

Ellandra looked at Mavrell with menacing eyes and said, "Are you prepared to deal with the entire host of the Citadel Mavrell? As you can see you are grossly outnumbered, no matter how much power you possess. You will fail."

Mavrell ascended five feet in the air, and with an echoing wail that reverberated across the arena he unleashed a wave of currents into the crowd. Mixed with writhing mixtures of purple, green, and black, they pulsed with pale light and power.

With renewed purpose, the host of the citadel raised their staves in unison, and the energy hit a barrier. Then they advanced on Mavrell at once. The formation of the fire Kynd to his left, the water Kynd to his right, the earth Kynd at his back, and the air Kynd in front of him. Again they raised their staves in unison, and the power of each element formed a set of four walls around Mavrell. The Twykk rose from their symbiotes, and formed a circle in the air above the formations. With joined hands they sent ripples of aetheric energy throughout their circle, and a downward funnel of the energy emerged from the circle and enveloped Mavrell.

Mavrell was beset from every side. Rushes of water crashed into him, and wreathes of flame circled about him. He began screaming and wailing, unable to quench the power that was obviously much greater than he was. He began shaking and convulsing, and within him the tremors sent cracks through his bones and tears erupted in his muscles. Still he wailed louder, and yet still he attempted to maintain the Undoing.

Sweat poured from the pores of every person in the onslaught against him, and it seemed that their power was weakening. Shara shouted over the tumult, "We must not give up hope. Stay focused, or all is lost!" From deep within them they found strength to carry on, and strength to deepen their connections with the Twykk.

When it seemed they could maintain the stream of power no longer, Mavrell began convulsing violently and a sickening storm of dark energies was torn from his body by the aetheric funnel. His staff splintered and shattered, pieces of it flying in every direction. The hair on his head went from dark brown to shock white, and he crashed to the floor in a pile of shattered humanity.

The formations of the Kynd broke off the power, and all went quiet. After a few minutes of staring at the figure cowering on the floor, shouts of victory rose from the relieved crowd.

Shara broke from her comrades and cautiously approached Mavrell. Ellandra followed after her and held her back. As Shara turned Ellandra said, "Be careful young lady. Not all is certain as of yet."

Ellandra went up to where Mavrell lay on the stone floor. His robes were a tattered mess. The skin on his body was thin and wrinkled, and looked as if it barely hung upon his bones. His long white hair was thin and sparse. He was now an old man whose youth had been stolen from him by a lust for power. A power he had obviously not understood. What was most unsettling of all was his eyes. Once they had held the deepest blue, and then under the power they were more brilliant still. All that remained under the heavy lids of his eyes were pure white balls, whiter than the purest pearl. He would never see again.

In a barely audible semblance of voice, he spoke. "Imp…impossible. What has happened to me?"

Ellandra answered, "In your quest for power, you failed to appreciate the complementary power of the separate elements Mavrell. Fire balances water, water balances fire, and on occasion they must subdue each other. This is true of all the elements. It appears that when you mingled them, you quenched their individual properties. You were then unable to combat the sheer force of the pure power of the elements."

"I want to die." The request could barely be heard.

Celestia spoke up as she approached, "No Mavrell, you will live. As long as the fates determine for you, you shall live. But you shall live without power, a destitute man and a beggar. And when you pass on, you will be granted communion among the elements, just as Crispin and Voltanis have done this day."

He began to weep, and as he did so the crowds of the citadel dispersed. Delegates of the air Kynd gathered what they could of the ashes of Crispin and Voltanis into clay jars, and then followed the rest. The arena was empty, save for the shell of a man weeping at its center.

An hour later he was still lying there, in fits of sleeping and waking, when someone approached. Shara came up and knelt by his side. She crept close to his ear and said softly, "I forgive you." She then pushed a stone cup of water toward him, helped him wrap his hand around it, and left with Mek following close behind.

The next day the hosts of the citadel converged in the courtyard of the citadel. A square had been cordoned off with a burning flame set at each corner. The two delegates from the air Kynd stood in the center holding the clay jars of ashes.

They set down the jars, backed away and raised their staves to the sky. They then brought them down slowly in formation. The winds descended, gathered the contents of each jar, and gushed them into the air. The torrents would carry them across the globe to become one with Antharos. One with the elements. Voltanis and Crispin would find rest. This was the knowledge and tradition of the Aether.

Shara Daro stood looking on with the rest of the guilds, fully clad in their cloaks and staves upraised in tribute. Their Twykk sat atop their right shoulders with heads bowed. Shara stood at the front of the crowds as an honor to a heroine. The threat of the Undoing was extinguished, a new day was dawning, and she was given much of the credit. A renewed purpose was in motion to bring vitality to Antharos.

When the Honoring Ceremony ended, the courtyard emptied. Shara still stood alone with Mek, looking out on the vast expanse of water. She felt the pulse of its power within her, and was at peace. She turned to Mek, he nodded, and they returned to the citadel. It was now time to begin a new work. A work that would shape the future of their existence.

~

"Mmmm, yes, that Mavrell character should have known better than to tamper with the proper order of elemental magic. You certainly have been to many different worlds, Traveler. What is your purpose?"

"Oh nothing really. I simply observe and make note of progress on the different worlds."

"How so? You carry no parchment, nor tools of a scribe."

"My mind is all I need. You of all creatures know, the sentient mind is a powerful thing. Powerful enough to store vast amounts of knowledge if unencumbered."

"Yes, but even the greatest of minds has limits, Traveler. Indeed, you are an intriguing one."

Without stopping to wonder if he would be allowed to leave, the Traveler assumed he must continue entertaining. "On to the next tale then."

CHAPTER SIX
CURIOSITY

Madder Sweeney woke to the incessant barking of his dog. The sky was gray and overcast, giving the impression that he was still supposed to be sleeping. He had not slept well that night either, which was evidenced by the twisted mess his shirt and boxers were in. He barked back at his dog with an incoherent jumble of words as he rubbed his eyes furiously to try and erase the lingering fatigue. Sweeney was an ordinary guy, with an ordinary job, and an ordinary life. His dog Wake was also ordinary, but had a highly extra-ordinary bark, to his chagrin, which is how the dog got its name.

After a few very uncomfortable stretches, Madder pried himself off the bed and sluggishly made his way to the bathroom. He stood in the dark for a few minutes, cursing against the inevitable, and then turned on the light. He squinted for a few minutes and then stared. "What a horrid mess!" He said to himself as he gazed at his appearance in the mirror. His long, shoulder length hair was wildly disheveled, his eye sockets were sunken pits that screamed for sleep, and the eyes within them were even worse. His complexion had obviously seen better days as well.

He set to work vigorously scouring his teeth with a brush for all of thirty seconds, rinsed, and swallowed. Realizing that he had swallowed, he mumbled an assortment of vulgarities, and trudged off to the kitchen to eat a mash of eggs and whatever else he could concoct.

After inhaling his breakfast and drinking his normal morning sludge, which he always tried to convince himself was coffee, he fired up his laptop to check the morning news on the internet. After what seemed like an hour, the laptop was finally ready to be used. He thanked whatever gods above that he had the day off, and did not have to rush around. Being late to his own life was perfectly acceptable.

Sweeney was the ever so dutiful assistant manager of Pitter's Consignments. Between his manager barking at him like his dog, and the customers doing the same, when he finally got a day off he pretended the world did not exist. On rare occasions, one of which would be today, he liked to frequent other consignment stores. This was partly to see what little gems he might be able to find, and partly to see if there might be better places to work. He never completely liked consignment work, but he was good at it despite the way his manager barked.

He quickly threw on some pants, straightened his shirt, and embarked on the overcast world beyond his front door. As he prepared to get on his bike he realized the tire was flat, for the third time in a week, so it was apparent a good pumping would not suffice. *Oh well*, he thought, *the shopping district isn't far*.

After a couple of hours, and more exercise than he had really wanted, he finally got to town; the same old ordinary town of Lizard's Bluff. Something was different though, or so it seemed. It just…felt different.

As he walked down the sidewalk perusing the usual assortment of storefronts, he noticed something new. There was a new store in town. *The Curious Curiosities of Crispus Crik*, the sign read. Madder stopped in front of the store and just stared stoically at the sign as if he himself could have passed for one of the curiosities. He finally realized how stupid he looked and shook the glaze from his face and opened the door.

It was as if he had walked into another world. Everything smelled musty and ancient, and the shop was lit by candles on sconces that lined the eaves. On every shelf lay some of the most unusual things he had ever seen. The owner, who Madder could only assume must be Crik, came out to greet him.

"Greetings my intrepid friend! I am Crispus Crik" he squeaked in a heavy Mediterranean accent, sounding like a mouse with bronchitis. "Imagine your luck at being my first patron."

"Hi," Madder said sheepishly.

Crick was a sight to behold. He was likely older than horse drawn carriages. He wore a pea green Victorian shirt with billowed sleeves, and leather laces at the cleave. His pants were equally as billowed, but cherry brown in color. He wore no shoes, and likely never did judging by how calloused his feet were. He was bald from his head to his chin, and he wore a fedora adorned with a pigeon feather. He looked like something out of the Silverstein poems Madder read as a child, and Madder thought that Crick seemed more unusual than the items in his shop.

"Feel free to look around," Crik squeaked again. "I have a wide assortment of enjoyable items, and at the most reasonable prices of course."

Madder smiled and nodded, and walked casually around the different displays. One shelf was full of ornate wooden boxes of all shapes and sizes, with curious inscriptions imbedded in the wood. Some shelves had odd looking books that had vellum covers and some type of calligraphy. The titles were even stranger, such as *The Rudiments of the Icchus Dracu* or *The Runes of the Ancient Filioi*. Other shelves had various different kinds of unusual trinkets and jewelry. All of a sudden something caught his eye. A simple hooded robe of some sort was hanging on a hook in the wall, set off by itself in a corner. As he got closer and examined it, he was definitely intrigued. The silvery colored material was smooth and soft like silk, but yet smoother.

He looked for a price tag, but found none, so he took it with him to where Crik was standing. The odd little shop owner was immersed in his ledgers, and more or less oblivious to anything else.

"Excuse me," Madder said, "Mis…ter…Crik? I really like this cloak but could not find a price. Could you tell me how much it is?"

Crik's eyes went wide and cockeyed, and he directed a mischievous look toward Madder as he answered. "That cloak? You want that cloak? Oh no my friend, you don't want *that* cloak."

Madder, rather taken back, pressed on. "Actually I do, yes, very much. Why would I not?"

"Well, a bright young man like yourself has his whole life ahead of him. That cloak will only cause you trouble," Crik whispered hoarsely.

Trouble? I might enjoy a bit of trouble, Madder thought as he persisted, "Thank you for your concern Mr. Crik, but I would like to make my own judgment call."

"Very well," Crik said. "Don't ever say I didn't warn you though. The cloak will cost you twenty dollars. I would charge more, but the trouble you will have would make you hate me for it."

"What could be so bad about a hooded cloak?" Madder asked the funny little man.

Crik laughed a high curdled laugh and said, "Oh you'll find out when you put it on young man."

Madder paid the twenty dollars, grabbed the cloak, and cautiously went out the door and started to make the long trek back. After walking about a block he realized he didn't know how to clean the cloak, not that he was accustomed to following laundry directions to begin with. He turned around and walked back in the direction of the shop.

As he returned there was no store to be seen. The lot was empty and furiously overgrown with weeds. It bore no evidence that anything had been there except for a few dogs. Madder couldn't understand. He held the evidence in his hands, but it was as if the shop had never existed.

He arrived home at lunch time and fixed himself a sandwich, if one could call it that. What might be expected of a bachelor's concoction, it was a slice of ham between two stale pieces of bread with mustard that Madder called a sandwich, although many might disagree with him.

As he was chewing his food, looking rather like a dog gnawing on a bone, he began to wonder if he had dreamed the whole thing. He would look at his cloak, then back at his sandwich, and then back at the cloak again. Each time he expected that the cloak would not be there, but each time it was, and so he finally resigned himself that it had not been a dream.

He stopped eating his sandwich, deciding he didn't want to hurt his teeth anymore, and inhaled a glass of water. He then grabbed the cloak and sat down on the sofa with it. He smiled at it for a moment, and then got up to try it on.

What happened the minute he put it on was anything but ordinary. He instantly felt like he was being sucked through a vacuum and into a wind tunnel. After what seemed like only a few minutes, he came to a spinning stop and collapsed on the ground. It was another few minutes before his head stopped spinning enough for him to vomit. He swore to himself that he had eaten stale bread for the last time.

He staggered to his feet and had just enough time to quickly look at his surroundings, when he felt a hard crash against the back of his head accompanied by a severe pain. Suddenly everything went black.

He woke up about…well honestly he didn't know when it was. He started to sit up, but the way his head screamed when he did, made him think twice about that effort. He was laying on a cobblestone floor, and he was surrounded on three sides by a cage of thick iron bars. There was a cobblestone wall behind him with a small barred window resting in the eave, and there was a torch in a sconce on the wall that bathed his quarters in a dim light.

"Arrested," he muttered to himself. "Great! I've gone from average loser to hardened criminal all in one day."

Something was different about this cell. He was pretty sure the cells in police stations were somewhat more modern than the one he was currently in.

He was gradually able to bring himself to a standing position, and looked out the window. The sky was dark, and there was a torch-lit trail leading up to the wall where he was. He moved to the front of the cell to look out, and stumbled before he reached his destination. He fell face first to the floor and felt a sharp pain in his ankle. He looked down and saw that he was shackled to the wall by an iron chain about five feet in length.

He sat back up on the hard, cold floor and waited. It was all becoming clearer now that the trauma to the back of his head was brought on by being hit with something from behind. His stomach began rumbling like a mild aftershock, and he began to crave a sixteen-ounce, medium well ribeye steak. He wasn't sure why it was steak, but apparently his stomach went all out when it came to imagination.

A few minutes passed and he heard the fall of heavy boots on the floor approaching his cell. The light increased significantly as the person approached carrying a very well-lit torch. He squinted his eyes to adjust to the extra light, and when he looked up his visitor slowly came into clarity. He stared with his mouth loosely hanging as he pondered what his brain told him his eyes were seeing. *A Roman soldier?*

"*Quid defluis?*" The soldier said.

At that point he bemoaned himself for never taking Latin in high school, though he never dreamed he would need it, and certainly not in such a ridiculous situation.

"Ummm, do you speak English?" Madder asked.

The soldier gave a puzzled look for a moment, and then rolled his eyes and opened the cell. He grabbed Madder by the arm and hoisted him up, then he bent down and unlocked the shackle around Madder's ankle.

"So you speak Anglicus do you?" The soldier asked, though it was not a question. "Shall see how well you speak for your freedom."

The prison house was cold and dank, and as they walked Madder pulled his hood up and his cloak around him to warm himself. When he did so he felt the vacuum again, wrenching his stomach free and pulling him along with it. From out of the vacuum he crashed into his sofa, tipping it over backwards and landing himself flat on his back on the ceramic tile.

He laid there in disbelief for a while, and then noticed one of the pillows from the sofa was lying next to him. He grabbed the pillow, cuddling up to it like a child, and was instantly asleep.

He woke on what he assumed was the next day, pried himself off the floor, and fumbled around among the scattered sofa cushions for his watch. When he finally found it, it was as still as a rock. "Great!" He shouted out loud. "I can survive time travel, but my watch can't!" He threw it across the room, knocking over his parents' photo with precise accuracy.

He then headed for the kitchen where he had plugged his cell phone in. He flipped it open, and was instantly bombarded by a notification that he had missed about twenty calls. Half of the calls were from his workplace, which he had apparently avoided for a whole work day. After wading through the incessant screaming (and barking) in his voicemails, he concluded that the basic message was he would no longer be welcome at Pitter's Consignments.

Now that Madder had come into possession of an insane amount of free time, he started thinking long and hard about his plan for the future. After doing said thinking for all of five minutes, he decided to read for a bit. He had an old history book on Egypt that he hadn't picked up in a while. Madder had always been fascinated with Egypt, but had always found this book rather dull and boring. After dusting it off and attempting to read a chapter, which he was failing at, he closed the book and started thinking about the cloak. What must it be like to experience Egypt in all of its grandeur?

The thought hit him like a baseball bat to the back of the head, as many of his epiphanies did. He could experience ancient Egypt firsthand, and all he had to do was put on the.... cloak. He felt a knot form in the pit of his stomach just thinking about going through that again. But, seeing as how he had plenty of time, he decided to give it a shot.

He went back to his sleeping spot on the floor, and picked up the cloak. It was in perfect condition, apparently the one piece of clothing that would never need ironing if he did decide to do it. He fixed Egypt, and more specifically the Pharaoh Rameses the Great, firmly in his mind. He then wrapped the cloak around his shoulders, and the hood over his head, and pulled it close around him. Again he felt the sickening lurch of time sucking him away.

When he flew out of the portal he crashed hard against what he soon discovered was the head of a statue. As much as he tried to hold on, he proceeded to slide down and landed face first on a hot desert slab. He picked himself up and brushed the coarse sand off the cloak. He gazed out at what he assumed was a section of water from the Nile river.

As he turned his eyes became the size of two large white eggs as he stood facing the temple of Abu Simbel, and the four ornate statues of Rameses the Great. He had seen plenty of pictures, but there was nothing compared to this.

He stood transfixed for a while until he started to become very thirsty. He hadn't planned very well, or he would have thought it a good idea to bring water on a trip to the desert. He looked around to see if there was any other water source than the blatantly obvious. He knew the water of the Nile was sacred, and he really didn't want to risk being struck down by Ra. Madder didn't really think Ra existed, but didn't really want to take a chance. And besides, the Nile was almost certainly polluted.

He waited until he could no longer bear the thirst, and began climbing down toward the water. When he reached the edge of the Nile, he looked sheepishly into the sky and said, "Ra…forgive me. I'm thirsty." He felt a little stupid, but wanted to be more safe than sorry.

He knelt down, and closing his eyes he took a long slurping drink. The water was surprisingly cool, and very refreshing as well. "Maybe it isn't polluted," he said to himself. "In fact, maybe I'll live forever." Thinking more about it though, he wasn't sure he wanted to live forever.

He took another long drink, and as he got up he heard arguing up above the ridge where the temple was. With painful effort, he climbed back up and hid just under the overhang of the cliffs. He lifted his head just enough to peek out over the rise, and saw two men in long gowns, sandals, and wearing turbans. They both carried bundles of tools, and were looking around as if to make sure no one saw them. Thieves! It had to be, Madder thought.

Every few minutes they would argue with each other in some language Madder couldn't make out. *Must be locals*, he thought. As the thieves entered the main vestibule of the temple, Madder crept up on the structure and grabbed the steel mallet out of one of the bundles, and hid between the two statues on his left. He thought that at least if he tried to do something, the gods of Egypt may look more favorably on him about drinking the Nile water. A silly thought, but reassuring in any case. One of the thieves came out to get his tools, and while he was distracted looking for his mallet, he heard some fool shout out "for Ra!" before the lights went out.

Madder stood over his captive with a huge dorky grin, holding the large mallet in his hand. The end of it was stained with blood, as he had hit the poor fellow a little too hard.

After a few minutes the other thief came out, most likely to find out what was taking the other one so long. Madder swung just as the guy laid eyes on him, but he missed. The thief took the opportunity, and kicked Madder dead in the face. He lost control of the mallet, and hit the stone slab hard. The thief came on him, and madder swung his foot out and tripped the man. They both got up at the same time, and in a fit of fear Madder slapped the thief across the face. The thief stared at Madder in disbelief, laughed maniacally, and then grabbed the mallet and came after Madder again. Madder took off running along the enormous courtyard of the temple, wrapped his cloak and hood tight about himself and was gone.

Madder plunged back into his home, this time landing on the bathroom floor. This was good since Madder could make it to the toilet in time to throw up. After he was done, he crawled to the bedroom, drawing strange looks from Wake, and climbed into the bed to sleep.

He was running and running, being chased by a mummy that was carrying a large steel mallet and screaming at him. He bumped into something big and black, and he looked up to see a gigantic scarab staring him in the face. He screamed and started running back the other way, and just when the mummy would've caught up to him, he woke up. He opened his eyes groggily, and was staring into the eyes of something else big and black…and hungry. All it took was one bark, and Madder jumped out of bed and went to fetch the dog food.

After surviving his dog's breakfast demands, Madder walked lazily to the bathroom and climbed in the shower. The water felt extremely good to him as he let it run the length of his body. He must've taken some time, because the water all of a sudden got cold. Cursing fluently, Madder quickly soaped down, rinsed, and climbed out. Since he was now shivering due to the cold water, he was quick with drying and dressing as well, and made his way to the kitchen to check the morning news on his computer.

Madder loved to read international news, and it just so happened that there was a breaking news article about a recent archeological find. His eyes began to widen as he read the article about a huge treasure trove inside the temple of Abu Simbel in Egypt. The article was full of the usual hype, but one thing stuck out to Madder. The second article stated that highly revered sites such as Abu Simbel were among the most likely to be looted by thieves, but the treasure they discovered was largely intact.

Madder stopped reading. His mouth was cocked to one side, and his eyes were bulging as if he was in shock. *No…it couldn't be* he thought to himself. He shook off the daze and closed his laptop.

Frustrated, Madder grabbed his cloak and took Wake out for a walk. The cool morning breeze felt pleasant to Madder's face. He felt as though he had not been out of the house for days, and had cabin fever. Wake was walking happily along, head held high, and his tongue lolling lazily out to one side of his mouth. Suddenly the dog seemed spooked and took off in a swift run. Madder was pulled along as he helplessly held the leash, and cursed the animal with several choice words for doing this to him.

Wake finally pulled up short, panting heavily. As Madder was catching his breath, he was thinking about trying the cloak out one more time. He was also thinking that maybe he should've got a horse instead of a dog. He walked back to his house with Wake in tow, let the dog in, and then went back out again for a walk by himself.

After about a mile Madder stopped and looked down at the cloak he was mindlessly clutching in his fist. He threw it on like he normally did, pulled it taut, and instantly felt the rush of the time vacuum.

Once again the vacuum threw him out onto solid ground. "I've got to find a less painful way to arrive," he grumbled to himself. As he got up and brushed himself off he noticed a pile of hay off to his left. Letting his cynicism fly, he said, "Because of course I could never land there. No, that would be too easy."

He looked around to try and discover where he was, and noticed he was in an elaborate marble structure. Roman style columns throughout, and gilded gates. As he turned he came face to face with…a horse. The horse nickered softy at him sprinkling him with spittle. The horse's trough was also made of marble, and the entire stall was of ivory. There were several purple blankets the texture of velvet, and various dishes of uneaten food lay about. The most curious item in the stall was a golden bowl with a deep red concoction in it.

Madder bent down to examine the bowl, and took a whiff of the contents. "Wine?" He said. "Who gives a horse wine?"

As Madder was looking around the stall, and admiring the level of detail taken to care for a horse, the horse had decided he did not care much for his new visitor.

All of a sudden the horse reared forward and kicked Madder square in the rear end. Madder let out a loud yelp of pain, and began scrambling to get himself out of the stall.

The horse turned in the direction Madder was heading, and once Madder exited the stall the horse reared forward and kicked again. This time the force was enough to propel Madder headlong into the eastern wall of the stable, and he slid to the ground crumpled like an empty sack.

The horse whinnied loudly as if laughing at Madder, and soon the sound of at least half a dozen men could be heard outside the stable. "Don't tell me this horse has slaves too," Madder said to himself. He knew, of course that it could just as easily be armed guards that would love nothing more than to interrogate a stranger to their grounds.

Madder tightened his cloak and hood around him and vanished into thin air. This time he arrived outside his house. He was tossed against his front door, which unhinged from the weight of force and fell flat on the entryway floor along with him on top of it. *On second thought, I think I'll stick with a dog*, he thought.

He was in so much pain from being kicked by the horse that he could hardly walk, so he headed straight to the bathroom, drew a bath, and soaked for an hour. As he dried off, he looked at the clock on his nightstand. Eight O'clock at night. *Time travel sure isn't very organized*, he thought.

He went to the kitchen, made himself some dinner, and sat at the table in front of his laptop. Pulling up an internet window, he quickly typed in the query Marble Horse Stall. At the top of the result list was an article about the Roman emperor Gaius Caligula.

As Madder began reading, he discovered that what he had seen almost completely matched the description in the article of how Caligula treated his favorite horse. According to some accounts the emperor had even made his horse a senator. Whether this was done as a practical joke, or because he was insane was under dispute. Madder smiled wryly, thinking it was probably a little of both. "Apparently I pissed off the Imperial steed!" he said with a chuckle.

He was exhausted, so he closed the laptop and headed to bed. He was determined that he would return the cloak first thing in the morning.

When Madder awoke, the clock by his bedside said ten o'clock. Wake had not come in yet, which was peculiar, but he welcomed a reprieve. It was short-lived however, for Wake soon bounded into the bedroom and tackled Madder before he could put one foot on the floor.

After feeding his dog, and nearly being dog food himself, Madder poured some cereal and inhaled. He quickly showered, dressed, and headed out the door with the cloak in hand.

He arrived in Lizard's Bluff in less than ninety minutes, and headed to the lot where he had originally found Crik's shop. As he approached, it was obvious that the lot still showed no evidence of Crik's shop having been there. It was just as bare as before.

Madder walked to the edge of the curb and sat down, staring with rapt fascination at the trash trapped in the street gutter.

Suddenly someone tapped him on the shoulder. He turned around and looked up, staring into the peculiar face of Crispus Crik.

"Good day to you, my friend! Why you sit on the curb like a fire hydrant? You'll be a dog's water spot before you know it," he said and then laughed boisterously.

"Actually," Madder said carefully, "I've come to see you. I would like to return this wretched cloak to you. It has caused me nothing but trouble."

The sound of Crik's laughter was so loud that it startled passersby, who looked in Madder's direction with disgust. "Hm hm, I warned you did I not my friend?" 'That cloak will cause you trouble' I said."

"Yes I know," Madder said. "You warned me and I didn't listen. I was looking to add some flare to my otherwise boring life, but I think I would rather not now." He continued, "In the last three days I have been a prisoner of Rome, got in a scuffle with Egyptian grave robbers, and gotten kicked in the ass by a high ranking Roman horse. I think I'm ready for mediocrity again."

The look on Crik's face infuriated Madder, as the smile on the strange little man got increasingly wider. He eventually burst out in another bout of laughter, and after containing himself somewhat he put his arm around Madder and turned him around. The shop was right where it had been, oddly enough.

"So you're ready to give up the cloak, eh?" Crik asked. "Well, I normally don't allow returns, but I like you. And…I know that cloak, so I no blame you." He gave Madder back the money, and continued looking at him intently.

Madder didn't like the look. *What is this guy's problem?* He thought.

After a few more moments Madder couldn't stand it anymore. "What is it Mr. Crik? What are you looking at me that way for?"

Crik chirped in his squeaky voice, "Oh not to worry my friend. It's just that…well…the only people that can ever find my shop are those that come to work for me."

"Work for you?" Madder sounded incredulous. "What do you mean?"

"That cloak," Crik said, "is one of many that belong to those in my employ. You see, I sell curiosities. My workers travel throughout time collecting items for my shop."

Madder was dumbfounded. "Why did you sell me the cloak then?"

Crik laughed heartily again. "I wanted you to satisfy your own curiosity, and I had to protect my investment. What if you never came back with it? They are extremely rare."

"What if I don't want to work for you?"

"That is your choice my friend, of course. But, you are not currently employed Mr. Sweeney, and you have nothing holding you back except your dog."

"H..h..how do you know that? And, how do you know my name?!"

"It is my business to know about potential workers, Mr. Sweeney. Now here's the deal, you can accept my offer and travel the world through time, collecting rare little oddities. I will pay you handsomely, and train you to use the cloak with more efficiency. Or," he paused briefly, "you can decline my offer, and go back to your mediocre life. It will make no difference to me, my friend. Do what your soul tells you, but you must decide now."

Madder considered the offer while roaming around the shop looking at all the fascinating items. He was good at working consignments, and he had no doubt he would be good at curiosities as well. What is more, he would be able to fulfill his dreams of traveling the world, with the added bonus of reliving history. Crik was right. Nothing was really holding him down except Wake, and he could always return to his dog as if no time had ever lapsed if he knew how to use the cloak properly. He was an only child, and both of his parents had passed, so he really had no reason to decline.

After a few minutes he returned to the counter, and Crik looked up at him, eyeing him ominously. The question was in his eyes, though he kept silent. *What will you do my friend?*

"I will accept your offer Mr. Crik, but please allow me to tie up a few things at home."

Crik wrapped Madder in his arms, jumping for joy and squeezing him until he almost went blue from lack of oxygen. "Very good my friend Madder! Tie up what you will, and be back here at this same time in the morning. You will then begin embarking on adventures beyond your dreams!"

Madder returned home, gathered up a few things to bring with him, and put some things in storage in his garage.

He arrived eagerly the next morning to begin his new position. Crik was waiting for him as promised, and as they entered the curiosity shop together, Crik enthusiastically detailed to him the first adventure of his new career. Madder would retrieve a trinket from a certain Czarina of Russia from the late 1800's. The door to the shop closed, and a vacant lot could be seen by dozens of passersby.

~

"I once had a meal…er, I mean, a visitor who possessed one such garment. He was a crafty one, but I eventually…well. Keep going, Traveler."

"I am certain my next story will peak your interest, great Talindor. It involves a race similar to your own."

"Get on with it then, Traveler."

CHAPTER SEVEN
FORSAKEN

Sorina was one of many women engineered in the Firileen race. Only in existence for five hundred years, the Firileen were from the Torlune mountain ranges, and were a genetically engineered race bred for servitude to the ruling viceroys of Montessa Prime. Though Sorina was Firileen, one thing made her different from most of her female contemporaries. She bore the shroud.

Though human in their basic makeup, the Firileen were a highly modified race. They could live to be thousands of years old with only slightly visible age. Both the men and the women, although clearly distinguished by normal characteristics, were bred to be infertile. The men were essentially created to be eunuchs, and the women would never pose risk to any they served since they lacked the ability to reproduce. The Firileen women, or Evenni, were sold to the kingships as serving wenches or courtesans. The men, called Annos, served as royal guards to the viceroys.

The women averaged a somewhat normal height of six and a half feet, and were lithe and limber, adept at any task assigned to them. The men averaged a height of at least seven feet high, and had an extraordinarily high concentration of muscle tissue. A man would easily weigh three hundred pounds in muscle mass alone. With no exceptions the men and the women alike had dark olive complexions and silky dark hair.

The one thing that only Annos were created with was the shroud. Dark scales of various colors that started at the neck and proceeded in patches down the trunk of the body. It was the mark of honor, the mark of a Shift-mage, for so they were called.

On rare occasions the women would exhibit this trait, and like many others before her, when Sorina reached the age of five and the shroud was discovered, she was banned from society. It was a mark of disgrace, and those women unfortunate enough to bear it were labeled Forsaken and branded with the symbol of shunning.

The Forsaken resided in the underworld of Montessa. Other than the Torlune mountains, Montessa was the only other inhabited collection of systems on the planet Aduwain. It consisted of five ruling kingships, each in control of its own province.

The Kingship of Kish was the most prominent in Montessa. It was ruled over by the tyrant Gayus Pryn, who was well known for his barbaric treatment of the population. Pryn was largely responsible for the existence of Montessa Minor - a vast underworld of vagrants, thieves, and rebels who sought to bring freedom and equality to Montessa Prime.

Montessa minor was a desolate wasteland of catacombs populated mostly by common folk who were trying to reform society, but there was also a small population of Firileen who had been freed from their conditioning and joined the rebellion.

The Forsaken were the most prominent beings in Montessa minor. Though rejected by most of their own and the higher echelons of society, they were revered as deities by inhabitants of the underworld.

Sorina was now approaching the witching age, twenty years to be exact, when her powers would be fully awakened. Warda, the first of the Firileen women to be found deformed, was the witch-mother of the Forsaken. When the outcasts arrived, she was the first to welcome them and see that they were properly cared for and raised. She had taken a personal interest in Sorina as she began to grow and blossom, and had been grooming her to assume the role of a warrior priestess.

Sorina had proved to be very deft in her training, and a very powerful shifter as well.

The month of Manos was waking, and the ceremony of Evenlight was upon them. The ceremony was a confirmation of adulthood and entrance into goddess-hood.

Sorina walked briskly down a long corridor attended by her maidens Reena and Alette, who were trying desperately to keep up. Warda had summoned her for a final observation before the ceremony.

"Come," Warda said as she heard the swift knock of a nervous young Evenni at her door.

Sorina opened the door, and bid her attendants wait outside. "You sent for me Mother?"

"Yes child, I did. I want you to shift for me so that I can inspect your form and stance once more before Even-light."

"Mother, I have already done this several times for you," Sorina protested. It was true. The witch-mother was very watchful that everything proceeds just so. Even when it came to the behavior of the honorees.

"Yes, I know Sorina, but only once more. You know how important this is to me, and it is important for you as well. Come into the dome."

The dome was a preparation room set off of Warda's quarters. It was used to prepare for major events and rites in Montessa minor, and was solely under the control of Warda. Though the ceremony, like other events, would be held in the theatre, the Dome was ideal for preparation because it was private.

As they entered the Dome, Warda pointed to the far side. "Over there now, just as before, and remove your cloak and garments."

Nudity was not frowned upon in certain circumstances, and never was among other Firileen. And, though the rest of the world saw the shroud of the Evenni as a disgrace, those of the Forsaken all wore it proudly.

"Very good child. Now…make your shift."

Sorina closed her eyes, stretched out her arms, and focused all her attention on her core energy just as she had done numerous times before. The scales along her body glowed white and blinding, and then the shift began. She let out a loud wail as her whole body lengthened and expanded, for the pain was intense.

Her neck grew long and thick, her face stretched out into a snout, and her mouth grew full of sharp fangs. Her eyes, once a pale green, were now a piercing, fiery red, and her ears grew into fleshly daggers that towered above her scalp. Boney knobs protruded in a line from her forehead all the way down her snout. Her arms and legs grew thick, and she could feel the muscles tightening and expanding. Her shoulder blades erupted into an expansive wingspan, and the scales that covered her body flowed over her massive alternate form like free flowing water.

When the shift was complete, her wailing turned to a piercing wave of vibrational energy that echoed throughout the dome.

The ancient Evenni looked on proudly at the way Sorina transformed so gracefully. She clapped her hands twice and exclaimed, "You are indeed ready for your presentation tomorrow, child. Though they deny it, the shifting of the Annos pales in comparison to the beauty of ours. Revert back now, and go. You must be fully rested for the event."

Sorina did as she was told, returning to flesh and clothing herself again. The transition back was always a relief to her body. It was almost soothing in a way, but it left her feeling achy and sensitive to the touch, and her skin felt disconnected from her now smaller frame. She bid the witch-mother farewell with a kiss on each cheek, and smiled daintily as she left the room. With her maidens trailing behind her, she made the return to her room.

Night drew its dark canopy around the sky of the world, as the two luminaries cycled and dimmed their lights.

King Pryn stood on the balcony overlooking his private courtyard, watching as two of his women danced under the darkened light. Mesmerized as he stared at them, a knock came on the door that snapped him alert.

"Enter already," he growled in anger.

The chief of his royal guard entered his suite. "Good night master," he said.

"What do you want Hestus?" He said, as he continued staring down from the balcony.

"The outcasts are having their Even-light ceremony tomorrow. My brothers are wondering how long this will be allowed to go on, and I do not doubt your subjects wonder the same."

"Are you presuming to tell me my duty, slave?"

"No master. It's just that, well, it is a reproach on our kind. The whole purpose of our creation was to separate the roles, and…"

Pryn turned on him. "I know perfectly well what the purpose was, Hestus! You will not tell me how to handle my rule! Now, go!"

"Of course, lord. My apologies." He bowed as he walked out and closed the door.

It was true that the ceremony was an abomination. Over 500 years of order had been maintained by the obeisance of the Firileen. The blatant rebellion of the rejects and their followers had been an open sore that was gradually getting worse and festering. The Firileen males that forsook their stations and went to the catacombs rejoiced in being dominated by the women. *The women were supposed to be the companions, not the other way around!* He thought to himself as he gazed down at his courtesans again.

What was worse, the Evenlight ceremony made goddesses that were a threat to his rule, and though it angered him greatly, Pryn was at a loss for what he should do about it. He knew that if something was not done fast he would lose his prominence among the other five kingships.

He called down into the courtyard, "Evenni, to me! I am ready to retire."

Hestus sat in his armchair by the fire, sipping spiced wine. He had been loyal to Pryn ever since the tyrant had come to rule over twenty years ago. They were a cruel twenty years, yet he had served faithfully according to his purpose in life.

Two guards walked into the room. "You called for us, Hestus?" Doth asked.

"Yes, Doth. I want you and Errod to attend the Evenlight ceremony tomorrow. So much of what we know of it has been pieced together from different accounts. You will go and report back to me."

"Did these orders come from the King?" Errod asked.

"No, but I have no doubt he would approve. The information may give him a better idea of how to handle the situation. He hides it well, but I know he fears a danger to his rule."

"We will go sir," Doth said.

Hestus nodded, and shooed them away. He had never given orders that did not come directly from the king, and he was not sure what it would cost him. He had not taken flight in many moons due to the pressure of military demands. Tonight must be different. He shed his robes as he went out to his terrace. He woke the beast within, and as the dragon shroud overtook him, he leaped into the air with a mighty downbeat of his wings. The cool night air wakened his flesh, as it beat against his flapping wings, and it brought renewed vigor to his mind. *How could the outcasts call themselves dragons if they had never experienced the glory of flight?* He thought to himself, and it outraged him.

He soared upward and down, for a long time. The thrill held him captive until suddenly he saw the light brightening on the horizon, and decided he must return. As he flew back, he cursed himself that he had not taken the opportunity for rest, but the sky had beckoned to him.

The great theatre of Montessa minor was filled to overflowing with those who were variously perceived as the scum of the realm. Men and women of the poor classes, rebel Firileen men, and hundreds of Forsaken were in attendance. Two visitors also looked on. A deafening noise spread across the crowd as everyone was talking excitedly about the event they were to witness, for many had never experienced the Even-light ceremony.

A great and majestic dragon flew into the theatre and lighted on the stage. The splendor of her presence crushed the noise of the crowd into silence. Folding her wings behind her, she shifted, and two attendants brought forward her robes to wrap her in.

"Welcome, citizens, to the ceremony of Evenlight. Today we witness the aging of many of our younger Evenni. It is truly a time for celebration. Those who bear the shroud bear the honor of the shroud!" Her voice could be heard clearly with perfect precision.

"Those who bear the shroud bear the honor of the shroud!" The people chanted back in unison.

A long staff of knotted acacia wood appeared in Warda's hand, and she waved it in a circular motion around the canopy of the theatre. From out of nowhere flames of white light appeared to brighten the proceedings. She then turned her staff toward the center of the platform and a bright blue flame flared up and sat hovering in midair. It was the eternal flame of the forsaken ones. The Even-light.

Sorina and twenty other young women her age lined the left face of the platform, eagerly waiting for their time under the flame. One by one they took the stage, and as they stood under the flame they grew into their brilliant reptilian form. With wings outstretched and neck stretched toward the hovering flame, a roar with mighty vibrato erupted from the depths of their throat.

As each one did so, the flame burst forth in wild colors of bright red and green, and shot down into their bodies. A bright red glow of light showed within their bodies, and they opened their massive jaws to let loose shimmering waves of flame. The crowd went wild with chaotic joy.

Sorina was the last to rise the platform. A hush fell over the crowd as they watched her every step. Not only was Sorina a favorite of Warda, but the citizenry adored her as well. Even despite the shroud, her sheer beauty was, in their eyes, unmatched among the Evenni. She disrobed and stood nervously in front of the crowd.

As she stood under the flame, and centered her focus, the change came fast. Faster than she was prepared for. The muscles rippled and expanded across her body, and her wings fanned out with a mighty wind that threw the entire first row of onlookers off their feet. When she reared her head to gaze into the Evenlight it expanded in matter of seconds and possessed Sorina.

Gasps of wonder shook the crowd as the scene settled. The Evenlight was gone. Sorina, lying naked in her human form on the ground, could hardly move, but her body was glowing as if consumed by the light.

Doth and Errod looked at each other, confused as to what they had just witnessed.

Warda joined Sorina on the platform and helped her to her feet, grabbing her cloak and wrapping it around her. She then turned to the crowd, and with Sorina's hand clasped in hers she raised it skyward saying. "Today marks an unprecedented change in our coven. The Evenlight has chosen Sorina as the new witch-mother of our kind. The Evenstaff shall pass to her, and as my light diminishes, her light will shine brightly."

The triumphant clamor that arose was deafening. From all around the theatre shouts of euphoria burst from the crowd.

Sorina's head turned in shock as she heard the witch-mother's announcement. "Mother, what do you mean?"

"Not now child. I will explain to you later. Enjoy your fanfare."

As the cheering and celebration went on around them, with large platters of food being served and flagons of wine flowing freely, Doth turned to Errod and said, "We must get out of here and report to Hestus." They left the theatre quickly, exiting the catacombs. As soon as they were above ground their arm and leg muscles rippled out into giant reptilian limbs, their wings fanned out, and they flew swiftly back to Rangor Keep. When they arrived they landed quickly and clumsily on top of the largest battlement. They took their human form and ran in haste to warn Hestus. They found him training in the arena, and whispered the news to him.

Hestus was outraged and unnerved at the news, and he dropped everything and went to inform his liege-lord.

Pryn was finishing a hearty boar stew when Hestus rushed in. Pryn rose and yelled, "Are you mad?! What makes you rush in here like a wild bull and disturb my meal?!"

"My King, the Forsaken have a new witch-mother. The ethereal fire has anointed her so."

Pryn stood so fast the table shook, and his tankard of ale toppled and spilled.

"Where did you get this information, Hestus?!" He bellowed.

"I sent two of my best to the ceremony as spies."

Pryn was turning dark red at this point. He wasn't sure what angered him more; the fact that Hestus went over his head, or that the Forsaken had a new queen. He decided the latter was worse.

"Summon the guard," he said as bits of food flew from his mouth. "We will meet in the war room after the meal at first light.

Also, send out the pigeons with an urgent message to the other four kings. They are to come for a meeting in the great hall in three days' time, and bring their best warriors and guards with them."

Hestus nodded and left.

Pryn was not sure what the new development meant, but it was an omen for sure. An omen that he must make work in his favor.

As the luminaries brightened signaling a new day, Warda summoned Sorina to her quarters. The new witch-mother arrived quickly and Warda bade her sit down.

"Mother, I cannot take this role from you," Sorina whimpered.

"Nonsense, Sorina. The Even-light has chosen, and it is a power older than you are.

Besides, I am over four-hundred years old and the coven needs new blood. Do not be dismayed though: I will be here to guide you. I will always be a witch-mother."

"You knew this would happen, didn't you?"

"I had a vision, yes, but I knew not when."

She stretched out her hand, and the acacia staff appeared again. "Sorina, this is the Evenstaff. When I was cast out, it came to me. I know not how, but I awoke the next morning to find it by my side. I placed my hands on it, and the Even-light claimed me, and it spoke to me somehow of the future of the Evenni who bear the shroud. It is now yours."

Sorina hesitated, a deep fear growing inside her.

"Sorina, step forward and grasp the staff with your hands. I will release, and then it is done."

Sorina walked carefully forward, and placed both of her hands on the staff. A tingling sensation rushed up her arms and traveled her whole body. It was like the charge she got from her garments when they had rubbed against other fabrics.

Warda knelt on the floor and bowed her head. "Hail, Sorina; witch-mother of the forsaken coven." She said.

Something sunk inside Sorina. "Please Mother, how will I lead the shrouded sisters?"

"With honor," Warda said. "A breaking point is coming, Sorina. It is important that we be the mending force and not the breaking force. These Evenni respect you, and the rest of the underground looks to us for protection, as deities to them. Trust your instinct."

Sorina nodded, and barely smiled.

"Now go child, there is much for me to do here. These quarters will belong to you soon, and I must pack my things."

"Thank you mother," Sorina said as she went to leave.

"No, I insist, thank you…mother," Warda said with a lyrical laugh.

All the Annos of Kish, some one hundred guards, gathered in the war room in answer to King Pryn's summons. They were posted throughout the room, standing and sitting around the large oak table. Hestus stood at the head of the table next to Pryn. Pryn was obviously agitated.

"It has come to my attention," he began, "that a successor to Warda has been named."

A murmur broke the silence and spread like water throughout the room. Pryn slammed the flat of his hand against the table.

"I am speaking, and I expect attention! If I had been around when the first abomination was created, I would have demanded execution, and then enacted laws that continued the practice. At least I relegated them to the catacombs when I came to power. This is our opportunity to exterminate them."

One of the Annos spoke up and said, "My lord, they may be deformed, but they are still Firileen. You would have us eradicate our own kind?"

"If it comes to that…yes. It may be sufficient if we kill their witches. Perhaps that will send a message that the rest should submit to their place in society."

"How will we stand against the power of the Evenlight?" Another asked.

"Do you have a fear of fire?! You are of the shroud are you not?"

"Yes Master, but our weapon is sound not fire."

"The vibrational sound we emit is formidable," Hestus cut in. "None can withstand it."

"It is decided then," Pryn said. "The royal guard of Kish, together with those from the other provinces, will invade the catacombs and do the deed. This will happen in a fortnight."

The silence was thick throughout the room, and Hestus grew impatient. "What say you?" He said.

"I serve!" One said, and the same exclamation came from every voice in the room.

"Excellent! Dismissed," Pryn said.

As the doors opened, a young boy who had been listening bolted and ran into the library. He hid behind a stack of old volumes as the noise of the guards bickering gradually got further down the corridor. He quickly found the window that led outside and climbed over the sill. He ran for a mile, and finally came to the wooden door that led down into the underground.

Sorina was moving in to the witch-mother's quarters. The servants had brought all of her belongings, and she was just beginning to settle into her new quarters when a loud tapping came at the door.

She opened it and the frantic little boy barged in. "Where is the witch-mother?" He panted.

"I…am the witch-mother now," Sorina said as her face flushed. She did not feel ready for any of this.

The boy paused, looking away and then back at Sorina. "Um, m-mother, I have overheard a meeting in King Pryn's war room. He is sending the Annos to kill you!"

The words took a while to sink in. *The males are going to kill us?* She couldn't understand why. "Do you know why they are doing this, uh…?"

"Azum is my name, Mother. Not really, although I did hear him call you abominations."

"I see. Thank you Azum. Leave me now, so that I may think on this."

The boy ran out as quickly as he had come.

Sorina was troubled, and she was greatly relieved when Warda arrived. She explained the message the boy had brought her, trembling greatly as she did so.

Warda sat silent for several moments before speaking. "Pryn is an arrogant and pretentious sot! However, he is also a brilliant strategist, and has the other provincial kings wrapped around his ego. They will no doubt follow whatever plans he might have. Our brothers of the shroud are mighty as well. They lack the flame, but their emanation can be equally devastating."

"What is the power they possess mother?"

"They are able to emit vibrational sound. Sometimes, if they are very skilled, it is so powerful it can quake the land or shatter bones. Those who are here among us will no doubt come to our aid though."

"I'm frightened, your eminence."

"As well you should be, Sorina. However, you are a warrior priestess now. What is more, you are the witch-mother, and you possess the Evenstaff. It is not just a ceremonial instrument, but an equally powerful tool of destruction. Use it, but use it carefully and with wisdom."

Sorina nodded, and hugged Warda.

"Come Sorina. I will be at your side as you address the sisters. They will look to you for leadership."

The Forsaken had been summoned to a gathering inside the massive dome. In one corner a rough-hewn stone rostrum jutted out from a platform of rock. Sorina and Warda stood side by side behind it, and Sorina looked out across the dome at the massive gathering of Evenni. As she stood there, as though frozen in time, Warda laid her hand gently but firmly on her shoulder. A wellspring of courage came to life inside Sorina, and the Evenstaff appeared in her hand.

"Sisters," she called out. "I have been informed that King Pryn is organizing an assassination attempt on my life. To be sure it will not stop there. He will want to eliminate queen Warda here, and the rest of us as well."

She paused, letting the awe thicken in the air. Where was this strength coming from? "He perceives us to be abominations, but we know better! Those who bear the shroud, bear the honor of the shroud! We are not abominations, but equals!"

Shouts of triumph and revolution rose up in a deafening cacophony. The thrill of their reaction strengthened her resolve. "We must be on the defense, not only for our kind, but also for the other outcasts of our society who reside within our walls. Sisters, prepare yourselves. If it is destruction he wants, we will serve it to him!"

Thick clouds of moving forms darkened the sky as beasts of the shroud flew over the plains toward Kish, casting their shadows along the ground like shades of evening. Those at the fore were ridden by the other kings of Montessa, and one legion from each province followed in tow.

They arrived at the castle upon the midday hour. The kings dismounted, and their mounts transformed and took up formation to stand guard during the deliberations.

King Pryn sat at the head of the table in his war room and watched the other kings stride in.

King Anibaster entered first. He was tall and lean with a long arrow point beard and curled mustache. His head was shaved bald save for a strand in the back that trailed down just past his shoulder blades and was tied off with a string of hemp. He approached Pryn and made an extravagant bow, and the king thought to himself, "what a pompous ass."

King Simor came shortly on the heels of Anibaster. Always the follower, one would think he worshipped the king of pomp. He was a short and stubby man with rosy bulbous cheeks, rather reminiscent of a chipmunk hoarding nuts. His long flowing robes were much too long actually, as he was constantly holding them up so he wouldn't stumble over them.

The next to enter was The Sage. His actual name was Denalo, and though he was king, he rejected his title as a stand for humility. He earned his fool name for his constant intellectual blathering and trite sayings. He was of average height and plain to look on. He wore the same one-piece robe every day, and he smelled of incense and cloves. There was a reason the other kings, and no doubt his citizens, kept their distance.

After several minutes passed, and the other kings had taken their seats, the final king walked in. Demmet by name, he was fond of making an entrance. Like Denalo, Demmet was of average build, but the similarities ended there. He was by no means demure in his presentation. He entered the room with more pomp than Anibaster could have hoped to muster in a year's time, and the Evenni consorts on each arm gazed at him as though he was the answer to all the problems of Montessa.

Underneath all the pretense, however, he feared Gayus Pryn. Pryn knew it, and reveled in it. Demmet sat down gingerly and shooed away his companions, sending them back outside to wait among the guards.

Pryn sat staring at Demmet and said, "are you finally ready to begin?" Demmet looked stricken, as if he would lose his last meal, and a dastardly grin broke open on Pryn's face. He stood quickly and began walking around the room as he talked. "You all know why I have summoned you here. A new witch-mother has come to power, and no doubt Warda still maintains her influence, so the threat to our rule is doubled. The key to their power is rumored to be a wooden staff that harnesses extraordinary power. We must usurp the Forsaken before they do the same to us. With any luck, we will wipe out the rest of the underground scum in the same blow."

"May I share something with you Gayus?" Denalo said with the usual air of gravity in his tone.

Pryn rolled his eyes and motioned Denalo to continue.

"As you know, the people watch how we treat those of the underground. Many share their feelings about the society we have created, but still remain loyal to us. How would it look if we were to engage in a mass extermination? Prudence rewards those who exercise it."

"My good fellow, I think you've been inhaling a bit too many fumes from those herbs you burn," Pryn said with a subtle laugh.

The other kings laughed along with him as the Sage's eyebrows arched downward and his face turned the color of burgundy.

"Of course *we* are with you, Gayus," Anibaster exclaimed in a patronizing yet cautious tone. Simor just smiled and nodded the same. No one bothered to wait for Demmet's assent, who always deferred out of a desire to save his own skin.

"Well then, my prudish little friend, it seems you are outnumbered here. Either join us below, or fly back to your royal tent and cower beneath your pillows!" Pryn watched with glee as Denalo's face went ashen.

A knock came at the door, and without waiting Hestus opened it and strode up to Pryn. Anyone else would've been slain on the spot, but though Pryn was aghast, he knew something must be important for Hestus to barge in.

"My lord, we have a visitor. Sorina, the witch-mother of the Forsaken coven is here. I would have executed her, but she invoked the right of parley."

"You see gentlemen," Pryn said curtly. "The sore begins to fester! By all means send her in, Hestus."

Sorina stood outside in the reception yard, flanked on either side by her guards Serra and Mila, with Warda close by as well. It wasn't often they went above ground, and the chill breeze floating in from the ocean enlivened her spirits.

The boy Azum had notified them that the council of kings would be meeting, and It had been decided that she would hold council with them in what would hopefully result in a mutual understanding. The reception that she had received, almost being killed by the chieftain of the guard, had somewhat lessened her expectations.

The doors opened, and pointing a long bony finger inward, Hestus ushered them in. Sorina commanded her flanking guards to remain, and then went inside. As Warda followed her, Hestus stepped in to block her.

"Only the witch-mother will be allowed inside," he said with a smirk and heavy disrespect.

The smell of sweat and smoke was so heavy in the room that Sorina almost gagged, but she kept her composure. She was not willing to give any indication of weakness to these brutes.

"To what do we owe the displeasure of your visit?" Pryn bellowed; condescension thick within his voice.

"I wish to arrive at an understanding. Discrimination has always been the rule of the realm, and I know how you feel about our kind. You feel we were mistakes, and you treat us accordingly. You must feel that certain of your citizens are also mistakes, for you treat them the same way. You think you are the rulers of Montessa, but I assure you that the Evenlight rules all, and the Evenlight makes no mistakes."

"Your particular brand of sorcery holds no sway in the upper realm. No matter how much you repeat the prattle of your predecessor, the fact remains that you are Forsaken. What's more, you pose a threat to our rule. One that we will not tolerate." He motioned to the guards that had followed her in and said, "Seize this filth, and remove her to my dungeons!"

The Evenstaff appeared and Sorina grasped it in both hands. Holding it upright, she channeled its energy and arrows of flame shot out toward the five kings and the guards. The arrows came to a stop mere inches from their throats, and just hovered in midair.

"You would break the sanctity of parley, King Pryn? How shameful! Well, if that will be the way of it, we'll see you in the catacombs. But beware, when the shroud takes over, the beast's appetite is not easily slaked. Are you prepared to feed us?" Sorina smiled playfully, as fire from the Evenstaff burst the doors, and she rushed out to join her companions. The arrows of fire vanished.

The rush of wind as the door exploded had scattered the guards closest to the building, allowing the Evenni to shroud themselves and take flight with a mighty scream.

Pryn came rushing out in a fury. "What are you fools waiting for?! Go after them!"

The shifters of each province changed at once and took to the sky. Hestus transformed as well, leaving a storm of dust in his wake as he flew to the fore to lead the chase.

Sorina's great wings sliced the air as they moved back and forth, up and down, increasing her speed through the air. Warda flew right behind, and Serra and Mila trailed.

They were nearing the area where the entrance to the underground waited when the host of Annos sounded behind them. As their male counterparts opened their massive jaws, a sound erupted from within them that was so deafening it was almost unbearable. The sound sent Sorina and her attendants into delirium, and they began plummeting to the ground in a free fall.

Just before hitting the ground Sorina came to her senses, and rushed her wings forward to push herself away from a crash. Serra and Mila recovered in time as well, but Warda was not so fortunate. The force of the soundwave had ruptured the tissue in her ears, and she hit the ground with such force that cracks began forming in the parched earth. Within moments she returned to her normal form, and lay motionless on the ground, naked and unconscious.

Sorina shifted as well, and ran over to Warda. Picking her up, she ran frantically for the entrance to the catacombs. Serra and Mila stayed behind to hold off their attackers, hoping to give Sorina enough time to go underground.

Thoughts bombarded Sorina as she ran. Why had she gone to the meeting? Why had she assumed they would listen to reason? She had endangered them all, and she had underestimated the power of her Firileen brothers.

Serra and Mila watched as twenty or thirty royal guards landed on the plain. They were outnumbered, but they would not give up. In unison they let loose their molten rage, and turning as they did so, great streams of blistering flame threatened to blanked their adversaries. The flames were so hot that several of the male beasts were crisping and wailing under its power. They failed to maintain the shroud, shifted back, and were consumed. Piles of ash rested where they had once fought.

Sorina reached the entrance to the catacombs and three of her sisters were waiting for her. Two of them made haste to bring Warda to the healers, while the other, named Halla, fetched Sorina fresh garments.

"Halla, summon those of the Annos that have sworn loyalty to us. We will need their might to hold our defenses."

Nodding, Halla left immediately.

Sorina went swiftly back to the scene of the attack. Serra was backing up frantically, trying to hold the remaining Annos off. Mila lay dead upon the ground. Her humanoid body a bloated heap, cracked and bleeding, as if some unseen power had ruptured her from the inside. The sound!

As Sorina rushed forward, the Evenstaff now in her hand, she shot the Evenlight forward into the center of the commotion. A fiery boil appeared in the soil and exploded outward, sending the other dragons back several feet.

Hestus quickly changed and raised his fist to halt another onslaught. Turning to the others he said, "Five of you return to Kish and summon the remaining forces to our side. I will remain here with the rest."

They took flight immediately, returning whence they came.

Hestus turned back around. His long black hair, streaked evenly with silver, glimmered in the light of the suns. He stood in battle stance, his male form rippled with bulging muscles and his skin was taut. He was a great fortified tower, made as of steel. He was flanked by three dragons on either side, one of which carried a thick jeweled scabbard five feet in length. He reached over and unsheathed a great terror of a blade.

"This was a gift to me from the maker," he called out to Sorina as she stood staring at him. Her eyes were blazing with the same ferocity as the Evenstaff. "She gave it to me when I came of serving age. Before this day is done I shall run you through with it, but not before I have tired of dancing with you."

He rushed Sorina with uncanny speed, colliding with her in intense rage. She fell to the ground hard, and the wind left her lungs. Hestus laid both of his massive hands on the Evenstaff, but as he did so the staff erupted in flame and seared the skin from his hands. He ripped them away, shrieking and skating with rage as he did.

Sorina bolted up from the ground, her eyes still alight with flame, and aimed her staff directly at Hestus. "Were you not aware? Only the witch-mother can touch the Evenstaff." She swirled the head of the staff in a circular motion, creating a sphere of flame that grew quickly in size and intensity.

Seeing what she was about to do, Hestus resumed the shroud, towering over Sorina as the bulk of his reptilian mass filled the spot where he stood.

Sorina continued conjuring until a ball the size of a small pool in circumference hovered in the air, undulating with untold power. She let loose the sphere, and it careened into the massive beast before her. He loosed a deafening howl as the flames gnawed at his leathery skin, and began beating his wings heavily in an attempt to fan away the worst of it. His screams caught her off guard, making her disoriented.

The other six dragons let loose their weapons of sound, shaking the foundations of all of their footholds. As they did so however, the Evenstaff flared to life and shielded her from the debilitating and possibly deadly sound. As they charged toward Sorina to relieve her of her life a tumult arose from the underground and began reaching to the surface.

The entrance began spewing forth dozens of those rejected by society. Many of the Forsaken were present, as were Firileen men that had sworn fealty to the Evenni of the shroud. Many human men and women had joined the fray as well, carrying clubs, axes, or whatever else they could get their hands on.

Halla was among the Forsaken who had joined the fray, and she went quickly to Sorina and whispered something in her ear as tears streamed down her face.

As Sorina listened, her countenance changed and a boiling rage turned the color of her skin a deep crimson mixed with gray. Warda was dead.

She threw off her garments and instantly loosed the beast. She screamed a frenzied call to battle and the rest of the Firileen answered her call. As they shifted their skin the rest of the citizens moved quickly away to avoid getting trampled under the massive limbs and claws.

Before the guardians of Montessa Minor could unleash their rage on the opposing dragons, a mass of reptilian power arrived from afar and converged on the battlefield. Forty dragons had come to add to Hestus' force, and the foremost dragons were mounted by the five kings.

The rage burned within Sorina, but she withdrew slightly and watched the scene unfolding before her.

Gayus Pryn climbed down from his dragon and raised both arms as if to show he meant no harm. He stopped and stood mere feet from Sorina and the host behind her. Hestus, now human again, walked up and stood beside him. There was a grotesque grin of satisfaction on his face, and his blade rested comfortably by his side.

He thinks this is the end, Sorina thought to herself.

"Witch-mother, the game is at a close," Pryn said. "Surrender to us, and we will allow your people to escape your fate."

Sorina came forward inch by inch, her massive wings folded back and the same familiar fire ablaze in her eyes. As she came close enough to touch Pryn, she snorted a massive gust of smoke in his face. Pryn began fitfully gagging, trying to relieve his lungs of the congestion. As he did so, Sorina turned to face Hestus.

Hestus beamed a great smile, and his eyebrows arched downward as he gazed into Sorina's eyes. "I grow tired of our dance," he said, and he grabbed the mighty sword with both hands and drove it in the direction of her gullet.

He wasn't fast enough though. Sorina dodged the blade as she vaulted to the left of Hestus, and as he began to retract the blade and turn again to face her she snapped at him with her massive jaws and severed his right arm. A chilling scream exploded from his lungs, as crimson blood streamed from the stub that was once his arm.

His hand fell to the ground still gripping the sword. Despite the horror, he concentrated with all his might to bring forth the beast. It was useless. The shroud had been separated when he lost his arm, so that he would never again wear its honor.

"What have you done!" Pryn shouted. "You lay your kingdom desolate by this action!"

Sorina sounded the battle cry again, and pandemonium broke out. Flames shot everywhere, and cataclysmic sound covered the area as the dragons turned the standoff into chaos. The other four kings deserted Pryn as they made haste back to their mounts and ordered them to leave. The last sight Pryn saw before being set ablaze by one of the Forsaken was King Denalo running away like a frightened pig running from a butcher. The lower half of his robe had caught fire, and he desperately tried to put it out as he ran.

Chaos broke out all over the plain. Sorina took out two of the Annos with one massive bolt of flame from her cavernous jaws. It pierced right through their chests leaving a massive bleeding hole, and the great beasts collapsed in a heap of death. She then charged another one. The two opponents locked in battle, shoving and clawing at each other.

Dantelus, for that was his name, swiped at her with jagged claws outstretched and caught the flesh of her face, tearing fearsome gashes as it finished. Sorina shrieked in pain and anger. As she shook off the daze, dark blood trickled down from the wound.

Sorina grabbed one of Dantelus' arms and drove it claw first in the hard soil, while holding his other claw in her iron grip. As the bones cracked under her weight, she held it in place with her hind paw, bringing her claws back up to gouge out his eyes. She then slashed the muscles in his wings, and flew off with him until she held him over the chasm. There she dropped him for a timely death, and went to rejoin her comrades.

As her mistress continued to resist, Serra also took out two more dragons, emboldened by her grief at Mila's death. As she did so however, she was taken by surprise. Another of the Annos swooped down from the sky, landing on top of her, and relieved her of her throat.

From all around them Annos that were loyal to the Forsaken joined in the fray, directing the full volume of their sonic weapon toward the invaders of their home. The accompanying humans joined in as well, attacking with the various weaponry they had brought with them. Some of these met with success, and others with demise, but many of the Montessan guards perished or broke under the weight of the onslaught.

Battered and weary, Sorina took human form again and proceeded to retrieve her robe and clothe herself. Blood still trickled from the unsightly gashes on her face, and as she walked a slight limp was barely noticeable. She summoned the Evenstaff holding it aloft, the fire within it a beacon of dread, and she gave a mighty shout of such power that it echoed across the canyons and rippled off the nearby waters. Upon hearing her shocking cry the battle came to a standstill. The royal guards began backing off, and silence spilled over the plain. The battle was over.

The twin lights were waning and changing into their cloak of night. Many Firileen, returned to their base form, lay dead or dying on the battlefield. Some from ruptured ears, or entire bodies. Others having been stricken by axe or arrow. Many would never be able to invoke the shroud again. The enemy that still remained alive had surrendered to the Forsaken, bowing their massive heads with wings outstretched flat upon the ground. An act of fealty. Likely they did so to preserve their lives, but whatever the reason it was enough.

Sorina walked over to where Hestus lay bruised and bleeding, his power brought to an end. "Warda is dead because of you and your lackeys. I should kill you where you lay," she said.

The news rushed over him like a knife slicing him open. He and Warda had been two of the first Firileen to come into existence, and despite his forsworn allegiance, he had secretly always fancied her. Tears welled up in his eyes at the thought, and the weight of it was so much for him that he began to faint.

Sorina noticed his change in demeanor, and the blood oozing from his severed appendage. She brought the flame of her staff to light and set to closing the wound with the flame as he screamed in agony. "I see you cared for her? Well then, living shall be your curse." As she said it she walked away from him.

Over the next few months Montessa Prime became the home of all the outcasts of Montessa Minor, Firileen and human alike. The provinces would be unified at last.

Sorina became the witch-mother and queen of the realm, and formed a permanent alliance with human kind to serve as co-regents. The Firileen who had sworn allegiance continued to serve as the royal guard, and the women who were not of the shifting kind were allowed to continue their various types of servitude, as long as they were treated with the utmost respect and dignity. The woman known only as the Maker was granted a home within the province of Kish. The breeding factories of the Torlune mountains were destroyed and the workers relieved of their duties. Never again would Firileen be bred.

Sorina stood in the balcony of Rangor Keep, where Gayus Pryn had once stood. As she looked out into the courtyard, she lifted her eyes to look at the light of night. As she gazed at its splendor, a swell of pride brought a smile to her lips. A new era of peace was dawning in Montessa. As surely as the twin lights changed their powers from day to night, so also peace and purpose would shine brightly. She would rest easy this night.

~

"Curious indeed! There are those of your kind that can become drakken-kind? Surely you jest, Traveler."

"You have my word on it. I have seen it with my own eyes, and it was then that related the tale to me. I have simply related it to you in my own way of telling. Talindor, could I perhaps refresh myself from my water skin? I am rather parched."

"Of course, Traveler. I do want you properly hydrated."

I'm sure you do, the Traveler thought to himself. He pulled his water skin from the latch on his belt and drank deeply. The room was exceptionally warm with the dragon's breath, and he wondered how much longer he would have to endure it."

When he had finished, and replaced the water skin, he launched into another story.

CHAPTER EIGHT
BENDERS OF LIGHT

As the early morning mist was settling on the foliage under the twilight of the waning moon, a shimmering figure passed along a deserted road toward a small town. His presence would have escaped any passers-by due to a certain peculiarity. His feet would have appeared like the path he walked, and other parts of his body blended with his surroundings.

Kirian Blackhorn had first discovered his bending abilities when he was twelve. He was playing Terraball with some friends when all of a sudden a sharp pain ran through his head causing him to pass out. From the perspective of his friends, they witnessed the horrifying disappearance of their friend, and were certain that he had been abducted by otherworldly forces.

By later that same day, the entire area was swarming with peace-keepers, psychics, and shamans. His parents were beside themselves with fear. When Kirian came to, and saw all the commotion, he got to his feet and went over to his parents.

"Mom, what's going on?" He said.

When his mother heard the voice next to her, but could not see her son, she fainted on the spot. Kirian grabbed her to brace her fall, and as he did he began shimmering and suddenly everyone in attendance at the fiasco was able to see him. After an exhausting amount of questioning, and both physical and psychological examinations, Kirian was finally able to achieve a certain sense of normalcy in life.

Over the years his ability afforded him some very unique experiences. He saw people at their deepest and darkest moments. He shared in their joys, their mistakes, and their sorrows.

One day he was walking along Vestabore street, and heard a scuffle not far from where he was. He decided it might be interesting to find out what it was all about, so he cloaked himself and quickened his pace to where everything was happening. As he got closer he could hear the terrified sound of a woman being accosted. He bent down and picked up a rather jagged rock from the stone way, and toyed with it gently in his hand to determine the best amount of force to use when throwing it at someone.

As he turned the corner he noticed a stout man of about forty years positioned a foot's distance from a young woman. He was holding an arm-blade to her throat. Arm-blades were the perfect weapon for taking someone unawares. Comprised of a sheath where the blade was embedded, and a spring trigger to reveal it at the appropriate time, the blades were fashioned with a cuff that straps to the forearm.

The man had obviously done a good job of catching the woman off guard. She was a simple woman, and proper, but also rather naive. Kirian came closer, enough to be sufficient for a good aim. He reared back his arm and catapulted the rock at the back of the man's head. The rock struck true, and the man howled in pain.

He turned this way and that, looking for his attacker, but his vision was rather blurry from the pain and the tears, and of course Kirian was well concealed. Kirian positioned his tall bulky frame in front of the woman, so that when the man turned back, he assumed she had fled and made a hasty departure himself.

Kirian never revealed himself to the woman, and she ran away as fast as she could as soon as her assailant left.

Kirian followed the cruel fellow at a safe distance until they arrived at his home. The dwelling was several hundred years old, and extremely run down. The living conditions sparked a small twinge of pity in Kirian as he watched the man desperately look around to see if he had been followed, and then enter the shack.

The pity didn't last of course, for Kirian immediately submitted an anonymous tip to the peace-keepers with the fellow's location and physical description.

Later he read in the local bulletin that one Tillius Krum had been apprehended the exact same day, and charged with abduction and ongoing torture of several unfortunate women.

The best part about Kirian's ability, in his mind, was that he never had to wonder what anyone thought of him, for he was present when people talked about him behind his back, and they never knew he was there. He did, however, need to be cautious if he had gas.

A few weeks back he had happened across a group of men his age at a local ale house. He was relaxing in a corner with an amber hued ale, which was rather abnormal for him as he normally preferred thicker brews. This particular day he felt like something a little lighter.

He had seen these men before. They frequented many of the same establishments that he normally went to, and their favorite thing in the world, it seemed, was to drink and discuss the nature of human existence. He had decided on this day to engage them in their discussions. They talked for a few hours before Kirian decided to leave, or at least pretend to leave. He could sense something was amiss when they spoke to him.

When he was easily out of sight, so that they would not know he had not left, he cloaked himself and slowly walked back and stood close to where his group of so-called comrades were talking. They were on their third round of intoxicants, and sufficiently inebriated to be somewhat louder when talking.

He was immensely entertained, if not also somewhat offended, by their complete retraction of everything good they had said about him before. They used terms such as idiot, daft, thick, and other not-so-niceties to describe his stupidity. He especially enjoyed the look on their faces as he let his guard down, and began to materialize before their eyes.

He spoke briefly, saying "What an amazing portrait! I had no idea you felt quite that way about me." There were looks of shock and horror on their faces, even fear, before they finally dropped some coin on the table and left as fast as they could.

Kirian was now twenty–five, and he was very adept at cloaking. Because he was quite introverted, he spent a lot of time using his gift. In fact, he spent too much time using it. However, he was about to have an encounter that would upset his perfect little world.

He came to a stop just outside the town. There was a woman standing opposite him in the road and It was clear that she was staring straight at him. She waved flirtatiously in his direction and smiled. Could she see him? Was she a Cloaker too? They stared at each other for a few minutes, and suddenly the woman began approaching him. She was average height and petite, with wavy brunette hair, and light olive skin. As she got closer, her scent reminded Kirian of fresh coconut. She approached him and held out her hand, saying "My name is Lyvia, what is yours?"

Kirian was rather dumbfounded. She could see him. "My name is Kirian," he said finally, "Kirian Blackhorn. Are you a...uh..."

"A Cloaker?" She finished for him. "Yes I am. Otherwise, you know I would likely not be able to see you. There are others of us you know. Would you like to meet them?"

Kirian thought long and hard for a few minutes before answering her. He had grown so accustomed to being alone. More and more every day, he spent withdrawn from people. Not only people in general, but even those he cared most about.

He loved his parents with all his heart, but they had never really understood his gift. Ever since his abilities were awakened they had kept a certain guard up with him, as though he were a freak. They accepted by default the existence of the clerics and the shamans, so how was he any different?

He knew deep down that they loved him, but it seemed they did not really know what to feel. He was sure they were at the very least afraid of him. He longed to have people in his life who understood him. He longed to have a real sense of family like he had always heard about, and like he had with his parents before the incident.

He had thought before that there must be others; there had to be. He was not prepared for such a sudden discovery however.

He replied with obvious hesitation, "Ok, I'll meet them. However, I want it on my terms."

"Of course," Lyvia replied, "where and when can we make it happen?"

Kirian wanted a public place that also offered plenty of privacy. If there was trouble, he wanted the commotion to be obvious. He knew the perfect place. He had been there many times, and it offered the perfect balance of having crowds and offering privacy. The main floor was open and airy, yet the patrons were seated in booths with high walls that erupted into a canopy. Plus, it was off the beaten path, and so no one who knew him, or the others for that matter, would likely happen there.

"Meet me at The Skeptics Cauldron tomorrow, at the midday meal hour," He said.

Lyvia replied excitedly, "Until tomorrow then, Kirian Blackhorn. Luck to you!" She then ran off into the town.

Kirian thought about following her, but then decided against it. He was emotionally drained from the encounter, and wanted to return home. Kirian lived in a medium sized cottage in the town of Mantalla. It was a fairly upscale market town, always bustling with merchants, tradesman, thieves, and cutthroats; the normal fare. The Blackhorn cottage was in the suburbs of town, gently tucked away.

He arrived home just in time for the evening meal. His mother had just finished preparing the food, and his father was sitting in his armchair reading the local bulletin, and smoking his reed pipe. Disease had caused his eyesight to fade dramatically over the last few years, and so his free hand was frequently holding a looking glass, especially at moonrise. Kirian laid a gentle hand on his father's shoulder. His father looked up at him, and after a toothy smile he returned to his squinting.

Kirian then went to the cook room to see his mother. She had lined two massive platters with equally massive amounts of food. Roast chicken and pork, boiled and spiced potatoes, fresh sautéed spinach and asparagus tips, and freshly baked oat loaf were the main fair. As always she had made enough to feed a small army. The best part was the platter of cherry tarts his mother had made for the end of the meal. She was currently filling their goblets with a rich, dark wine.

He walked over and kissed her on the cheek and patted her back. She looked at him and smiled longer than his father had. She handed him a tart and whispered, "Don't tell your father now." He wouldn't of course. Horus Blackhorn had always been more proper and ordered than his wife Tynia, and would be aghast if someone ate food outside the proper order of the meal.

As they were eating Horus, as was typical for the evening meal, shared some news from the local bulletin. "It seems the peace-keepers apprehended another vile citizen today. Said they received an anonymous tip. That's a stroke of luck, that is. Maybe we should fire the peace-keepers and hire the tipsters, eh eh." Horus always seemed more amusing to himself than anyone else, but at least it kept him amiable.

Kirian wanted to share some news too, which was not typical for him at mealtime. He was not sure how to begin. He normally sat and quietly ate his food, and only gave yes, no, and other assorted answers when engaged by his parents. The more he thought about it the more intimidating it became, so he decided to just come out with it.

"So I met someone like me today," he began. "It was kind of strange actually. She was staring right at me while I was doing my hiding trick, so I knew she must be like me."

The silence was so thick that a two-handed broadsword could not have cut it. Horus and Tynia seemed frozen in time as they stared at Kirian with their mouths wide open. They had assumed that there had to be others like their son, but had refused to entertain the thought for too long, and they had never shared their assumptions with Kirian.

Tynia was the first to speak up. She set her utensils down next to her food and said, "Kirian, your father and

I want you to have friends, but we would prefer that you not surround yourself with others who have your abilities. Who knows what kind of trouble a group of you could get into." Horus simply closed his eyes and nodded the whole time.

Kirian considered his response carefully before saying, "Mother, you have raised me to be cautious, and I am. I have arranged to meet her group tomorrow at the Skeptics Cauldron to find out more about them. You know that is the perfect place for meeting people you aren't certain about. I won't do anything foolish, and you know I would never do anything unl……"

Before he could finish his father spoke up. "Kirian it is not you we are worried about, but these other people. You don't know what their intentions are. We have done our best to help you conceal yourself, so that you would not be a public nuisance, but that may not be the case with this group. If they were to commit a crime, you could be guilty by association."

"What if they use their gifts to help people?" Kirian asked. "I have used mine for that purpose, and they may be of that mindset as well. I *will* meet them tomorrow." He had never been so determined and strong willed with his parents before, but he decided it had to end. He was tired of being alone and misunderstood.

They finished the meal in silence. Kirian was glad that he had eaten his tart before the meal, because he certainly didn't want it now. He was barely able to consume his main portions. He excused himself from the table, still extending affection to his parents, and retired to his room.

He flew in and out of sleep that night. When he woke the final time, it was in a cold sweat. He slowly moved to the lavatory, poured some water into the washbasin, and dunked his face in the water. The clear, lukewarm water relaxed him as it trickled down the contours of his face.

He grabbed a cloth from the basket to wash himself with, and after drying off and dressing himself in a lightweight leather jerkin and breeches he went outside. He looked longingly into the sky. If only his gift was flying, he thought. Judging by the position of the sun, it had to be mid to late morning. It was time to be getting on to the Cauldron.

Kirian's family owned a couple of horses. He preferred walking, but today seemed like a good day for a ride. He threw on his riding cloak and headed out to the stable. He saddled up his favorite horse, named Dayskipper, and led him out of the stable. He mounted the horse, and brought it to a slow but steady gallop. The day was getting warm, and Kirian was glad to have the shade of the cloak.

When he arrived it was nearly the meal hour. He tied up the horse at one of the posts adjoining the Cauldron and went inside. The tavern was empty except for a few of the regulars that he would normally see there. Lyvia and her entourage had not arrived yet, so Kirian acquired a large booth, and waited.

It wasn't long before Lyvia and the others arrived. They came in on a large carriage pulled by great-wolves; giant wolves the size of bears that were common to the northern lands. The reigns were controlled by a sizable, stalky man of about thirty-five years with a scar from his right temple to the left corner of his chin. Judging from the looks of it, he had owned the scar for many years.

Lyvia's other companions were two other men, two women, and a young boy.

When they entered the Cauldron, Kirian rose and motioned to them. Lyvia's face lit up like the hues of the rising sun, and she walked briskly over to the booth. She squeezed Kirian's arm affectionately, and then proceeded to introduce her companions. "The big one here, who I am sure was the first one you noticed, is Brindle Urgas. We call him Scar, for obvious reasons, and he wears it like a badge of honor. The young pup here is Yustas Wyrn, or Yuey as we call him. My other mates are Brock Leigus, Yustas' older brother Yulius, Meegan Sether, and Talyn Brese."

Feeling a bit overwhelmed, Kirian motioned for his new friends to sit down. One of the attendants approached their table with a nice hot loaf of bread, and gave them the food list for the day. They each ordered a tankard of ale, and then proceeded to hack off a slice of bread and slather it with the creamy spread that was in the adjacent bowl. They sat in silence for a few minutes, eagerly studying Kirian.

Lyvia could tell that Kirian was tired of being studied, and so she decided to be the first to speak. "So Kirian, how did you first discover your abilities?"

For the next hour, Kirian related the tale of how his abilities awakened. His new found friends sat in raptured silence as he told of how he had discovered his ability, the frantic search to find him, and the reactions once he reappeared. The group was hanging on his every word, partly because deep inside they were each reliving their own experience.

When he had finally finished, he sat back in a slacked position as if an enormous weight had been lifted off his shoulders. Why had he been so open and vulnerable with people he barely knew? He admitted that much of it probably had to do with Lyvia. She was very attractive, and had a disarming charm about her.

Scar was the first to reply. "Kirian we all had different experiences, but one thing that is the same with all of us is that we found out in very public and embarrassing ways. Lyvia here wants to bring you into our small group. Let me be clear about one thing though. We are not a guild or a club that you join on a whim. We were given this gift to be used. We can walk about unseen, and that has huge advantages."

It was becoming clear that Scar was the de facto leader of this little band, or at least he took it upon himself to be. Kirian tuned himself out to the rest of Scar's lengthy discourse, pondering to himself whether it was wise to tell them of the various situations where he had used his cloaking abilities. Suddenly he noticed that they were all looking at him again.

"I'm sorry," Kirian said. "I got lost in thought for a few moments, and I must admit I didn't hear some of what you said Scar. This is all very new to me, as you can probably guess. I am not used to being around others like myself. I have had numerous opportunities to use my abilities since I discovered them, and in most cases I would say I used them nobly, but I have made mistakes along the way as well. I am tired of living a mediocre life, and I would like to get to know all of you more. Would I be welcome in your group?"

They all took turns glancing at each other as if silently asking each other the exact same question. Lyvia then said, "Kirian, I think I can speak for all of us in saying that encountering you was no accident. We call ourselves Watchers, and we believe we are here for humanity's benefit."

Watchers. Kirian knew the term from ancient mystic religions he had studied. A sort of guardian spirit being, and a fitting name for their group he thought.

Lyvia continued, "If you want to be part of something more meaningful, then we would love to have you join us.

There are many more of us than just our group, but as you would expect, many of them have less than honorable uses for this gift. We affectionately call them vultures, because they prey on the 'lesser humans'. So, we see our protective mission as two-fold, really. The first part is keeping the peace of course, and the second is guarding society against the vultures."

A wide smile broke across Kirian's face as he listened to Lyvia explain their purpose. It was as if he had found a home at last, someplace to belong. He also liked that he would no longer be alone in his efforts to watch out for the less fortunate.

They all ordered some food and ate eagerly together, making idle conversation. When it became obvious that the sun was reaching its final zenith before the waning of the daylight, Kirian decided he had better return home. They dropped some coin on the table, said their goodbyes and began to leave. Everyone that is, except Lyvia. She whispered something to her girlfriends as they walked out, at which they giggled together, and then she grabbed Kirian's arm on the way out.

"Kirian," she began. "Could I ride with you?"

Kirian was visibly caught off guard. He liked Lyvia, but was not used to a lot of attention from the opposite sex. He answered guardedly, "Uh…of course…yes."

He helped Lyvia onto Dayskipper's back, and then mounted the horse himself. They rode for a few miles with a deathly awkward silence. The sun was setting rapidly, streaming orange, gold, and purple hues all across the dimly lit sky. Kirian thought that he should say something, but Lyvia beat him to it.

"I'm sorry I made you uncomfortable," she said. "I fancied you at our first meeting, and I wanted to get to know you more. I thought a quiet ride back with you would be the perfect opportunity. I'm sorry if I imposed upon your kindness."

Kirian was quick to reply. "No, not at all. To be honest, I am glad to have a riding companion. I fancy you as well, though I was nervous to say so. I don't have a lot of experience with beautiful women. I was always nervous that if they knew me, and knew about my ability, that they would completely reject me. So, I never bothered. None of the women I have known have my ability though, so this is different." He laughed nervously.

Lyvia smiled, with an obvious blush to her face. They rode in silence for a while longer, and suddenly they came upon the carriage of her companions. The great wolves were gone and the carriage abandoned. It was also obvious that there had been an ambush of some sort. Kirian reigned in his horse, dismounted, and bolted for the wreckage. Lyvia cloaked and sat in utter fright.

The carriage was in shambles. The reigns and harnesses were shredded, the spokes of the wheels were broken and splintered, and the great wolves were nowhere to be seen. There were splatters of blood in various spots in the dirt, but there were also numerous footprints, which would indicate that some of their comrades had at least been taken alive.

Kirian tried to remain calm for Lyvia's sake, but he couldn't help but be concerned for the others. When he returned to where Lyvia and the horse were waiting, he cloaked himself as well. They had to find the rest of the group, but had no idea where to go. When cloaked, not even a person's footsteps could be seen. There had to be a way though.

"I need to get you home," Kirian said.

Lyvia would hear nothing of the sort. "Nonsense! I am going with you. I can handle myself just fine, and you need some backup."

Kirian guessed there was no point in arguing. "Alright," he said. "One thing we must do is go by our respective homes and let our families know we will be out more tonight, but do not let on to my parents what has happened. They will go straight to the peace-keepers."

"I won't," she agreed. "However, there is no point in going to my home. I have no one except my friends." She began to weep as the emotions were still fresh. "I was orphaned when I was eight years old. I have no other family left to rely on."

"Not to worry," Kirian said, embracing her gently. "I won't abandon you, and we will find our friends."

They watered the horse at a stream a couple of miles north of the wreckage, and then made haste for Mantalla. They both knew that time would not be their friend in this situation. They tried to lighten their emotional load a bit by joking that this was not quite the circumstances under which they had hoped she would meet his parents. They also discussed plans for an explanation of why they would be out so late on this particular evening. As luck would have it there was a gypsy show in town, so they decided they would use that as their excuse.

They arrived as nightfall was just setting in, and as they approached they noticed that the door was ajar. Kirian peered inside and slowly walked in. There was a cup of garlic tea sitting cold on the counter. Garlic tea was a favorite of his mother's, and the cup never stayed full for long. There was a half-eaten cherry tart sitting by the candle at his father's armchair, which was something else that never happened under normal circumstances.

Kirian called quietly for his parents, and then he heard a rumbling in the closet. When he opened the door, he found that both his parents had been gagged and tied together. He mused that at this point the story about the gypsy show would not likely hold much water. He had to wonder if this was related to the attack on the carriage, or simply a random, unrelated occurrence. Whatever the case, the attackers were no longer there as nearly as he could tell.

"Lyvia, you can come in now!" Kirian called. He could hear her rushing nervously into the house, and slamming the door behind her.

They untied his parents, who were an emotional mess, and Kirian made his mother a fresh brew of garlic tea, and made sure his dad was set with a fresh cherry tart. Then, they settled in around the table to discover what was happening. They told Kirian's parents about the incident with the carriage, and his parents told them about their ordeal as well. Two men of roughly thirty years of age just appeared in their home, who then cloaked and tied them up before they even had a chance to understand what was happening.

"Did they say what they were looking for?" Lyvia asked.

Horus was the first to answer. "They were looking for a group of people called watchers, and they thought that Kirian might be one of them. You aren't, are you, son?"

Kirian thought for a few moments about how he should answer. Either way his parents would eventually find out, he assumed, and so it was better that they should hear it from him.

"I just met with the Watchers, dad," Kirian said. "And, yes, I feel like I can be part of something bigger by being with them. I was meant to do this. I am sorry to get you involved like this. The ones who attacked you are likely from a group with abilities like mine, but who use them to terrorize and destroy. They have taken my other friends, and Lyvia and I need to find them. Did they say how to contact them?"

Upon hearing this, Horus turned about five shades of angry, belligerent, and downright distasteful. He stood up, looked Kirian straight in the eyes, and let an open palm fly hard across Kirian's face. The news apparently didn't go over as well as he had hoped.

"How dare you, boy!" Horus exclaimed as spit flew from his mouth, and spread in five different directions. "You have exposed us all to freaks like yourself."

Kirian stood up immediately, and with a surprising calm, he set his father straight. "Actually, dad, they have likely been watching the house for a while. The way they pulled this whole thing off shows that they have been planning it for a while. So, if you are done throwing your tantrum, I need you to tell me whatever they told you."

Kirian had never stood up for himself before, and the look on Horus face as he replied showed it. "Well…I…uh, I don't…, they mentioned having something you wanted in an abandoned building on the outskirts of Trellia. They said it was urgent that you find them there."

Trellia was a small town a few hours north of Mantalla, and had been abandoned for fifty years. It was never clear why it was abandoned, but half of the population had vanished and the other half had cleared out in less than a day. Most were so anxious to go that they took no possessions with them except the clothes on their backs, and in some cases the family pet.

Kirian grabbed his dad, hugged him tight, and after doing the same with his mother he and Lyvia made preparations to leave. Tynia gave them a rucksack full of food for traveling. A loaf of oat bread, assorted dried fruits, and some cherry tarts. She kissed Kirian on the cheek, then turned and glared at Lyvia with a scowl on her face that would have closely resembled a hag in labor. Lyvia looked away with tears in her eyes. Tynia then pushed them out the door, and abruptly closed it behind them.

Kirian looked at Lyvia with apology in his eyes, and they walked off to the stable. They brought a bag of oats for Dayskipper, who was still visibly weary from the events of the day, and rode out on him into the blanket of night.

The night was pitch black, perfect for their situation. Cloaking abilities aside, those of their kind could still see them, and so travel under cover of darkness would draw less attention. The night was still young, and so they rode at a slow pace to give Dayskipper some time to recuperate.

Lyvia had wrapped her arms around Kirian from behind, and fallen asleep against his back. He was rather glad for the silence, especially because he knew it would not last long. Once they arrived in Trellia, things would get more chaotic.

When they began nearing Trellia, the darkness was still surrounding them, so they took the opportunity to make camp. They found a copse of trees next to a stream close by, and they dismounted Dayskipper and guided him over to the stream.

Dayskipper drank heartily, and then collapsed in the grass and grazed for a bit. Kirian and Lyvia also collapsed in the grass under the shade of a massive oak tree, and were instantly asleep.

The rising sun gradually signaled their bodies to awaken, and after stretching profusely they mounted Dayskipper again and made their way into the abandoned town of Trellia.

There was a deathly pallor to the town, and yet they could feel the eyes watching their every movement toward the center square. The town had one solitary street running right through the middle of it lined with what might have been shops on either side. Behind the shops were clusters of cottages and shacks, long abandoned stables, and patches of granaries.

When they reached the other end of the forsaken town, they came upon a three story building that may have once been used for a courthouse of some sort. This was the only building in the whole town that stood apart. The brick was stonewashed, and no visible signs of disrepair existed at all on its facade. There were, however, spots of freshly dried blood ascending the steps. It seemed that this must be the place.

As they approached the building, the great double doors swung inward, and a menacing figure exited the building and began making his way toward them. He was large and imposing, and wearing a woolen pullover shirt cut off at the shoulders. He had shoulder length brown hair that hung in messy tangles, and was clean shaven. Shards of shale were attached to a metal hook in each of his ears, and he wore a weather worn patch over his left eye.

There were others with him as well. Three other men and two women who were dressed in a similar fashion to the brute, but none were as clean shaven as he was.

Kirian spoke first. "Who are you, and what do you want with our friends?"

The hulk of a man bellowed a derisive laugh before answering. "I am Gert and these are my companions. You don't need their names, but you know us as…what was it you called us? Vultures? Yes, vultures. How appropriate. Vultures love being in the presence of a kill.

"Now you have a choice kid. You and your friends can join up with us, or you can die standing against us. People like us were meant to rule others, so don't be a fool."

The venom in his reply was unnerving. His companions just stood there glaring. One was carrying a quarterstaff, and another a farmer's scythe. They were obviously planning on brutality.

"Sorry friend, I feel like being a fool today." Kirian kicked a huge cloud of dust into Gert's eyes, grabbed Lyvia, and they cloaked and made a dash into one of the abandoned building just west of the courthouse. Gert and the others were screaming curses, and Gert himself began barking orders.

Kirian knew it wouldn't be long before they were found, so he tried to think of a way out of this mess. They had to get into the courthouse and find their comrades. It would take their combined efforts to take down the vultures.

A thought struck Lyvia all of a sudden. "Kirian, the day I saw you, I didn't notice you until you were in my line of sight. I never mentioned to you that it works this way, but surely that is how it works for them too."

Kirian hadn't ever realized that. They cloaked themselves and moved carefully out of the building, creeping along the side and across the way to the side of the courthouse. They continued moving along the outside wall, and up the side steps. The old wood was battered and breaking, and when they took the steps their weight made the steps creak loudly. The vultures jerked around at once, re-converging on the courthouse, just as Kirian and Lyvia ran inside.

They found Scar and the others just up the stairs on the second level of the courthouse. They had been beaten severely and each lay unconscious, strapped to a table.

Kirian thought it best not to waste much time, so he barred the door and began trying to loosen the straps. Lyvia began doing the same.

They had just loosed all their friends, and laid them gently in a corner, when suddenly the room filled with the Vultures, and this time there were more of them. Kirian counted at least twenty.

Vultures is an appropriate name, Kirian thought. *They hover just like them.*

There would be no getting out of this Kirian realized. Everything he could do, they could do. Then he noticed Lyvia. She was crouching on the floor behind one of the tables and pointing at the stove in the corner of the room not far from Kirian. The Vultures must've had a meal here, or had some inane desire to keep the room warm, because there was still the slight flicker of a fire that could be seen through the crack in the cage door.

There was also an oil pot next to the stove, no doubt to quicken the flames. Kirian darted to the corner, grabbed the oil pot, and swung it in with his arms letting the oil fly toward the group.

While the Vultures scrambled to figure out what to do, Kirian grabbed a shard of tinder from the stove and threw it in the direction the oil had gone, which was all over the floor and some of the Vultures as well.

The room lit up with flame within seconds of the shard hitting the oil, and shortly after the room lit up with shrieks as well.

Luckily enough, the rest of their group was regaining consciousness. Fire was made of matter just like anything else, and they were able to cloak and pass through the flame. They made their way down the stairs and out of the courthouse as quickly as they could, and started heading for the spot where they left Dayskipper. The others were awake and somewhat mobile by now, though some were slower due to their numerous injuries.

Their fortune didn't last long, as a handful of the Vultures had discovered a way to avoid the flames as well, and they gave chase a few minutes after Kirian and his friends had left the building.

When Kirian saw them coming, he quickly turned to the others and said "We need to hide now! They won't be able to see us unless we are in their field of vision."

There was a barn about a block from where Dayskipper was tied, and they quickly cloaked and ducked inside.

Scar turned to Kirian and said, "Listen, Kirian, there is another aspect of your ability you may not have come across yet. Not only can you cloak yourself and move through various types of matter, but you can also push things while cloaked. With all of our strength combined we may be able to bring this barn down on them if we time everything right, but we will need to lure them in."

"It's me they were initially after," Kirian said. "I'll draw them in."

His decision could not have had better timing. As if drawn to the scent of a kill, the Vultures found the barn. Only ten of them had made it out alive from the courthouse.

Kirian flagged them down. "I'm over here," he said, and then ran out the other side of the barn.

The Vultures bolted after him, but as they did the barn door slid shut. As they turned to go the other way, the opposite door slid shut as well.

The Watchers all cloaked themselves and focused all that was in them on the frame of the barn. Kirian watched intently for a few moments, and then joined his friends in the endeavor.

The whole frame of the barn began shaking, and then the shaking turned to quaking as dust shook from the cracks in the wood. They raised their arms and then lowered them in one swift motion, and the entire barn collapsed inward.

They hit the ground together in exhaustion just as a dozen peacekeepers rode into the area. They had been summoned to Trellia to contain a fire that had broken out, and determine the cause.

After the fire had been contained, the surviving Vultures were carted away by a second troop of peacekeepers that had arrived.

The troop commander questioned Kirian and his friends for over an hour, and finally determined that their story checked out. Another group of peacekeepers had found the wreckage of the carriage, and the evidence of a commotion, so there was no disputing the facts.

Scar and the other watchers rode back to [town], all except for Lyvia who stayed behind with Kirian. They mounted Dayskipper and made their way back to Mantalla.

When they arrived, apparently word had got around, and Kirian's parents were in a panic about what had happened to him. Tynia ran out to meet them and grabbed both of them in a suffocating embrace.

"Nice to see Lyvia is finally in your good graces, mother." Kirian mused.

They talked for a while and then turned in for the night. Lyvia was invited to sleep on a spare mat in the family area.

The next day, Kirian and Lyvia met their friends again the Skeptics Cauldron. They were all on the mend, and were laughing heartily with good conversation. They enjoyed a loaf of honey bread, a plate of boiled chicken, and a cask of rich dark ale together.

One threat was averted, but surely more would come. Now was the time to solidify their efforts for the good of their homeland. They were strong as friends. They would be stronger as comrades.

~

"I have never understood the fascination with various fermented beverages. Your kind certainly does have strange rituals. I also find that those who partake heavily of your drinks tend not to taste as good."

"Is that all you found of interest in my story Talindor?

"Apologies, Traveler. I can be easily distracted sometimes. Do tell me another."

CHAPTER NINE
HIPPOCHRYN

There are few who are lucky enough to get visited by the Hippochryn. Many have been in their presence, but usually are not aware of them. Most who lay claim to having seen them, are accused of dark magic or insanity.

There are those who have described them as human like, some male and some female, adorned in white battle raiment with great majestic wings protruding from their back on either side. They are said to have eyes as black as coal throughout, and long crystalline hair flowing down their back as though it were a waterfall.

There are also others who describe them as gigantic winged stallions the color of clear water, with a long flowing mane of crystal hair. Protruding from the skull is a single spiral horn the color and consistency of pure sea coral.

In reality they are neither, and both at the same time, though none have enough information to know for sure. Except one.

Sitrius Murr strolled barefoot at a casual pace along the oceanfront. He always took every opportunity to take in the full effect of nature upon his senses. With every step he dug his feet into the sand, letting the coarse granules lodge themselves between his toes and inside his toenails. The sand was cooler and crisper than usual, since it was the season of the ice tides. For two cycles every year the tides that blanketed the coastline of Tymor Bay combined with the runoff from the snow-capped peaks of Mt. Velitria far in the north. When these tides rushed in it left the sand feeling almost as cold and prickly as newly fallen rock snow.

As he reached the peninsula, he paused and stared out over the ocean. The ocean breezes caressed his dark olive skin, and he closed his eyes as if in a trance. As he inhaled, the scent of the breeze was immensely satisfying, and his shoulder length auburn hair fluttered wildly in the onslaught of the currents of air. He felt like he must surely be a creature of the sea. The screeching of gulls filled the air, and if he could not belong to the sea, then his second choice would have been to join the gulls in their reverie.

Sitrius had made it a ritual to take a refreshing swim with the sea lizards every morning before breaking his fast. His parents had always thought him insane, and warned him of various different ailments that would set into him if he continued the practice, but he never listened. It was second nature to him to be in the sea. He was about to shed his clothes and go for his morning swim, when he heard a huff of air a short distance from him. Startled at first, he crouched behind a large moss covered rock, and peeked out just enough to look toward where the sound had come from. What he saw was astonishing.

Standing at the edge of the water was the most beautiful creature he had ever beheld. It was a large stallion, the likes of which he had never seen, though he had heard the rumors. Its color was almost translucent, and yet not. Its hair was like pure white crystal that looked as if it might feel like satin to the touch. The hooves seemed like they could have been made of pearl. This was no ordinary stallion however. On either side of its body at the shoulder blades were the most brilliant wings he had ever seen. They were milk white, and completely unblemished. Atop the stallion's head was a single spiral horn that looked like pure coral, just like the tales had told. The creature's eyes were closed, and it was lazily drinking from the water of the inlet.

Sitrius rose up slightly from his crouching position, and moved gingerly across from where he was in a half crouching, half standing movement. He didn't want to spook it. As he drew closer, the stallion turned its head in his direction, and surprisingly returned to focus on the water without giving him a second thought.

He continued approaching, and when he had come mere footsteps away he knelt down and cupped his hands in the water. He raised the handful of water in offer to the creature, and as the water slowly seeped from his hands the stallion stared at him as if considering the offer.

Finally, it stepped forward and drank the water Sitrius had put forth. As it drank it stared at Sitrius. It had the most disturbing eyes. There was no color to them whatsoever, but instead the eyes were completely black throughout.

Sitrius reached out and stroked the stallion's neck. The skin was as smooth as sea stone, and slightly moist to the touch. He was completely mesmerized by this wonder of the gods.

Suddenly the stallion backed away, and Sitrius stared at it in wonder. What happened next he might never be able to fully explain. The stallion's bodily structure began to shift before his eyes. The circumference of the hind legs began to expand, and feet sprouted where hooves had once been. The trunk of its body reared and became a human like torso and chest, and the circumference of the front legs then expanded, and the hooves became human hands. Atop the shoulders sat a human head, much like his own. The main difference being the single white horn at the peak of the humanoid's forehead. The horn was not as long as the stallion's had been, which made Sitrius wonder if it had sunk into the crevice of the skull. Where the mane had been, was a waterfall of flowing white hair, which ran on as if forever down its back. And on its back the wings remained, protruding from the shoulder blades. As a man, the creature stood close to eight feet tall.

Sitrius sank to his knees, part out of fear and part out of sheer awe. He closed his eyes for a moment, thinking he might be imagining things. When he opened his eyes, however, the winged man still stood there.

They stared at each other for a few moments, and finally the mysterious being spoke. "I am called Gryn," he said. "What might I call you?"

Gryn's voice sounded as crisp and clear as the whispers of the ocean breezes. Sitrius was unable to speak for what seemed like ages, and then he finally found his voice. "Sitrius," was all he could manage to say.

Gryn spoke again. "Does this inlet belong to you, Sitrius? My apologies if I have trespassed on your borders."

"No…not at all," Sitrius answered. "I simply come here to enjoy the coastline and swim every morning. My home is not far from here, and it offers me a pleasant start to my day."

"I see," Gryn replied. "It is truly a pleasing area. I can see why you enjoy it." He paused for a moment, and then continued. "Forgive me Sitrius, but I need to speak with you of more urgent matters. I had to be sure it was you, before I divulged my reason for being here. I am actually here to find you."

Sitrius was again at a loss for words, though unvoiced questions ran freely through his mind. What is this creature? Where is he from? What does he want with me? Is he to be trusted?

The slightest smile struck the corners of Gryn's mouth, and he sat down on the sand with his legs crossed one over the other. "I can see I have troubled you," he said.

"Troubled me?" Sitrius said grandiosely. "Yes you have. What are you, and why are you here for me?"

Amused, Gryn offered a trickle of laughter. "Forgive me friend. We rarely engage at any length with those of your kind, and so I am sure I have caught you off your guard. The true name of our kind would mean nothing to you, but at times when we have met with those of your race they have called us Hippochryn. I believe it means something to the effect of flying horse man, does it not?" He laughed again.

Sitrius stared at Gryn dumbfounded, and then suddenly he felt at ease. "Why yes I think it does," he replied with a laugh. He joined Gryn on the sand, assuming the same sitting position, and they stared out over the ocean.

After a few minutes had passed, Gryn spoke again. "As to the reason I have sought you out, it is because of your family. Our race has had dealings with your parents before, primarily with your father Torren, and we bear you a certain trust."

"My father has never mentioned you except to tell me stories. Most of which I have heard from others as well," Sitrius replied. "Why would he never tell me?"

"Due to the mysterious nature of our kind, and the fact that we do not make ourselves known to just anyone, it was likely better for your father that we remain a myth," Gryn stated. "Humans often fear what they do not understand, and your father may have encountered unpleasant reactions to his tale had he regarded it as factual."

Nodding his head in agreement Guent Sitrius asked, "So what do you need of me?"

Gryn's expression grew very solemn as he said, "Just as there are those of my kind who, like myself, represent the forces of goodness and freedom, there are also those who wish to subvert that through manipulation and slavery. I am here to enlist your help, Sitrius. There is a mystical power in the human race that I, and those like me, cannot begin to channel."

Sitrius was very confused at this point, but he was sure more questioning would help. He looked over his left shoulder for a while, eyes fixed on the ocean. "You mentioned others, whom I assume are evil natured by your description. What are they?

"As I said before," Gryn began, "They are of my race, but a hunger for power and a fascination with the dark elements has corrupted them. They have become so permeated with them, that their form has changed significantly. As you look upon the brilliance and purity of my appearance, imagine a polar opposite to me, and that is what you would find. Their physical characteristics are basically the same as my own. They have wings, a horn, and take the form of what you call a stallion, but the resemblance ends there. Their brilliance is tainted, and their beauty marred. They have been called the pale ones, for they look sickly and diseased. Their wings are tattered, and their mane is wild and unkempt. Their skin is full of dark ridges, running like veins throughout. Visual proof that the darkness has enslaved them. They corrupt both my kind and yours, and they feed on those who do not conform to their rule."

Sitrius thought on this for a moment and said, "So should I assume that whatever you enlisted my father for, however long ago it was, did not succeed?"

"Oh no it succeeded, at least at the time. The pale ones had planned an uprising that would alter the fabric of existence as we know it if they had succeeded. I brought your father into it, along with others, to make use of the power that resides within your kind. Only that power was capable of stopping the uprising. Though he and his companions succeeded in halting the uprising, there was not enough collective power to completely subdue the dark elements and return the pale ones to their former splendor. So you see, they were only delayed, not defeated."

"Tell me more about this power you speak of," Sitrius said.

"You might think of it as an inner light. It is infused into every human being, and with it you shape your reality. Much of what you see around you has been given its form by your inner mind. Only you can discover the path to harnessing this power for yourself. I would rely on you to create a new, more positive reality."

Gryn rose quickly and exclaimed, "Now, Sitrius, we must be off. It is urgent that we begin preparing for the inevitable confrontation with the pale riders."

In no time at all Gryn had returned to his previous form, and turning to look at Sitrius he huffed at him and motioned with his muzzle toward his back. Sitrius had never ridden a horse before, and so he was hesitant to do so. Gryn reared back, lifting his front legs in the air and whinnying. Sitrius sighed in resignation and pulled himself up to sit on Gryn's back. He held on gently to the wings where they met at the shoulder blades. Gryn reared again and took off running up the coastline and into the hills.

They arrived shortly at Sitrius' small home, which was situated a little way inland from the sea. He got down and took a few minutes to steady himself. *If this is riding, what will I be like with flying* he wondered to himself. He had lived alone for the last ten years. His parents had disappeared, and no trace could be found of them. Stricken with grief, the one thing that had sustained him was the ocean, and now he was about to leave it all behind. He grabbed a bag and threw a change of clothing into it, and also a canvas wrap of fruits and fresh vegetables. Throughout his life he had been nourished on food from the earth and the sea, and had never needed to eat any kind of meat that fed off the land. He hoped he would not be forced to, and he was sure Gryn would share that sentiment.

He rushed out the door and found Gryn grazing in his garden. "Please don't eat my food. I worked hard to plant all that."

If it was possible for a horse to be embarrassed, Gryn looked it. Sitrius just laughed and said, "Don't fret over it."

He wrapped his bag around his shoulder and vaulted onto Gryn's back. After he had steadied himself they shot into the air, though it felt like he had left his stomach behind. He wretched over the side, and his mount made a noise that sounded like a laugh.

They flew hastily through the clouds and eventually began to approach a range of flatland encased in a wall of high mountain peaks. How many feet in the air they were was not clear.

As they drew closer, what Sitrius saw took his breath away. Whole herds of Gryn's kind were scattered across the plain. Some were chewing lazily on the lush green grass, some were resting, and still others seemed to prefer their human form.

Gryn began to flap his wings in a forward motion, slowing himself enough to achieve a perfect landing on a rough stone slab that would've easily held fifty of the beautiful creatures.

Sitrius stayed where he was for a while, staring at the ground to try and regain his head. When it became clear that he could not really do so, he slowly dismounted and collapsed to the stone beneath. When his stomach finally calmed, he looked up to see Gryn smiling at him from his human face.

Gryn reached down and helped him to his feet saying, "Welcome to Perennia, Sitrius. Now, we must hurry. My kin are anxious to meet you, and there is much to do. I must warn you that you will be somewhat revered among my kind. We have always taken great interest in those of your race, but it is rare to see one up close."

Sitrius didn't know what to say to that, so he didn't. They hadn't walked but a few steps before they were surrounded by crowds of the Hippochryn, all in their human form. They were breathtaking. Though some were surely younger than others, it was difficult to determine their age for they all had manes of the same color as that of Gryn. Some were male and some female, and just as with humans the women had a rare beauty.

One of the females spoke up. "Gryn, we've not much time. I have spotted the dark riders in my sight. They will rise up soon."

"Sitrius, this is Sorna. Only the females of our kind possess the sight, and she is one our chief seers."

"Who are the dark riders she speaks of?"

"They are human warriors who now serve the fallen of my kind. Their skills are barbarian in nature. They do not possess the same capacity of inner power that you do."

"Will there be more of my kind arriving?"

"We have a few already Sitrius, but that is all. You must lead them, for you have the greatest power among them."

Sitrius was so visibly distraught that Gryn did his best to reassure him. "Do not fear, Sitrius, we will also fight by your side. However, your kind will be the ones who turn the tide."

Sorna spoke again with a sense of urgency in her voice. "We must go now. I will take you to my sisters to make the necessary preparations."

Sitrius, Gryn, and the throngs of Hippochryn made their way to the base of Alletroya, which means the sacred rock. It was the central mountain in the range. A single entryway was cut out of the rock.

Sorna led Sitrius inside, while Gryn and the crowds remained. She led him through a long passageway lit only by solitary candles on the wall at every few paces. When they finally reached their destination they had arrived in a room with a fairly high ceiling, but only able to hold possibly fifty humans. There were seats carved into the rock all around the circumference of the oval shaped room, and in each of these seats sat a female Hippochryn with legs crossed and their wings tucked neatly behind them.

"Sisters," Sorna began, "This is Sitrius, son of Torren. He is the last to arrive of those who will help us."

Sitrius stood silent as the sisterhood looked him over. He felt extremely uncomfortable, as if he were on display in a lookery. Their gazes were piercing and probing.

"I will do my best to help." Sitrius said.

The sisters continued looking at him, until finally Sorna spoke again. "The sisterhood welcomes you Sitrius. I am the speaker. My sisters communicate with me telepathically."

Sitrius was relieved, as he felt maybe they despised him for his humanity. Maybe they did, he thought, and he would never know.

The sisters came forward and encircled him. They then laid their hand on him and began swaying. They reminded him of the tall, thin palm trees as they swayed in the ocean winds. Though they said nothing, there was a certain vibration that filled the room, as if they were chanting some ethereal incantation.

The vibration swelled until he felt a warming sensation begin to permeate his body, and then the warming became a burning that drove him to his knees in agony. Then, it was gone, yet something was different. He couldn't place it, or even say what it was, but he felt as if from a child he had reached adulthood again.

Sitrius stood, and at once he felt a tingling throughout his body. It was a similar sensation to what he felt when movement of blood lessened in his feet, but this was different, in that this sensation did not go away, but felt as if living energy was coursing through him. He moved to the wall to steady himself, and as he touched it the wall rippled as if it were a pool of water.

Sitrius jumped back in surprise. The wall had returned to normal, but he could still feel the sensation of its change.

Sorna laughed, and it sounded like a rush of wind. "Go easy, Sitrius. Yes, you can manipulate the fabric of reality. That is the nature of your power, but you have never done it before now. You will grow accustomed with time."

As they exited the mountain chamber, Gryn was waiting with an entourage of six other humans. "The hour is late, and I can already hear the rumble of hooves in the far distance. Sitrius, I want you to meet your comrades."

The first Sitrius met was Tirfa. She was tall and slender, but she had a ferocity buried under the surface waiting to be unleashed. The next was an older man, well past middle age, called Bratto. His age obviously had no bearing on his air of intimidation. The other four were two sets of twins, which surprised Sitrius somewhat. Rufus and Renn had lived eighteen years and fought like dragons. Tarin and Marca had lived twenty years, and obviously had a thing for Rufus and Renn, as they didn't give Sitrius the slightest thought.

Tirfa, however, eyed him playfully, and it caught him off guard. Sitrius had never been interested in intimate relationships, but he thought he might like to change that if given a chance with Tirfa.

"I am glad to know you all," Sitrius said "Do you all have the same ability to change reality?"

Gryn spoke for them. "They do Sitrius. Each has met with the sisterhood, and with the exception of intensity of the power, the power is essentially the same."

"What will the Hippochryn do Gryn?"

"We will fight on hoof and on foot, or take to the air. We will do what we must to further the success of your endeavors."

"And what will we be doing exactly?"

"Changing reality."

Sitrius didn't appreciate the cryptic response, but Sorna quickly stepped in.

"What Gryn is trying to say is this. Imagine the enemy is a wall, and touch that wall. You must change them."

"We will do our best, lady."

A meal was served, and Sitrius and his six companions sat around a makeshift fire eating heartily. There was plenty of boiled boar, vegetables and fruit, though Sitrius avoided the Boar. Boar were plentiful in the region, and they had a wild gamey taste that came as a shock at first.

Bratto was a game hunter, and regaled them all with a long and dreadful description of the various kinds of boar, and their diseases, as well as other wildlife that he was fond of hunting. He then started discussing their mating habits, followed by their eating habits.

"This one must've been eating pine branches. Game such as this tends to taste like whatever it ate. Imagine how you would taste, lad," he said to Sitrius with a loud guffaw.

Sitrius smiled a sour smile, and went on about his meal. He watched the twins as they ate. Rufus and Renn fought over the food as they seemed to fight over everything else. The boar was terrible...no, it was delicious. The fruit was dry.... on the contrary it was luscious. The girls on the other hand seemed to have more of an appetite for Rufus and Renn than the food before them, though it wasn't clear whether or not they reciprocated the affection.

"Where do you come from?" Sitrius asked Marca, who seemed to be the more mature of the two female twins.

"From the inland dunes. We live among sand dwellers."

"How do you survive? You may have access to food, but where do you get your water?"

"From the needle-bush. It is a plant that grows native in the sands, and it has a natural reservoir of water at its core. Harvesting the water takes great care though, because the needles weep a natural poison."

"What about the two of you?" He asked the male twins.

"We are from Deddus Prime in the east." Rufus said with a proud grin on his face.

"We work in the tree mills," Renn added. "Well, I work. Rufus, on the other hand..."

"Shut your mouth!" Rufus raged. "I do my share of the work!"

"Sorry I asked," Sitrius said with a smirk and roll of the eyes.

"What of you Sitrius?" Tirfa cut in.

"I am from a small village just inland from Tymor Bay. My parents have been gone for several years, so survival has been my study-master."

"Is the ocean as amazing as they say?"

"More so, actually. I can't imagine myself anywhere else. It is my life blood."

Tirfa smiled as she bit into her pear. She turned and spit it out. "Rufus was right, these are dry," she said, eliciting a laugh from Sitrius.

They finished their meal and Gryn led them to Verron Grove, a ring of stone arches that grew mysteriously out of the land.

"Here you will use the natural landscape to practice your skills. There is a deep magic in the stonework here, so there is no cause to worry that changes you make will be permanent. I fear you will not have long to study, so make the most of your time together. You may be more powerful in pairs or working all together, so do try that."

Before they could even begin a rumbling echoed through the mountain range, and then the rumbling become a thundering and whooshing sound. The thunder of hooves and the whoosh from a heavy downbeat of wings. But the worst of it was a nightmarish scream that seemed to reverberate all around them.

"It appears we have no time left at all. They are upon us," Gryn said.

Sitrius mounted Gryn, and the other six mounted Hippochryn as well. "Be on the ready friends. You are as new to this as I am, and I have a feeling we will not get a second chance."

The other Hippochryn heard the commotion as well and began arranging themselves into formations. The whole plain began to look like a sea of white leading all the way up to Alletroya.

The horrific creatures began pouring onto the plain by the hundreds, and Sitrius was struck with a surge of adrenalin that started the vibrations of his living energy pulsing within him.

Looking at them, it seemed as if the pure white sheen of the Hippochryn had been plunged into filth and darkness. He recalled what Gryn had said about them. *'They have been called the pale ones, for they look sickly and diseased. Their wings are tattered, and their mane is wild and unkempt. Their skin is full of dark ridges, running like veins throughout.'* It did not do justice to the scene before him. With each step they took, disease seemed to follow. The once lush grass turned to chaff with each hoof fall, and ashen cloud cover trailed in their wake. Truly there was dark magic afoot.

The sea of black arrived just short of a mile in front of the sea of white, and one of them came forward at a trot to the center of the field. It was an invitation to parlay.

The adrenalin was rippling through Sitrius as he rode Gryn forward to approach the blackened steed. There was a smell of burning ash and decay in the air as they got closer, and Sitrius felt as though he wanted to wretch.

When they came to a stop within a few feet of the beast, it changed to its human form. As elegant and comely as Gryn had been, and was still, this creature was his polar opposite. His robes were a blackened grey, frayed at the trails. His filthy hair was thin and frail and pitch black. He wore a sickening grin on his face that reeked of mockery. The only hint of resemblance was the eyes. They were exactly the same as Gryn's, and that made its visage even more startling. His rider was a woman, or what once had been a woman, and she stood next to him stoically. She was now devoid of any humanity. Her eyes were hollow and her skin was a stony gray. Only the dark power was keeping her alive now.

Sitrius dismounted, and Gryn changed form as well. "Thytus, you are not welcome here. Let us help you return to your previous form, or leave us in peace."

Thytus opened his mouth in a huge smile and a black tar like substance oozed from his mouth and down the sides of his face as he laughed at Gryn's demand.

"Oh Gryn, you never understood true power when you saw it. It is you who needs help. Or, you will when we have finished with you. Ask your sisterhood. Surely they have seen your demise."

Thytus stepped toward Gryn quickly, but before he could make contact Sitrius stepped forward and pushed him out of the way. Where his hand touched rippled, as with the wall, and Thytus recoiled.

"What has your human done?! What craft is this Gryn?!" He bellowed.

"This craft will be your redemption or undoing, Thytus. The choice is yours."

"No, the choice is yours Gryn, and you have made it. This day we dance the dance of death." With that, he grabbed his rider and flew away to rejoin his army, and Sitrius and Gryn stood waiting.

Gryn turned to the sea of white behind him. He raised his right fist in the air and cried, "Be ready guardians of Perennia! Battle is upon us, but victory shall be ours. All hail the Light-bringer!"

The clouds of ash were now covering the sky, and the smell of death accompanied them. The sickening scream erupted once again from the freakish horde as they sounded the battle cry in unison, and the thunder of hooves threatened to shake the foundations of the mountains as tidal waves of black and white rushed toward each other.

The clash of hooves and horns rumbled all around Sitrius and the other humans, and the storm of dirt and rocks and blood threatened to bury them. Across the cataclysm his eyes met with Gryn's, and one look was all that he needed to know what Gryn was asking. *Sitrius, we must end this now.*

One of the foul beasts came against Tirfa from behind, and would've trampled her down, but Sitrius rushed in and pushed her out of the way. He grabbed the hooves in both hands, and the vibrations coursed through the beast as the disease fled from its body. He looked back long enough to meet Tirfa's eyes. There were no words, but her gratitude was unmistakable. Bratto dove out of a horde of black flesh, and he and Tirfa bounded into the fray in a maddening frenzy of rage.

Sitrius turned to the others. Both sets of twins were in a stupor as they watched the scene unfold. "Twins! Look at me!" Sitrius barked. They did so without a word. "We need to act now! Are you ready?" They shook their heads in affirmation, but something told Sitrius they would meet an early death. He motioned them forward with him, and they rushed together into the battle with the energy pulsing and ready to burst.

Hippochryn were falling left and right. Some dark, and some white. Some had taken the battle to the air, and fell like rain. Others stayed on solid ground. Sitrius was grabbing the flesh of dark steeds left and right. With each touch came the familiar ripple, and then the beast fell. The others were all following suit, with the same result. He was pleasantly surprised to see all of the twins holding their own in the battle, forcing change on stallion after stallion with uncanny precision. He didn't take time to linger on the effects, or he would've been trampled.

One by one the dark Hippochryn fell at their touch, though it seemed the carnage would never end. Amidst the day's wreckage, he looked back and spotted the limp bodies of Rufus and Renn smashed upon the ashen soil. The plague would consume them soon, and their flesh would live again under its power. The weeping forms of Tarin and Marca hunched over their bodies as they cowered in fear of the enemy.

Sitrius bolted toward them, but was intercepted by a dark figure and pummeled to the ground. As he regained his breath, he looked up at the figure standing over him. Thytus took his human form instantly, grabbed Sitrius by the front of his tunic, and hoisted him into the air. From somewhere in the distance Sitrius could hear Tirfa cry out in panic, "NOOO! Sitrius!!"

The same sick smile returned to Thytus lips. "Such weakness, … such waste. You have fought for a lost cause, and now you will die for that cause. The pure ones truly thought you would best us?! Absurd!" A gale of laughter erupted from his mouth that sent chills up Sitrius' spine. A trail of what appeared to be black ooze trailed up the wretched arm of his captor and crawled onto the skin of his neck. Sitrius choked and gagged as the ooze began to drain the life from him. Sitrius was plagued by fear. Was this how he would die? Was this how the dark riders had been turned, and become mere shadows of existence?

Suddenly, Thytus loosened his grip and stumbled back. Sitrius fell to the ground, and looking up he noticed that Tirfa and Bratto had grabbed Thytus, but their grip had not held long. He shook it off and sent them flying to the ground several feet back. He was distracted though.

Sitrius summoned every ounce of strength and courage possible and lunged toward the creature. With both hands outstretched, he grabbed hold of Thytus and a massive ripple coursed through the grotesque form. Thytus shrieked in horror, and the calamity around them halted as those still living looked toward the scene in raptured silence. No matter how he writhed and tried to shake free, Sitrius did not let go. He had discovered unhindered power in his determination to help rid Perennia of this disease.

Sitrius had been holding on for merely minutes before the beast became as insubstantial as a mist of overheated water, and shimmered faintly before the darkness disappeared. He lay at the feet of Sitrius a broken mass. Though returned to his former purity, the scars of the dark elements remained. The tattered wings and sunken eyes never left, and sagging, sickly skin covered his body. He was a mere shadow of what he might have been before the darkness took him, and the shell of the woman that was once his rider had finally passed on.

Sitrius looked toward the mass of dark Hippochryn assembled in the valley and simply lifted his hands in triumph. His hands shimmered with the power like water lit by morning sunlight, and his eyes eerily bore the same trait. At that, all the dark ones in the valley began backing off.

The four remaining of his other six companions took their stand on either side of Sitrius.

Sitrius looked back down at the pitiful form of Thytus. His breathing was labored, and his eyes were glazed over. He tried to speak, but the ability failed him. As he tried to push himself into a sitting position he fell back against the ground and breathed his last. Tears wetted Sitrius cheeks as he realized he had probably used too much power against the dark energy within Thytus. It had been too much for him.

Sitrius wiped his face and looked back up to see the still massive crowd of black Hippochryn, all in their human form, slowly approaching their fallen leader. They stopped a few feet from where he lay and stood in silence.

Sitrius waited a few moments and then spoke. "You have seen what happened to Thytus. Do not let the same fate befall you. We have the power to either destroy you, or cure you."

One by one most of them walked forward and extended a hand toward the humans. They offered no resistance, and as Hippochryn hand joined human hand the curse began to lift.

There was, however, a small contingent that rushed forward in one final attempt to destroy the humans and gain vengeance for the death of Thytus. Their attack was thwarted by a group of the pure led by Gryn, and they were instantly slain.

Hours passed, and the restorative work was complete. They went quickly to where Rufus and Renn had fallen, and found their bodies beginning to twitch with dark life. Tarin and Marca laid their hands on them. Instantly the darkness was overcome, and their bodies went still. They burned the bodies, and the fires rose high as the honorary words, wails, and tears bid them farewell.

The Hippochryn prepared a feast in celebration. A massive stone slab raised up from the ground was filled with food from their stores. Fruit platters were filled with fresh papaya, tiranoes, terranials, apples, and melons. Numerous loaves of various kinds of breads were also provided, as well as abundant vegetation and herbs. To their chagrin, there was also more boar.

The humans ate merrily with the majestic creatures. Tirfa looked across the table at Sitrius, smiled gently, and just stared. Sitrius noticed the same ferocity in her eyes, but this time he knew she wasn't preparing for battle. She had conquest of a different sort in mind. He smiled back and averted his eyes back to his food. *Coward*, he thought to himself.

Gryn stood up and walked away. He headed toward a nearby outcropping of rock a few feet away. Sitrius got up and followed him, glancing briefly in Tirfa's direction to see that she still watched him.

Gryn smiled grandly as Sitrius walked up beside him. "You are free to go now my human friend. I will return you to your beach in the morning."

Sitrius looked down at his feet for a while and then replied. "I'm not sure I want to leave Gryn."

"Sorna and the sisterhood will not permit you to stay. We are still an exclusive community, except when the need arises to involve ourselves in the lives of those outside. I will see you again, but you and your friends may not stay."

"I love the ocean Gryn, but in many ways my life was very lonely."

"What of the woman Tirfa? She fancies you. This is plain."

"Yes, I…uh…I could tell."

"You would have no life here, even if you could stay. Make a new life for yourself full of human experiences. The love and embrace of a woman, the laughter of offspring, and the wonder of growing old."

Sitrius nodded, and went to rejoin the festivities.

Tirfa met him halfway. "So, I hear we are leaving tomorrow."

"Yes, Gryn just told me. Where is home for you, Tirfa?"

"I'm from all over really. Bit of a nomad, I am. And you, Sitrius? You said you lived close to Tymor Bay. Where is that?"

"It's in the province of Synia. I live in a small village called Teyanid."

"I know of Synia. I would love to visit Teyanid."

"You're welcome to join me if you like?"

Tirfa's gaze as he said it weighed him down, and she came up close quicker than he was prepared for. She looked into his eyes as if searching to find out if he was serious. "Yes, I believe I will join you," she said.

Sitrius smiled and Tirfa grabbed his hand, tugging him away to rejoin the group.

The next morning, they all bid farewell. Bratto walked up with Tarin and Marca on each arm. It was quite the sight for women so young to be hanging on a man almost three times their age. Sitrius had to suppress a laugh.

Bratto walked up and slapped Sitrius on the shoulder. "Well met, lad. Pleasure fighting by your side!"

Sitrius returned the slap, and watched as Bratto mounted one of the Hippochryn, and then almost slipped off as the creature shot into the air.

The twins gave Sitrius and Tirfa quick, yet stale hugs, and then they left swiftly as well.

Gryn and Sorna walked up to Sitrius and Tirfa. Sorna had a stern look on her face that quickly changed as she greeted them. "The sisters and I are deeply grateful for your work yesterday. Be well."

Sitrius and Tirfa bowed, and Gryn stepped forward. "It is time," he said. Within seconds he had changed form.

Sitrius mounted Gryn first, and then hoisted Tirfa up behind him. She wrapped her arms gently, yet tightly around his waist with a playful look in her eye, which made things more than a little awkward for Sitrius. He heard the same sound come from Gryn that sounded like a laugh.

The air became warmer as they descended from the high and lofty mountain ranges of Perennia, and into the regions of the land that rested closer to ocean level.

They landed at peak time on the beach where he and Gryn had met, and again it took Sitrius a while to gain his bearings on land. Tirfa just laughed at him as she dismounted, and stood upright as if she had never left the ground.

Gryn took human form and drew them close to him in an embrace. "I wish both of you the very best that human life can offer. Do not fret. You may very well see me again sometime. Until then, I think you can both handle things from here." He raised an eyebrow, and grinned at them slyly. He then returned to his animalian form and took off with a rush of wind that blanketed Sitrius and Tirfa heavily.

Sitrius grabbed Tirfa's hand and they walked down the beach together. As they stood looking out over the ocean, Tirfa turned to look at Sitrius.

"This is amazing! I think I'd like to stay." She looked at Sitrius insistently and smiled.

"I thought you might," he said. "I would enjoy having someone to share it with."

He wrapped his arms around her and they sat down in the sand. They gazed out over the ocean as the sea lizards splashed and dove among the waves. Though they were completely silent, the silence spoke volumes about how bright the future looked.

~

"Bah! Love! Yet another human emotion that I will never understand. Utter foolishness if you ask me," the dragon brooded loudly.

"It is all in your perspective, really. It is an emotion that brings out the best and the worst in their race."

"And, what of these flying hoof footed monstrosities? How absurd!"

"The hoof footed monstrosities, as you call them, are known by various names among their kind. They are truly majestic creatures, but of course nothing in comparison to you."

"Mmm, a moment ago you spoke of humans as though you are not of their kind. The truth is now apparent. What are you, Traveler?"

"You might say I am akin to them, but of a different order. My kind are those who can wield the forces of the planes of that which does not exist, and manipulate that which already does exist."

"Truly? I have read of those who navigate the thin spaces of reality, but I was sure they were a myth, or at least no longer existed. I have never encountered such until now, Traveler."

"What is written about us may be myth in some parts, but yes we do exist. If, indeed, it is my kind you have read of."

He could see a glimmer of respect, however faint, upon the dragon's countenance. Talindor nodded at him without a word, and he searched his stores for another tale to tell.

"My story begins in a very different, much more advanced society than some you may have read of…"

CHAPTER TEN
KORRALIS

It was nearing midnight as the production came to a close. The crowd had just witnessed an amazing performance of Faust. The man who portrayed Mephistopheles, the main antagonist, did so with uncanny precision, and his deep bass voice had intoxicated the audience.

Aeron Krest and his wife sat toward the middle of the auditorium, which they felt was the best possible spot to get the most out of the experience. The acoustics in the auditorium were simply amazing. It was one of the old opera houses that seemed like it was a piece of time long past, trapped in the web of a modern metropolis.

As the final scene ended, the entire auditorium, almost in unison, erupted in a standing ovation that seemed to last for ten minutes at least.

They followed the crowd out of the opera house at a slow crawl. The exit to the building was out onto the balcony, and then down several flights of steps. It had been designed this way so that the opera house would take on the form of a traditional amphitheater.

As they exited the building there was some kind of commotion arising in the city. Everyone was looking into the sky and pointing, and as Aaron did the same he noticed what looked like an electrical storm erupting all across the sky. There were flashes of lightning bubbling like a volcanic eruption, and as it lit up the clouds he could tell they had turned a sickly, darkish grey. These same clouds had cast their pallor over the entire city, and who knows where else.

His curiosity peaked, Aeron stood on the spot in awe until finally his wife laid her hand on his shoulder and he snapped back to reality. She started to say something to him when people all over the area started screaming.

Aeron looked up again, and noticed a large rift opening up in the clouds. The light that initially came through the opening was blinding, but eventually faded into gray.

All of a sudden the head of some creature emerged from the opening. It came to a halt and began craning its neck in all directions, surveying the city. It looked human, although not. The skin was pale brown in color, and somewhat translucent. The mouth bore a sickly twist, and then there were the eyes. The eyes were hollow except for a bright blue flame that set the sockets aglow. The hair on top hung low, and was tight with curls.

After making its assessment, the head pulled back into the rift. A few moments later the creature fully emerged from the opening, and lighted on the surface by the federal building. It was easily eight feet tall, and it wore a long, crimson robe with a black rope wrapped tight around the center. Its hands were the same ashen color as the face, and the nails were completely black. There were no wings that Aeron could see. Worse than that, it had brought friends.

A dozen others just like it landed on the street, and utter panic broke out across the city. Aeron's wife began tugging at his arm and screaming as tears streamed down her face. But, he could not leave. He had vowed never to reveal himself to anyone, unless…unless *they* came.

He shook out of her grip and turned around frantically. "Honey, you have to get away from here now. I can't explain now, but you have to trust me. My destiny is wrapped up in what is happening today. I just…, I have to stay."

Just then a friend ran up to them, and Aeron sent his wife away with her, screaming and pulling away. He promised that I would contact her as soon as he could. He turned back to the situation that was unfolding in the wake of the arrival.

Aeron had been prepared for this from his youth; part of a long succession of his kind. He belonged to the League of the Dragon; an organization of mages with one purpose, and one only, to protect humanity from these visitors by sending them back and sealing the rift. At the moment the rift opened, Aeron's powers had awakened, and he knew he had to act quickly.

The last time the rifts had opened, the League had hoped that they were sealed for good. Today was proof that they were not. He clasped his hands together and focused his mind on one solitary destination.

The Sanctum.

All members of the league knew how to enter the Sanctum when the time became necessary. It was a construct of the mind that they simply had to fix in their thoughts. It was the safe house where they would gather to be briefed on the threat to humanity. Most of them knew little if anything about the visitors, but they knew the Immortal would fill them in.

As Aeron stood in silence his mind was instantly aware of new surroundings. There were several hundred in attendance in this ante-room of the subconscious. At the center of the room stood our founder. The Immortal. No one knew his real name, or if they did, no one spoke it. Perhaps it was sacred, or its utterance deadly, but for whatever reason, it was never mentioned.

The Immortal spoke solemnly, "You have all gathered to the Sanctum today because of an old threat that has reemerged in our world. Most of you are at least five generations removed from the last opening of the rifts, and I am sure none of you really understand what you will be dealing with."

What he said was true. Their training had been extensive and set at a gradual pace over the course of their growing up years, but they received hardly any information about what to expect should the threat become real. Perhaps it was because no one had first-hand knowledge.

The Immortal continued, "Our enemy is called the Korralis. They are a collective of beings from an unknown dimension that seek about the galaxy for worlds to plunder and control. Even now they are arriving in every major city of this world and have begun to seize control.

"The original League, servants of the last dragon, were the first to encounter these beings and drive them back. You all are their direct descendants.

"You must move quickly to avert this threat, and seal the rift. You will have no other access to the sanctum unless it becomes absolutely necessary.

"Once the rifts are closed, and the threat is abated, we will re-enter the Sanctum on the twelfth hour of the next day. Good day, and may the dragon be on your side."

Aeron opened his eyes, and observed the chaos once again. The Korralis were setting things in order for their rule, and they would move quickly, so time was essential. He headed for the Cellar. Cellars were underground bunkers where the league would meet to prepare themselves, and there was one in every city of the world.

He arrived shortly after the others. They had never met each other, but instantly felt the connection. The Cellar vault was opened, and they all went inside. The vault was simply stocked with Cornaceae staves, dogwood being a supposed favorite of dragons for its earthy properties, and military grade rubberized armor suits.

They outfitted themselves and headed for the rooftop of the abandoned building across the street.

The air had a rank smell to it, likely due to the destruction the Korralis were causing, and Aeron found it hard to breathe.

One of his new comrades, Safina, pointed toward the cloud cover. "They seem to be drawing their power from the electrical charge in the clouds."

She was right, the electrical storm that had begun when the event first happened was likely fueling the Korralis. Aeron only hoped that the rest of the League would notice the connection.

He suddenly remembered something his father had always said as he prepared Aeron for his destiny all those years. "Aeron, always remember this. When you are faced with a threat reverse the charge."

"Listen everyone," Aeron said. "If we can channel some of the energy into our staves, and feed it back toward the Korralis as a counterbalance, I may be able to reverse the charge of the electricity to throw them off balance."

"Say what?" A man named Devon asked.

"Fight fire with fire," Safina replied.

They all set to work chanting the spell of binding against the storm clouds, and streaks of lightning lashed out and bound themselves to the staves.

Holding the staves straight up, a bubble of chaotic energy formed at the peak, and with upraised voices the comrades shouted the energy back toward the rift.

The Korralis let out a shriek that could be heard across the city. It was as if a thousand infants had started screaming into a megaphone at once, and it was enough to break our concentration.

A stream of some kind of blue energy shot from the palm of one of the Korralis, and broke into streams that separately attached themselves to the heads of the city elders.

If they want control of the city, that is how they will get it, Aeron thought. The Magisterial building contained access to the entire network of things necessary to keep the city running.

It had been some form of mind control, for the elders focused all their attention on the Korralis, and then all of a sudden turned to face the League. Their eyes were as empty as a freshly prepared tomb.

The elders started marching toward them with murderous intent, and Aeron was determined that he would not harm them.

One of his comrades broke off the attack, and sent a stunning blast from her staff that caused the elders to pass out before they reached us.

The league renewed its fervor, and the storm's energy was reversed again, causing another shriek to erupt from the Korralis.

"Fifty of you double your efforts and hold the storm at bay," someone shouted out. "As for the rest of you, we need to redirect our efforts to hitting them while they're vulnerable."

Without taking time to decide who would do what, Aeron and forty-nine others broke off the channel and descended to street level.

When they reached the street, they looked up to see that the steady stream of electricity was holding firm. It wouldn't do so for much longer though.

"Ok, point your staves to toward the sky." The person shouted out again. "Since the moon reflects the sun, we need to draw that energy somehow to eradicate the cloud cover."

They all did just that, and an unknown force shot up into the sky and illuminated the moon beyond its normal capacity. It seemed that as they were drawing energy from the moon, it was in turn drawing more energy from the sun, and the resulting flash of moonlight was blinding.

It did, however, have the desired effect. The light from the moon burst through the clouds and could not be contained.

The Korralis were bathed in the barrage of light, and turned pure white. Aeron and the others rejoined the main force in the attack on the storm, and the resulting reversal of energy sucked the creatures back through the rift.

The force of their onslaught having completely reversed the powers that had opened the rift in the first place, it snapped closed with a sound like a sonic explosion.

They hurried back to the Cellar before they could be beset by throngs of civilians, and returned their items to the vault.

Aeron called his wife to find out where she was, and quickly hurried to the center of town. They had taken refuge in the women's bathroom of a delicatessen. He grabbed her, and embraced her tightly in a passionate kiss, and they walked slowly home as he told her the events of the day.

As he explained to her what he was and what he was involved in, she was hurt but not overly angry. She understood that he had withheld the truth to protect her.

The League reconvened in the Sanctum at Noon the next day, and the Immortal got right to business. "I would like to congratulate all of you on your victory against the

Korralis. Word of the method spread quickly across the globe to all members of the league, and the threat was quickly averted.

"It is hard to say how permanent the sealing of the rift will be, but you know your duty. You must train the next generations, so that there will always be those on guard to defend the world should the rifts ever open again. May the favor of the last dragon be on you."

As Aeron opened his eyes, his wife was staring at him. He smiled softly at her, and she smirked back at him. They left the house arm in arm, and went for a walk through the park close by. The fact that everything was back to normal was favor indeed.

~

"Humans and their playacting! Humph!" Said Talindor.

"You are quite easily distracted my friend. What about the rest of the story?"

"Oh yes…yes, quite nice. I like that 'League of the Dragon' business. Very nicely done, Traveler. So this was recounted to you from that fellow who was in the league, hmm?"

"Yes it was. Did I recount it well?"

"Indeed. Well Traveler, is that all you have for me? I am very famished, yes indeed."

"Not quite yet. Perhaps a little lighter fare would suit you."

"More humor?" The dragon huffed, and nodded for the Traveler to continue.

CHAPTER ELEVEN
UNINVITED GUESTS

It was a normal day like any other. CJ Drake woke to the sound of the alarm at six o'clock, and lay in bed dreading that he eventually had to extract himself from the bed and start getting ready for work. He pried himself up and sat on the edge of the mattress twisting and turning his back in various directions trying to get the knots out. When he realized he was having no success he stood up slowly, trying not to disturb his wife's slumber, and headed for the bathroom.

After showering and getting dressed, he made his way to the kitchen to begin his morning routine. Of utmost importance was making the coffee. Without that, existence as he knew it would cease. Next was preparing lunch, waking the children, waking the wife, and making lunch. Not always necessarily in that order, but that is a good summary.

After dropping the children off at school, he made his way back to the freeway to check off the next item on his list for the day, ... work. He worked in a cubicle, on the phone for hours on end, and the excited anticipation was simply boiling up within him. It would be a normal day like any other.

The freeway was unusually empty that morning, but he was grateful he didn't have to be held up by traffic. *Maybe they didn't get the memo about work today,* he thought.

He branched off to another freeway, and again it was the same. Hardly any cars or trucks to be seen. He did, however, see a huge congregation of helicopters flying over the area where I worked. *Must be something big happening over there today,* he thought.

He turned onto the street occupied by the company he worked for, and pulled into the security gate. There were no guards to be seen. He waited for a few minutes, and then continued on his way to the parking garage. He found a parking spot on the third floor and headed inside the building.

As he came through the turnstile, he saw a huge group of people congregated in the main lobby, and the security guards were all standing around trying to look like they were on alert. From the look on their faces they were more afraid than alert. What was more, there was an aroma in the air that was something like burnt marshmallows.

As he approached the lobby, CJ saw his friend Tracy and asked her what was going on. She didn't speak a word, but just grabbed his head and turned it to look out the doors into the courtyard. What he saw at that moment would have caused his eyes to fall out if they hadn't been attached to his optical nerves. My mouth hung open for a few minutes until I started drooling and decided to close it.

It was not a normal day like any other! There were dragons at his workplace!

There were three of them to be exact. A dark purple dragon was sitting on its haunches in the middle of the courtyard. It took up about half the area, and if it stood at full height it would have been taller than the main building. It sat munching on one of the trees on the east side of the courtyard, and what remained of a wooden table and chairs was splintered underneath its hide. It must've been flailing its tail about, because one of the glass windows on that side was shattered as well.

Then there was the dragon on the second floor terrace. This one was maroon in color, and some of its scales were newly scuffed up. When CJ mentioned that, hid friend

Neil said that the crazy thing had been rubbing up against the building and dislodging parts of the exterior wall. CJ laughed to himself. *How curious*, he thought.

This one was slightly smaller than the one in the courtyard, but what it lacked in size it made up for in temperament. He was extremely restless, flapping his wings all about and creating an enormous dust storm.

The third dragon, a golden yellow in color, was creeping around the construction site, which as CH could see was on fire as he looked closer. This might explain the burnt marshmallows. What was once an additional building and parking garage, would be gone by the end of the day at the rate it was burning, and after every few steps the dragon spouted a current of flame.

After a few minutes the dragon shot up to the top of the once future parking garage, flapped its wings to clear away the smoke, and curled up for a nap.

Well this sent everyone into a frenzy, although why it took that long for the frenzy to happen made no sense whatsoever. Maybe the shock had worn off or something.

CJ wondered how they had gotten there? Dragons were supposed to be a myth, although he had always secretly hoped they were real. He thought maybe the government had exercised a mass conspiracy to prevent humans from knowing about them. In either case he decided to do what any abnormal human being with only half his wits would do. He went out into the courtyard. *Maybe I can reason with the creatures, after all dragons can't be all that bad*, he told myself. Surely they were just confused.

CJ approached the purple dragon, who was laying lazily in the courtyard now, and chewing slowly on a tree branch it had torn off. As he got near, it looked at him with it huge yellow eyes, as if wondering what CJ might do. And then….it spoke!

"What think you to be doing, scruffy little thing?"

Scruffy?! It must not like my facial hair, he thought.

"Well, I work here, and I just wanted to ask you what you're doing here. You are scaring people."

"We not mean harm. We want to eat and rest. Long journey."

"But how did you get here?"

"That one wakes us," it said, pointing in the direction of a construction worker cowering behind a broken concrete wall.

"Uh, well. Ok, but you can't stay here. It's not safe for you or us. See those things flying in the sky up there?" he said, pointing to the helicopters. "Those things are going to tell the whole city that you are here, and people will come and take you away." *Fat chance of that being successful,* he thought.

"Where we go?" asked the dragon.

"There is water and sand west of here," he said, pointing in the direction he spoke of. "That will be a better place for you and those with you."

"I talk with others and decide."

"Well don't take too long. Do you have a name that I can tell everyone, so at least they won't be as afraid?"

"Name is Mertorampolistanortinga, and the others are...."

CJ cut him off before he could finish. "Umm, never mind. Can I call you Mert?"

Mert nodded.

He walked back into the lobby, and everyone was just staring at him. "What?" he said. "Someone had to do something."

CJ announced the dragon's name over the emergency intercom system at work, and assured everyone that they were friendly and would not harm anyone. After he finished making the announcement he came back out to the lobby. Everyone was watching intently at something happening outside. The dragons were huddled together, and appeared to be deliberating.

All of a sudden the maroon colored dragon crouched low, and with a mighty gust of wind it vaulted into the air taking one of the palm trees with it. The golden yellow dragon was next.

As Mert prepared to follow suit he turned around and looked through the window, nodded at CJ, and followed after the others. They were heading in the direction of the coastline.

The commotion eventually died down, and everyone settled into their work routine. After extensive interviews with the press, and a talking to from the general manager about his stupidity, CJ got back to work. The phones were extremely busy as usual.

On his break CJ thought over the events of the day, smiled, and sighed peacefully. *Back to a normal day like any other.*

~

"Do you mean to say that they had never seen my kind before?" Talindor inquired.

"It is true, I'm afraid. In truth, you are to them but a myth."

"A MYTH!! Preposterous!"

"So, to see one of your kind would be quite a spectacle, you see?"

"If you say so, Traveler."

The dragon began examining his claws, and looking at the traveler with rapt anticipation. It seemed there must be more entertainment.

"Next I will tell you a tale of a young man trapped by a crazed sorcerer."

CHAPTER TWELVE
THE ROOM

Shivers ran up his spine. The darkness of the room, combined with the winter temperatures brought a chill to his entire body. He pushed himself up to a sitting position and looked around. Everything was pitch black, so he could not get his bearings. Hunger pangs tore madly at his stomach, and his mouth and throat were parched.

Barrett Sandin could not remember how he got here. Wherever here was. He felt around on the floor of the mysterious room. It seemed to be made of layered stone.

A faint light came alive at that moment, and Barrett stared in wonder at his surroundings. The room was a perfect ten-by-ten square. In the very center of each wall were sconces, and in each sconce was a solitary torch. It was as if the torches had suddenly just come alive, for no one was in sight who could possibly have lit them. There was no door to the room that he could see. It seemed as though he were in some kind of prison, but for what he was not sure.

He slowly pried himself off the floor and stumbled around in the faint light trying to get his bearings. He was still dressed in his clothes from the day before. A black shirt with blue jeans, and a simple brown jackct.

He still found no door, and this concerned him. Without a door, how did he get in the room in the first place? As he staggered around, four large flying creatures appeared in the room. They looked like giant wasps the size of condors, and the stingers that protruded from their tail were enormous.

Barrett shrunk into a corner in fear, and then darted away when the swarm started inching closer to him. He scraped at the walls in hopes that he would discover a secret door, but no matter how hard he searched, no door appeared. He was already growing weary in his quest to avoid the beasts. At one point one got so close that he was able to rear his foot back and give it a swift kick out of his way. He then noticed something he had not seen before. He wondered if it had been there the whole time. It was a small broadsword with a topaz encrusted pommel, and a brightly shining silver hilt, and it was resting against one of the corners on the opposite side of the room. He made a mad dash for the sword, and when one of the wasps gained on him he lunged for it.

His fingers managed to touch the hilt and guide it into his grip. When he had the sword firmly in hand he held it at the ready. He had never wielded a sword, but he had to do something. The swarm honed in on him and made their attack. He swung the sword as hard as he could and it caught one of the wasps in the side of the neck. The body hit the floor with a thud. Green slime splattered everywhere, and the rest of the creatures became enraged and bulleted toward him. He swung the sword wildly in the air, killing another beast and wounding the other two. His breath was coming in pants as he slowly calmed down.

The remaining two creatures were after him again, but his energy was spent. He had resigned himself to his demise when the creatures suddenly vanished. His sword vanished as well.

There he was, alone in a room with four walls, and still no doors that could be seen. He scooted over to the corner to calm himself and collect his thoughts.

He suddenly became aware of a presence, either in the room with him, or outside watching him. He could not be sure.

A range of emotions racked his mind. Fear, anger, hate and despair were coursing through him as he pondered the unanswered questions of his situation. The presence felt strangely familiar to him, but he was not sure why.

After a few minutes the room went dark again. The sconces on the wall had gone black, and Barrett's head went black with fear as well.

The presence was there. He could feel it even stronger now, like some creeping specter breathing down his spine.

"Greetings Barrett," a voice echoed in the darkness. The voice was deep and scratchy, and filled with disdain.

Barrett recognized the voice, but he couldn't place it.

"Did you like my bugs, Barrett?" The voice said again.

Something sparked in his mind at that moment. His neighbor Tom Simillon was a bug breeder. Barrett had always thought him an odd fellow, and never entered his home because it was absolutely crawling with bugs of every kind. Some were his own breeds even.

He had always wondered what went on at that house. He would often see strange hues of lights through the windows, and smell the most unusual smells from time to time. The large bugs he had encountered in the room were not ordinary either.

Could this be Simillon?

"Tom? I..Is that you?"

The sconces flamed to life again, and Barrett stood facing someone dressed in a long black pants, and a black Victorian shirt that had been retrofitted with a hood. He had a sneering grin on his face that showcased a full set of darkly yellowed teeth. Obviously this man was deranged.

"Why Barrett, I'm touched. You recognized my voice."

"What are you doing Tom? What is this place?"

"Have you heard the term Oubliette, Barrett"

"The French term for a type of dungeon, yes."

"Well, Barrett, this my version of an Oubliette. The only difference is that I have created this room in a pocket between the physical world and non-physical, and it has no doors unless I create one. The only people who will ever know you are here are the two of us.

"My pets on the other hand are my own creation. I have immersed myself in the ancient art of Morphomancy, and have created vastly new species of bugs. It will revolutionize the world.

"However, people such as my ever so dutiful neighbor simply think I'm delusional, and should be locked away."

Barrett couldn't argue with that, although he knew it was best to keep quiet about it.

"What do you intend to do with me?" Barrett asked.

"Oh, I intend to keep you here. My pets need someone to play with."

"Magic is dangerous if you disrespect it Tom."

"Then don't disrespect me Barrett. I am one with my magic. You wouldn't want to be in danger."

He let out a loud bellow of laughter, and waved his hands. With that, the lights were extinguished.

Barrett sat in the darkness, aware that he was now alone…again. *What did he mean that he was one with his magic?* He thought to himself.

From everything Barrett had read, he knew that Magic required a source. Some draw their power from the elements, others from talismans, esoteric words, or written markings. *Did he mean that his source was….*

Himself?! Barrett thought with alarm. Surely Tom had not invested his own life force in the workings of these magics! The result would be a great deal of power, but if he failed in his plan it could take his life.

Barrett moved a little and the torches flared to life again. Each corner of the room was guarded by what looked to be an enormous scorpion, but the tails were longer than normal scorpions. If it wanted, one of the scorpions could reach him wherever he sat.

"Oh, whatever will you do Barrett?!" The voice of Tom Simillon echoed in the air.

All of a sudden the sword was in Barrett's hand again. Where it had come from he had no idea, although he thought he heard Tom gasp from wherever he was lurking.

One of the scorpions lunged its stinger in his direction. He hefted the sword with both hands just in time to slice off the end of the tail. He heard another gasp. This one more painful. *He did it! The fool must've sourced the magic from himself,* Barrett thought.

Another tail flew in his direction, but he dodged it in time. Then another came just as he got up and he blocked it with…. a shield.

From somewhere he heard Tom shout "WHAT!!" Then Barrett knew. Somehow, some way, he was bringing his defenses into existence. Perhaps out of a desire to protect himself, he was making his boyhood fantasies a reality.

Barrett had played knights versus marauders all the time as a boy. Wooden swords and the lid off of a tin can were the popular choices among he and his friends. When he chose his weapons, he didn't mess around, and today was no different.

Suddenly Barrett had an idea. He had taken archery classes as a teenager. No sooner had the thought entered his mind, then a bow appeared in his hand and a quiver on his back. He nocked an arrow, set it, and readied his aim.

The scorpions vanished completely, and Tom reappeared in the room just as Barrett loosed his arrow.

The bolt flew true, and embedded itself in Tom's left shoulder. Tom wailed in pain, staggering about the room. The flames on the torches kept flickering in and out of life, as if he was trying to squelch them with no success.

A door appeared in the wall, adjacent to the northeast corner of the room. Barrett wasted no time rushing out, although he felt horrible for leaving Tom in the room to bleed out.

It became apparent as he ran out into the street that the room was somehow a part of Tom's house. He was feeling guiltier now, and he spotted a foot patrolman on the other side of the street and frantically got his attention.

"What's the problem. Sir?" The patrolman asked.

"You'll find a man through that door who needs medical attention." Barrett said as he turned around and pointed back in the direction of the house. However, all that could be seen was the lawn on the side of Tom's house, and Tom himself lying face down in the grass.

Barrett continued, "He attacked me, and I fought back. Please don't let him die."

The patrolman rushed over to the lawn and helped me pick Tom up. He was bleeding profusely from his wound.

The paramedics arrived about fifteen minutes later, and took Tom off to the hospital. The patrolmen called into the office to get an insect control team dispatched.

The cover of dark had set in by the time all the festivities were over, and Barrett walked slowly up his front steps. Once inside his house, he collapsed on the sofa and pondered the day's events.

The bug guys had hauled off countless specimens from Tom's house. Every time Barrett turned around, he saw them coming out with more crates. With all the insects, it was a wonder Tom had room to breathe.

The authorities had ordered the house to be condemned and demolished within a week, and Tom was to be charged with reckless endangerment of the neighborhood.

As for Barrett, he had discovered a new gift. What he might use it for remained to be seen. Maybe he wouldn't use it at all. Maybe…

~

"Tom should've bred dragons, Traveler," Talindor mused. "Then that imbecile, Barrett, would never have bested him."

"Well, perhaps fate was on Barrett's side then."

"Perhaps, yes."

The Traveler got to his feet and stretched. The sound of bones crackling and popping echoed in the chamber as he did so, and Talindor's eyes went wide with amazement. "I am growing impatient and bored, Traveler."

Amused, the Traveler grinned. He was beginning to like this dragon quite well. He resumed his seat on the floor, took a deep breath, and launched into another tale. "I think you will find a strange tale from a realm known as Saxos entertaining, my immense friend."

CHAPTER THIRTEEN
RATS

Pyper Hamlin was a ruthless and maniacal dictator. His penchant for the dark arts had wreaked havoc on the realm of Saxos for over fifty years. When he first arrived in the area his magic had seemed frivolous and fun. He would conjure streamers of various colors out of thin air, much to the delight of the children. He would even conjure shoes for the frogs, which caused all kinds of craziness to ensue, for frogs were never meant to wear shoes.

The tides began turning after lord Hamlin had been living in Pied Lake about ten years. He happened on a grove of acacia trees, situated in the Stilly valley. In the middle of the grove was an altar, and upon the altar a black onyx stone. Dazzled by the stone, Hamlin immediately grasped it. Black, raw power shot up through the veins in his arms, as he would describe it, and the magnitude of his power increased tenfold. No one ever saw the stone, but there were whispers among the townsfolk that the stone must have fused with his very soul.

As his power grew more and more arcane, terrifying events began to take place. A plague of boils swept the villages as a result of deranged incantations that he had uttered, and many of the children died as a result. Next came a famine, and large portions of crops suddenly died. Hamlin had forged a lute out of one of the trees from the grove, which was imbued with his power as a result, and he began to play hauntingly dark music on the lute in the wee hours of the morning.

On one such morning a local farmer woke to an infestation of rats in his grain storage vats. This would devastate the local agriculture if it was not taken care of at once. It was no secret that rat feces would permanently destroy any consumable food products. The farmer was at a loss for what to do, and so he sought out Pyper Hamlin. Hamlin was more than happy to oblige, as he loved to show off his powers and gain recognition. When he arrived at the farm, he began to play his lute. As if they were a group of soldiers going out to war, the rats departed the small farm in perfect single file, mesmerized by the melodic tune of Hamlin's lute. Over two thousand rats vacated the farm that day.

The farmer was ecstatic of course, but then the shoe dropped. The farmer never intended to compensate Lord Hamlin for his trouble. He insisted that he consider it part of the greater good. Hamlin was furious, and conjured a plague upon the farmer's land. All of the grain in his vats instantly turned to ash, and ever after it was a barren wasteland. That was only the beginning of his fury.

Hamlin took up his lute again and played a different tune for his captive rats, one that would change their very genetic code. The rats took on human stature and grew to over eight feet tall. Their frames filled as more muscles and sinews rippled and coursed through their insides. Their internal organs expanded and bulged. Their teeth grew to over six inches long, and their eyes took on a hideous green glow. They became some of the most ferocious creatures known in the world of rodents, and yet they were still completely mindless. Hamlin was their mind, and they were bent on serving his will.

Hamlin conjured suits of plated steel for the rats, and staves which emanated with electrical energy, and with a horde of two thousand monstrous rats, the realm of Saxos fell under the rule of Lord Pyper Hamlin.

On the fifth day of the third month of the…well anyway, Brindon Horth woke in the hayloft of his family barn. It was daybreak, which was evident from the annoyingly bright array of sunshine bombarding the boundaries of his corneas. Brandon was one of many in the realm who distributed propaganda for Hamlin's regime, and upon returning to his homestead and feeding the animals, he had apparently crashed in the loft.

He climbed down, eager to start his extremely busy day. Unbeknownst to Lord Hamlin's rat-men, as he liked to call them, Brindon was hatching a plan. Not that they knew any better; anytime he approached one of them all they did was snarl at him and go about their business.

Hamlin had built a fortress against the shores of Lake Ferwost. Brindon was related, three generations removed, to the mason who designed the hideous structure. When he discovered this, he had thought it high time to make a familial visit to dear old…whatever he was.

After some idle chit chat, and snooping around while he was supposed to be relieving himself, he left the visit with an additional copy of the drawings. Now, two years later, the fortress stood. Brindon only hoped no modifications had been made, other than the usual assortment of hexes, poisons, and death traps. Hamlin, he was sure, would take no chances.

Brindon had planned long and hard for this moment. He had spent long hours with the local Alchemist, his co-conspirator to concoct the most dangerous of toxins…rat poison. He would often laugh, for it was so simple and yet so deadly. The trick was producing it in mass quantities. They now had enough to feed three thousand giant rats if they needed to. He only hoped the rats were mindless enough not to see through the ruse.

As soon as the night fell Brindon, dressed all in black from neck to foot, donned a black hooded cape. He strapped a Lintarian scimitar with a hilt carved from dragon bone to his belt, and headed out. He saddled his horse, securing a large bag full of poison pellets, and sped off to the lake. He rode hard and fast, and as he did so he collected his thoughts. Would Hamlin perceive a danger approaching? Would all his planning be for nothing? "Calm," he told himself. "Must remain calm and focused."

He arrived at Lake Ferwost in just under an hour. The light of the moon shone an eerie glow upon the lake as the waters rippled in the night breeze. He fingered the small vial of anesthetic vapor serum in the inner pocket of his cloak, just to make sure it was there. He grabbed the bag of pellets and began to creep around the edge of the fortress toward the front entrance, which surprisingly enough was guarded by only two of Hamlin's beasts.

He crept up behind one of them, opened the vial, and dashed gracefully in front of it allowing the fumes to find their target. The rat hit the ground with a barely audible thud, the other rat charged Brindon almost immediately, but he grabbed one of the grotesquely large biceps and swung himself behind it. Producing the vial again, Brindon allowed the fumes to do their magic.

He then proceeded to heave open the large wooden door just enough to squeeze through, and keeping to the shadows, he distributed the poison pellets throughout the main corridor of the fortress. When he was finished he noticed that there was a large bell at the center of the corridor against the far wall. He ran over to it, rang it vigorously and retreated again to the shadows.

The rat hordes streamed down from the upper levels, drool streaming from their mouths, to see what was going on. No sooner had they congregated in the lower corridor, but they noticed the smell of something enticing. Drawn to the pellets, they immediately began feasting over the morsels. One by one the beasts dropped like flies, and Brindon ascended the stairs feeling quite impressed with himself.

He found Hamlin's quarters quickly. The name plate on the door which read "Lord Pyper Hamlin, Sorcerer, Ruler, and God" kind of gave it away. Hamlin was many things, but he was not modest. With a wry smile on his face, Brindon turned the handle and strode confidently into the room.

Lord Hamlin was sitting in an armchair in front of a small stone furnace lit with a roaring fire. He beamed a great smile as he turned to face his assailant.

"I knew it was only a matter of time," he said, followed by a hearty laugh. "Please, be my honored guest. I will serenade you with my music."

As he picked up his lute, Brindon rushed forward and grabbed it. He then smashed it on the floor and tossed it into the flaming furnace.

Hamlin was noticeably impressed with his zeal, and offered Brindon the armchair opposite him. "You know of course that the lute was not the source of my power." He continued.

Now that was something unexpected. Brindon never knew the source of the power, but only assumed it was the instrument. Hamlin leaned forward to stoke the fire with his magic.

Brindon thought long and hard about how foolish he had been. He had fallen into a trap he had set for himself. In the shadows, two rat-men stood by at the ready. No hexes and poisons were needed to trap Brindon, just his own naiveté. As he was vexing himself, he noticed something. He had always seen Hamlin wearing gloves in public, but now he wore none. One hand was a putrid gray in color, and was riddled with black veins. The hand that touched the magic stone.

He stared at it more closely and noticed a slight discoloration at the center of the hand, even a slight bulge. Could it be? Was the stone embedded in his palm?

Brindon slowly reached beneath his cloak, and fingered the hilt of his scimitar. He lashed out with an angry cry and severed the hand from Hamlin's arm. A blood curdling scream erupted from Hamlin's mouth at the shock of losing his hand, and also from the surge of power that instantly went out of him. Brindon had happened on Hamlin's one vulnerability, and just in time too. The Alchemist had raised a mob from the towns in Saxos, knowing that Brindon was attempting a one-man invasion, and they had congregated around the perimeter of the fortress.

Realizing that Hamlin was now helpless, Brindon helped him up and led him out of the fortress. He handed the beaten soul over to the mob, who would take him to await trial. The scourge of Saxos was defeated, and the misfortune that he had caused was completely reversed.

Brindon made his way back to the horse, and as he walked two rats scurried past him along the ground. A slight chuckle escaped his lips at the sight, and he was still laughing as he mounted his horse and rode home.

A week-long festival ensued after Hamlin's defeat. Brindon was crowned the town victor, and much music and merriment filled the air. It was the sound of hope; the sound of joy. It was the sound of safety and peace.

~

"I feel as though I have read that tale before, or at least something like it," the dragon said. "After all, I do have many books of folklore at my disposal you know."

"I've no doubt there are different tellings of it. Oral tradition is a vital tool in the progress of a society."

"And also in the downfall of a society, would you not agree?"

"How so Talindor?"

"Consider your recounting of the world that considered my kind a myth. Those dragons could have easily wreaked terror on that world, and been fully within their right to do so when faced with a clearly inferior race."

"Inferiority is in the eye of the beholder, great one. I won't wrangle over opinions though. I have one more tale to share with you, and then you must release me."

"We shall see, Traveler. We shall see."

CHAPTER FOURTEEN
DRAGON-FALL

In the far reaches of the Brakk galaxy, on the planet Gajne, a war was brewing. Long ago a race of immortals known as the Kan'Shah, revered by humans as sorcerers, created a race of dragons. The intent was that humans would use them to traverse the planet to engage in trade with other human nations, as well as travel abroad in the galaxy, for only the dragons had been given the genetic makeup to survive the atmosphere of deep space.

Some from the human region of Gajne were trained to ride the dragons for transport and diplomatic purposes. In the human tongue they are called Mandos, and they were trained for this task from a very young age. When traveling outside Gajne they donned special armor forged on the planet Lumina to protect them from deep space.

The dragons were enormous beasts and a wonder to behold. The largest dragons, which averaged at least eight tons in weight, had wingspans of up to a mile long. Atop their lithe, towering necks rested a large skull with enormous horns protruding out atop their ears, and at various other places depending on the dragon.

Each had a great hideous maw filled with dozens of jagged teeth, and at the other end a lengthy terror of a tail riddled with deadly spikes. Their forelegs and calves were as big around as the trunk of an ancient oak tree, while their haunches were twice that size. Their paws were large and muscular, with dark black daggers of bone protruding from their digits. Their bodies were completely covered in thick scale of various different colors and hues, with the exception of the undersides, making them almost invincible. They could easily hold a small troop of

Mandos, although they typically had two handlers at the most.

The dragons were originally created morally neutral and immutable. The Kan'Shah however were not, and their creations were tainted by their own propensities for good or evil.

One hundred years after the creation of the dragons, tensions had begun to run high. Within Egstat, the realm of dragon kind, infighting had begun. Kerrag, one of the high dragon lords, had begun to show signs of a growing evil within his being. He began to hold a congress within the catacombs of the dragon realm where he sought to sway other dragons in favor of an uprising. The goal of the uprising would be two-fold; to usurp their human masters, and to ultimately overthrow the control of the Kan'Shah.

Another of the high dragon lords, Khelest by name, came upon the congress and heard the rumblings of revolution. Kerrag attempted to sway his comrade to their cause, but was unsuccessful. Khelest immediately notified the Kan'Shah, and they dispatched a contingent of their finest sorcerers from the Void to parley with Kerrag and the other rebellious dragons in Egstat. Upon their arrival the delegates from the Void were slaughtered to the last. Their bodies were flayed and strewn on an open field to rot.

Upon orders from the Kan'Shah council that the rebel dragons were to be brought to justice living or dead, Khelest gathered the entire host of two hundred dragons loyal to the peace, along with several battalions of the dragon riders, to disrupt the next congress. Among the host were the other high dragon lords that had been given providential governance over the affairs of Egstat.

Khalvrog of Reun Keep, Kardest of Trym Keep, Krytest of Borlon Mountain, and Klyntar of Marstek End.

The next congress was to be held a fortnight from the day of the slaughter, and Khelest was determined that he and his host would be prepared.

When the day arrived the dragon host assembled on the plain of Mortak, at the foot of Borlon Mountain. As they prepared to take their flight to the congress, Khelest reared up, with his majestic wings fanned out, and gave a triumphant cry that silenced the mighty host that was scattered across the valley.

"My brothers, today we must do a grave thing," Khelest began. "We must fly to where others of our kind are assembled to disrupt the realm and uproot them from their plan. We have been commanded to let live those who will live in peace, and bring death upon those who persist in this hideous endeavor."

A deafening silence erupted across the great valley as the weight of what Khelest was saying set in. There were many assembled who had never considered the extreme actions that may be required of them.

"None of you assembled here are without choice in this matter," he continued. "If you withdraw from this mission, none here will think the less of you. These are your fellow dragons you are being asked to confront, and none here would blame you for shrinking away from such a task."

A loud rumbling spread among the host as they discussed the ramifications among themselves. It was no small task to potentially destroy their own kind.

"I would ask that the lords of the legions join me at the front," Khelest requested. The other four sped their way and lighted on the grassy area where Khelest was speaking.

Khelest began the call off. "Those of Reun Keep who wish to join us, take your place on the plain with your liege, Khalvrog. Those of Marstek end may attend lord Klyntar. Those of Trym Keep will attend Kardest the true. Those of Borlon Mountain are to attend to their lord Krytest. Those of Twilight Cavern will join me. Riders of Gajne, attend to your mounts. With our wisdom, and our might if wisdom fails us, we will crush this rebellion before it poisons our world."

A unanimous and victorious quake of noise erupted from the assembly and reverberated across the Borlon range. The giant swarm of reptilian strength lifted from the plain, leaving a mighty dust storm in their wake, and made haste to the catacombs where the rebellion met.

They arrived as the twin suns were approaching their zenith. All was quiet as the peacekeepers entered the room where the congress had been meeting. The host spoke enthusiastically with each other, wondering if Kerrag had seen reason and ended his murmuring of mutiny.

Khelest wondered the same thing, but was also extremely wary. Kerrag had never displayed a change of mind. He always stuck to the plan, and Khelest doubted that this time would be different. That being the case, he was perplexed as to where they were.

All of a sudden an enormous host, almost as enormous as that which Khelest had brought, rushed the voluminous arena.

"I knew you would come…brother," Kerrag bellowed with a hint of pride at having the element of surprise. His deep crimson covering was brilliant, even in the shadow of the cave.

"Stop this madness Kerrag!" Khelest boomed. "We were created for a greater good. We were created for service, not for power."

A rumble of laughter lifted from the cavern before Kerrag silenced it. "Be still, comrades! Khelest the foolish is speaking. What say you to his demands?!"

Things were worse than Khelest had hoped, as was evident from the unified dissension that came in reply from the rebel dragons.

"You have your answer! We will not be ruled!" Kerrag exclaimed. "You may join us in this endeavor, or flee this realm. Any other choice will destroy you and those with you, Khelest."

"We stand our ground, and we will halt your plan peacefully or with bloodshed," Khelest warned.

A heated flare rose in Kerrag's nostrils, and smoke trickled out from his snout to dissipate in the air. It was all the signal the others needed, for all at once a hideous noise split the silence as all the rebels in unison let loose a roar that shook the whole cavern. The resulting vibrations were so powerful that cracks began forming in the walls and the canopy of the room, dust began erupting from the cracks, and the dragons under Kerrag's lead swiftly exited the catacombs. As the room emptied, some of those with Khelest escaped with their lives, while others were buried under the rubble as the entire sequence of catacombs collapsed inward. Of the high dragon lords, only Khelest and Khalvrog made it out alive. Kerrag and his minions were nowhere to be seen, but it was clear who had won the upper hand on this day.

The survivors surveyed the area, looking for the battalions of Mandos that had ridden upon them. They had commanded them to wait outside the catacombs as a backup force should some of the evil dragons escape. Now, they were nowhere to be found. After about the span of an hour, a dragon with a dazzling deep purple coat lighted near Khelest bearing news.

"My liege," he began, "My name is Karnoom. I served under lord Krytest. I believe I have found the Mandos."

Taking to the air, Khelest said "Show me."

They landed a few miles away where a large pit had been dug. In the pit stood a large mound of something that had been charred beyond all recognition. Though by sight they could not recognize it, the stench of rotting flesh gave it away. The pile of carnage, still smoldering, was all that remained of the Mandos who had come with them.

With deep sorrow, Khelest bowed his long neck to them, and bellowing a mournful cry, he and Karnoom flew off to rejoin the others.

Upon returning, they assessed their losses. All totaled, one hundred dragons fell that day, and only a handful of Mandos still remained in service. At least one hundred dragons had joined Kerrag.

"We must return and regroup," Khelest said to the survivors at last. "Kerrag will not stop here. You heard what he said. Those who stand against him will fall. We must prepare ourselves, and we must also tell the remaining Mandos to flee back to their cities. They will be safe there for now at least. Let us be off!"

Karnoom was dispatched to summon the remaining Mandos, while the rest of the dragon horde made haste to gather at Twilight Cavern. With so few of them left lord Khalvrog deferred his rule to Khelest.

Twilight Cavern was set within a range of mountains known in the humanoid language as the Crag of Fire. The cavern was aptly named, for when the sun set just below the horizon the light reflected off of the minerals imbedded in the cavern walls, giving off sparkling light arrays of various colors such as green, and yellow, and red. The resulting radiance was more spectacular than a starlit sky.

With barely over one hundred dragons left, the amount of empty space in the cavern made their losses more apparent.

The rumble of nervous dragons obsessing over what would happen next was deafening. They all knew that there may yet be many more losses, and none of them wanted to meet their end prematurely.

"Silence!" Khelest bellowed. "We can thwart Kerrag's plan, and perhaps even still win him to our side, but we cannot do it unless we are of one mind and one purpose."

As he paused, Karnoom lighted in the center of the cavern, dipping his head and wings to Khelest. "The Mandos have retreated lord, as you ordered, but what will happen to the trade routes?"

"The humans are resourceful, and will no doubt have set up several stores in case of an emergency situation. We must now be concerned about the survival of our own race."

"What of the Kan'Shah council, Khelest?" Khalvrog asked. "What jurisdiction do they have in this matter?"

"If I may lord Khelest?" said Karnoom. "The Mandos have dispatched a communication to the Kan'Shah regarding an update on these affairs. They will be aware."

"Brothers, we are dragons!" Khelest continued. "We are fierce in battle and strong in flight, and we will stop this madness however possible."

A great roar of unity went up, and each great beast spewed white hot flame in affirmation of their leader's words.

~

Deep within the Void the entire host of Kan'Shah had gathered for The Shunning. There had not been a ceremony like it in two thousand years. Malkus, chief of the sorcerers of the void, presided over the ceremony. Destus, the accused, stood on a platform before Malkus, shackled in bonds of pure energy.

Malkus raised his hands for silence and began to speak. "Destus, you stand accused of violating the sacred trust of the Forming Rite. Because of your intentional act, you are party to the slaughter of numerous dragons and humans at the hands of the beast you helped form. I have received official word of this from Gajne. What say you?"

Destus was grinning as the charges were read. "I have always believed in the freedom to choose one's path. If we have that right, and humans have that right, why should dragon kind be any different? Of course I never wished for such negative repercussions, but such is the risk with true freedom."

"The dragons were to be morally neutral. We knew there would be some mingling, but you deliberately chose the base path. This is treason in the eyes of the council, Destus. You know the punishment for such a crime is banishment to the Nekkr."

Malkus lifted his eyes from Destus and addressed the assembly. "You have heard the charges, and also the response from the accused. We have now only to carry out or belay the punishment. What say you?!"

From most of the thousands gathered, black orbs of energy alighted above their heads in affirmation of the punishment. Those who wished to dismiss or modify the punishment sent up an orb of golden energy.

Malkus nodded. "As with all of our decisions, the majority carries."

He set his eyes on Destus. The silence echoed throughout the arena, as they all waited for the final sentence to fall.

Destus looked deep into Malkus eyes, never shifting his gaze, though a subtle fear started welling up in him. He began to perspire.

"Destus, elder of the Brekken order, you are stripped of your power and authority for crimes against the order and against the galaxy. You are hereby banished to the non-existence of the Nekkr, and will never reenter this realm unless a specific purpose mandates it."

The black orbs, which had rested above the heads of the majority of the elders, traveled to the center of the arena and fused into one giant central orb. Then it changed and flattened out into an orifice of black matter; a portal opening into the nether world of the Nekkr.

Instantly Destus was robbed of all power and all form, and a wail erupted from his body that slowly faded as he changed. All semblance of matter flushed away from his form until what was left was a pulsating cloud of spirit matter that still retained some shape of his former self. It was then assimilated through the portal, into the Nekkr, and the portal blinked out of existence.

After the assembly had dismissed, the high elders stayed behind to discuss matters more.

"What will we do about the rebel Dragons, Malkus?" A well-worn sorcerer asked. Artius by name, he was short and stout with black leathery skin and wide beady eyes.

"Do? We do nothing. We tried getting involved and a handful of our order were slaughtered! We do nothing. They will work it out themselves."

A sorceress named Falcha spoke up. "Malkus, the chaos will be devastating. We cannot expect primal minds to think logically and reason out their differences."

"Their instincts are primal, yes, but wisdom still exists within them. We must hope that the remaining dragon lords exercise that wisdom, for it is apparent that Kerrag is bereft of it."

"How many dragon lords yet remain?" Artius asked.

"I understand that only Khalvrog and Khelest remain, and their hordes are severely depleted."

"Will we not at least keep an eye on things from the gazing pool?" Falcha asked, always one of the more compassionate of the order.

"I suppose it wouldn't hurt." Malkus gazed around at each of the High elders with a commanding look that would disarm even the most powerful. "I charge all of you to keep your personal feelings out of this. No interference."

They all nodded in agreement. The dragons would be on their own, and Gajne would quake with the fallout.

~

Days had passed. The expectation of war hung as thick as a blanket of fog on the morale of those opposing Kerrag. Khelest stood perched just outside the mouth of the cavern; his shimmering turquoise wings folded back against his hide, and his head raised to the sunlit canopy of sky - lost in thought.

Khalvrog approached from behind. "My lord, fear is running high within the horde. The beckoning of death seems to be all they hear."

A low rumble of consternation escaped Khelest. "I am aware of it, comrade. This will be a dark day that may see many of our kind die. Even you, or me, or both of us."

"I am prepared for this death, if the fates would have it."

"As am I, Khalvrog. However, it is Kerrag who must fall today. We must see to it."

"Yes, perhaps the others will return to their former glory once he is no longer in the equation."

Khelest nodded his head quickly in affirmation, and lifted his eyes back to the canopy. What he saw made the fires burn within him.

A dark cloud was breaking the horizon; monstrous and moving closer with great speed. Kerrag and those loyal to him were advancing; a maelstrom of death, preparing to swallow them whole.

Khelest let loose a loud screech with full vibrato that echoed throughout the crag. The alarm alerted all his kin to prepare for battle.

Spilling from every crevice, what was left of the dragon horde made their way to the highest peak. The mountain had once been a volcano, and had since crusted over with age forming a bowl shaped crater at the top.

They gathered together in the crater and waited with rapt anticipation as Kerrag and his forces approached the mountain, the twin suns reflecting off their scales in a shimmering rainbow of color.

Khelest turned to his comrades and spoke with a clear yet commanding tone. "Those of you in the rear, ascend to the wall surrounding this crater and perch yourselves there as an elevated assault. As for the rest of you, spread out from each other. A closely huddled force will be easier to press upon for the kill. We must not give them that opportunity."

Some called out, "What of the Kan'Shah? Have they not heard of our plight?"

Khelest lowered his head with eyes closed, "They have heard, I do not doubt. They are not coming. Make haste to your placements. Now!

No sooner had they attained their posts, then they were surrounded by their enemies.

"The hour grows late, Khelest," Kerrag bellowed, "and I am ready to be done with you. You have rejected me once already but I am…" he lingered on the words letting the tension build, "merciful." A ripple of laughter scattered across the host that had accompanied him.

"Mercy?!" Khelest protested. "This … is … *mercy* to you? You have slaughtered Kan'Shah, humans, and dragon kind alike. None have escaped your thirst for bloodshed, and you speak of mercy?!"

"The time for servitude is over, Khelest. We will now be those who are served; we now rule!"

"You intend to rule as a tyrant, fool that you are! I will not stand for it! The original order must be preserved, or all of Gajne, yes even the galaxy itself, will fall into chaos."

"So, you shall not be persuaded. Death is your suitor this night, then. So be it. Brothers," he turned to the others, "your kindred have rejected our rule. Descend on them!"

The evening sky erupted in a storm, as blood-bent dragons rained down upon their kin. Those at higher stations who followed Khelest also descended, careening into the enemy at full force. Fire erupted all around as dragon clashed with dragon, and the ascending smoke made the volcano seem alive again.

Talon and tooth met with flesh, ripping and tearing as roars of triumph and anguish sounded across the crevice.

Swirls of color and death filled the sky as some took their battle to the air. As one dragon bested another, the victims fell like stars to the solid rock below.

Screeches echoed throughout the crag as the shock of battle accelerated. The beasts were falling left and right, and blood flowed as lava. Some lay dead, others severely wounded with torn wings and festering burns. Neither side was exempt from the carnage.

Deep within the void the reassembled sorcerers looked on in horror as their creations tore each other apart, slowly ridding the galaxy of the once majestic race.

The battle wore on for hours, when at last only a small band of the mighty creatures remained, and the enemy outnumbered the allied force.

Khalvrog charged against two dragons that were flanking Kerrag, who was locked in battle with a quickly weakening Khelest, and impaled them one after the other through the throat with his mighty spiked tail. Another rushed toward him, and he vaulted into the air, grabbing his assailant with the full grip of his talons as he ascended.

Now fully airborne, the two tore into each other. Chunks of dragon flesh fell to the ground, as blood rained down from their wounds. The young and feisty attacker let loose a wave of hot searing flame against Khalvrog, just as the elder dragon was opening his great maw to do the same. The young dragon's bevy of flame met its equal, and gases within the atmosphere exploded all around. Khalvrog did not let up, and eventually the young one was overcome. He plummeted to the ground in a heap of charred and dying flesh.

When Khalvrog descended, Karnoom lay on a pile of rock against the wall of the crevice. He was barely moving, but two dead dragons lay at his side. Their wings had been ripped from their sides, and their necks bore the visible gashes from his jagged claws. Indeed, Karnoom was a force to be reckoned with.

From somewhere behind them a volley of fire blanketed Karnoom's head, suffocating him and burning away what life remained in him. As Khalvrog turned, a huge purple hued dragon, whom he recognized as Krendor the Mad, stood poised and ready to deal a death blow to him.

As massive as Khalvrog was, Krendor was more so. His hind legs were as big around, and as thick, as the oldest of oak trees. Their musculature was so strong that he was able to rear on his hind legs indefinitely as if human. His coal black eyes, shimmering with flame behind, burned into Khalvrog. Like a king, the crown of his skull was layered with tooth like horns a foot long.

The gigantic beast charged at him with uncanny speed, and Khalvrog met him with every amount of equal strength. Blood was still dripping from various places on his body where scales had been ripped off and his hide rent. As the two locked in battle, Khalvrog released a mighty blow with his right paw full in the face of his opponent. His claws dug deep gouging through flesh, and destroying one eye.

Krendor loosed his grip and staggered back, bracing on all fours as he shook off the blow. Dark molten blood oozed from the dead eye, and a roar black with hate erupted from his massive jaws.

He unleashed waves of fire in rebuke, and as they hit Khalvrog he could feel his rough skin cooking. He leapt into the air to cool off, skyrocketing into the atmosphere above. The flame bath had cauterized his wounds for the time being, and he felt more alive. He changed course and dove for the beast, a meteor of raw power with death in tow.

He collided with Krendor truly, jaws tearing into flesh as some of his teeth broke loose from biting into scales. The warm, metallic taste of blood filled his mouth, but it was not just Krendor's blood that he tasted. Blood began pouring from wounds all along the length of his neck. He had been so enthralled in the heat of battle, that he had not felt Krendor tear into him.

The two mighty beasts slumped on the ground side by side. Blood spilled out of their wounds freely as their spark of life slowly dwindled out of existence.

Khelest and Kerrag had been battling wits and attacks for hours, and were each wearing thin. When he saw Khalvrog fall, Khelest went into a fit of rage and sent Kerrag flying into a rock wall. A layer of the wall shattered with the force, and a shower of rock fell. A large rock collapsed on Kerrag's head, knocking him unconscious.

Kiode, the dragon that had still been flanking Kerrag, bolted in a panic and flew fast in the direction of the caves of the Crag of Fire.

Khelest was right behind him, and gaining on him much faster than Kiode could fly. Khelest flew over him, and in a rush of wind he lowered upon the coward. He dug his talons in deep, piercing between scales into the tender meat of his back, and then returned to the crevice dragging the flailing and screaming beast with him. Blood streamed through the air as they flew to their destination.

When they returned to the crevice Khelest shoved the other dragon into a free fall drop to the ground below. As he landed the sound of bone shattering echoed in the now almost silent arena. Like a bird of prey, Khelest landed next to the fallen heap, and with one swift flash of iron-born teeth he ripped the gullet from Kiode's neck.

Deeply out of breath as his body started to recoup, Khelest glanced in the direction of Kerrag. He was sitting back on his haunches glaring at Khelest.

"So...brother," he began. "We now stand on equal footing it would seem. You have done me a great service today." A loud rumble of laughter escaped him.

"What do you mean, beast?!" Khelest bellowed. "You are a disgrace to dragon kind. I have done nothing for you. You have done this yourself!"

"You and your dead followers have eliminated all present," he growled, "leaving us the only two left of our kind." He allowed a lengthy pause, as he drank in the silence of realization in Khelest. "You have played into my trap, fool that you are."

"You orchestrated this to eliminate our kind?!" Khelest growled, poising himself to attack.

Just then a giant orb of light descended from the sky. Khelest backed away cautiously as his eyes were blinded temporarily by the light. Once settled, the orb of light took on a humanoid shape.

Khelest looked on in wonder at what was before him. "What sorcery is this, Kerrag?!"

Kerrag snorted in derision. "There are other planets in the galaxy besides Gajne, Khelest. You know this to be true, yes?

"The planet Lumina is the closest to ours, and is inhabited by others such as my friend here."

"What are you called?" Khelest asked the being.

We are collective. We are called nothing. Khelest received what it said, but never heard it utter any sound.

"They speak without words, and yet our minds know what is said. Wild and imaginative creations, don't you think Khelest? Courtesy of the tyrannical Kan'Shah!"

"Why is it..., or..., he here? Khelest asked apprehensively.

"The Luminatre are slavers and business dealers. They supply various needs to the galaxy, and have the power to withhold it as well. I made...a proposal." Kerrag made a low growl of pleasure, as smoke trailed up from his snout.

Khelest didn't like the sound of that. He cursed the elders of the void that they had abandoned the dragons to extinction, and wondered what part they had in the plan. He was now too weak to fight any longer.

"And pray, what would that proposal be, Kerrag?"

"The Luminatre will take you away from here. What they do with you is none of my concern, as long as they keep you alive. I am satisfied to be rid of you. I, in turn, will be given freedom over Gajne as the last of the dragon-lords." As he said the last bit slather and spit dripped from his mouth as though his thirst for power were manifesting itself.

"Why not just end me here and now, Kerrag!"

"No no no, you see I want you to live out the rest of your years knowing who it was that bested you." He let out a thundering laugh, and turned to the being at his side. "Be off with him."

Khelest took to the air backwards, still facing his would be captors, and loosed gushes of flame in what he thought was the triumph of escape.

From the hand of the Luminatre came streamers of light that twisted and wrapped around Khelest. When the wrappings had been finished he was firmly encased in a cocoon of pure energy that closely resembled a dragon egg. The cage was impenetrable. He had met his match.

The Luminatre became a great orb of light once more and hovered over to where the cocoon rested. The orb swallowed the cocoon with Khelest inside, and left the way it came.

Kerrag flew to the top of the mountain that nestled twilight cavern, perched on its peak, and echoed an earth shattering roar into the night. As darkness fell, the presence of darkness was also rising.

~

Malkus stood silent with Falcha by his side. The rest of the elders had dispersed to their dwelling, and Malkus gazed deep into the pool where they had seen everything transpire.

It was a dark day for the galaxy. Kerrag was cruel, and would likely terrorize the humans of Gajne. He was alone, however, and that might be something in the future.

"What now Malkus?" Falcha asked.

"For the first time in Millennia, I am at a loss."

"We were wrong to not get involved, Malkus."

"Yes, I see that now. The future is shrouded in shadow, so our sight is limited."

"Kerrag must be slain, Malkus. Khelest may be as good as dead, for who knows what the Luminatre will do with him. If they are to be extinct, let them be completely extinct."

"Yes you are right, Falcha. But, we must all think long and hard on this. He must meet his fate from a source he would not expect."

She nodded, and left him alone to think.

Only the Kan'Shah could hope to turn the tide of darkness. Malkus would call for decisive action at the next Conclave. He was determined to overturn the evil that had taken place, and he felt there was only one way. A way that would force him to break a sacred oath.

He gazed back into the pool, and attempted to look into the shadow of the future.

~

Just as the Traveler finished, Talindor reared up to his full height and let loose a terrifying and angry howl that shook the entire cavern, and bellowed at him. "How dare you tell me a tale of the destruction of my own kind, and then leave it so grotesquely unfinished! What happened, Traveler?! Tell me before I tear open your flesh, and crush you under my mighty paw!"

As the dragon accosted him, the Traveler jumped from his sitting position and raised his staff in defense. A large circle of pure light decorated with ancient symbols surrounded him. "You may not pass beyond this circle, great Talindor. As to the tale I have just relayed, I am afraid I never had a chance to complete the chronicle. Due to a ripple in the planes that I travel, I was ripped away prematurely and brought to your world. If you wish to hear the resolution, you must release me."

"Trickery!" Talindor boomed. "You deceitful germ! Your remains will rot here in my hole!" With that the great beast flew against the Traveler, fixing to pin him against the rock wall with its great horned skull. Upon entering the circle of power, a shock of power reverberated outward.

Talindor was thrown back against the entry of his hole and crashed to the floor. The foundations shook, more great cracks fissured in the cavern walls, and dust from the tumult clouded the room. Books flew off of the shelves and landed on top of the already large pile in the center of the floor. The magic of the great door was upset and it loosed from its hinges. The dragon looked on in awe and fury.

"I warned you, great one. Even with your powerful magic, the circle cannot be broken except by one of my own kind. However, I understand your frustration with me, so I have something to give you."

The Traveler raised his hand, waved it, and the shimmer-stones in his staff came alive with all the colors of a rainbow. A large tome, a beauty to behold, appeared in the air along with a quill that moved of its own accord. The quill flew through the air as each page of the book turned over. When all was finished, the quill disappeared, the book closed, and it floated lazily over to rest on the ground where the beast had fallen.

"What witchery is this, Traveler?" Talindor growled.

"This is my gift to you. It is a complete volume of all the stories that I have told you today. I also leave you with a promise. When I have finished recording the fate of the great Khelest, I will return to you. I also give you my name. I am called Valos. By the authority of the Kan'Shah I declare your reign here ended, and I bind you prisoner within your lair, so that you may reflect upon your fate until my return. With that, I bid you farewell."

The Traveler turned on a heel, extinguishing the circle. He waved his arms to the right, and with a mighty gust the great door flew open.

Not since the Traveler's arrival had the great dragon been so silent, for he had many thoughtful sounds as he heard the tales, but as the Traveler left he was speechless for the first time.

The Traveler walked slowly out of the mountain, and reset the door with his own enchantments. He shook with a chill as the warmth of the dragon's archive left him. He raised his staff, igniting his power again, and a great fissure opened before him. He grinned slightly, stepping through into nothingness, and the portal blinked out of existence.

Charles McGarry is an author, a blogger, and a truly unique individual. He is a free thinker, a futurist, and loves to think deeply about many issues. He was raised on a small hay farm in southern Utah. After high school, and floundering for a couple of years, he moved to Phoenix AZ to attend Bible college. He met his wife there and they were married in December of 2000. After graduating in 2001, he went to seminary and obtained his Master of Divinity in 2007. He pastored a church for three years, but eventually realized that his true purpose was to connect with people through writing. He is married to the love of his life and they have two amazing children and an adorable, and rather eccentric cat.

Charles enjoys all kinds of different movies and music, and is also a huge bookworm. His genres of choice are spiritual and philosophical non-fiction, suspenseful thrillers, Science Fiction and Fantasy. Charles is a huge fan of authors like Terry Brooks, JRR Tolkien, and Christopher Paolini, Dan Brown, Eckhart Tolle and Wayne Dyer. He is also enamored with ancient world history, especially Egyptology, and likes to play video games.

A proud health nut, Charles is a huge fan of Yoga, Tai Chi, and meditation for fitness and releasing stress. He also has a thing for dragons.

You can find his website at www.charlesmcgarry.net